LAND ^{OF} _{THE} BLIND

THE ATALANTA CHRONICLES

VOLUME ONE

LAND OF THE BLIND

THE ATALANTA CHRONICLES

VOLUME ONE

ANTHONY WOOD

HAT CREEK

HAT CREEK

an imprint of
Roan & Weatherford Publishing Associates, LLC
Bentonville, Arkansas • Heber City, Utah
www.roanweatherford.com

Library of Congress Cataloging-in-Publication Data
Names: Wood, Anthony, author
Title: Land of the Blind/Anthony Wood | The Atalanta Chronicles #1
Description: First Edition | Bentonville: Hat Creek, 2026.
Identifiers: LCCN: 2025951077 | IBSN: 979-8-89299-091-2 (trade paperback) |
ISBN: 979-8-89299-092-9 (eBook)
Subjects: FICTION/Westerns | FICTION/Action & Adventure |
FICTION/Historical
LC record available at: https://lccn.loc.gov.2025951077

Hat Creek trade paperback edition May, 2026

Cover & Interior Design by Casey W. Cowan
Cover Art by C. Michael Dudash
Her Life Was the Cowboy Life, 2022, Oil on Linen
Editing by Don Money & Rachel Santino

I dedicate this book to Wayne and Joan Davis for always "being there" with strength, love, and care to help so many people be safe and become better, including me. Joan, I'm happy to be your favorite son-in-law, even though I'm your only son-in-law. Smile.

AUTHOR'S NOTE

ONE OF THE great joys of writing Westerns and historical fiction, or any genre for me, is traveling and experiencing the places that I write about as I do research for a novel. Nothing replaces being in the place where my characters live, breathe and die as I craft the stories given me by Creator. Standing in the place where my ancestors and characters fought at Vicksburg, farmed in Louisiana, or battled outlaws in Texas, ensures that I "get the feel" of being onsite where events I pen happened, or as a fiction writer, imagine that could have happened.

For *Land of the Blind,* I thoroughly enjoyed traveling the Chisholm Trail north with Marion and Lummy, crossing the Red River and following the train route they took into the Indian Territory where they rode horseback through The Narrows, camped near Edwards Store, and then shot it out with outlaw leader, the Buyer, and his gang in Robbers Cave.

Visiting the places about which I write makes the world of my characters become more real for me. Because I take time to visit my writing locations, I hope the story becomes more real for you as a reader.

ACKNOWLEDGEMENTS

LOCAL, STATE, AND National parks, museums, historic sites, and those employed to manage and care for them are treasures we should protect at all costs. The names are too many for me to list for all the wonderful people who have assisted me when I show up by appointment or unannounced asking for help with my research. You are some of the kindest, most helpful professionals I have enjoyed sharing time with in my writing career.

One in particular, a member of the Choctaw Nation who works at Robbers Cave State Park in Oklahoma, stands out for *Land of the Blind.*

Andrew, thank you for being so accommodating, sharing wisdom and stories, answering my many questions, and pointing me in the right direction as I explored Robbers Cave for this western novel.

You are Andrew in this story.

In the land of the blind, the one-eyed man is king.
—Desiderius Erasmus, Adagia

LAND OF THE BLIND

THE ATALANTA CHRONICLES

VOLUME ONE

I AM MARION

A woman need not be weak in a man's world.

Before Dawn, August 24, 1886

I TRACK MEN. Cowards who believe women exist to serve their every need. Uncouth ruffians with little home training who think women are property to be twisted and turned any which way they want because they appear weaker. Heck, if we women were any weaker, we wouldn't have survived men all these years. But we have, and not just survived—we have thrived. They just haven't figured out what we already know—if it doesn't kill us, we get more determined.

Understand me—I don't hate all men. Meeting Rainy Mills and Lummy Tullos changed that. The way they dealt with Tom Kimbrell in that red sky storm battle to the death reminded me there are still good men in this world. They're cut from the same cloth as my Uncle Silas who rescued me from that whorehouse in Natchez, Missip, so many years ago. Imperfect men wishing for a perfect world. Fighting evil alongside Rainy and Uncle Lummy renewed my hope in the man part of the human race.

No, I detest the ones who steal, buy, and sell the innocent like cattle for profit, sport, pleasure, or just plain old down in the dirt meanness. I plan to stop as many of them as I can. Dead in their tracks. Dead if need be. Dead is *always* preferable. It makes claiming the reward easier.

And now I have a lead. Don't have a real name, just the Buyer, and not even a description. But the trail leads north from what little I've gathered.

Helping orchestrate the battle to save Tarle Tullos's wife, Caroline, a few days ago from that rascal Tom Kimbrell and his wicked old momma Aunt Polly with my newfound uncles Rainy and Lummy Tullos put me on the track of the demon leader I'm looking for. Yeah, I said it. Demon. I claim to be no angel. Never wanted to be one. Not with my background, but I'm on the avenging righteous side of things and well within the law to ply my trade. God makes angels, not men or women. He has to. Otherwise, we'd all be demons.

I had hoped to catch the demon who buys and sells women with Kimbrell and kill them all in one swoop. My performance in the saloon that night luring Kimbrell out into the alley—where he tried to rape me—was nothing short of a stupendous performance that would've even made Miss Lillie Langtry of the thespian crowd proud. But, I guess I really don't know anything about her except what they say in the newspapers. Maybe she's that good as an actress. I know I am, and what I did wasn't played out on any stage. It was real, and my calling in this life is solid as the rock I stand on now. And I got the information we needed to save Caroline's life before the Buyer took her to who knows where. Now I'm on the trail to God knows where to find the Buyer.

I will find him.

My name is Marion Tullos. I track men. It's who I am. It's what I do. It's how I live. And I'm good at it.

CLEANING UP AFTER A RED SKY STORM

Cleaning up after a storm isn't just about damaged property, trees, and such. It's also about damaged hearts.

First Light, August 24, 1886

I DRAIN THE dregs from my coffee cup and stash it in my saddlebag as a blue sky shows in the east. Cold coffee takes the joy out of the coffee experience. But cold is what I've felt ever since I left Mississippi years ago. Only lately have things warmed up.

Lummy strides over like a man headed to put out a fire. "Marion, I need to get out of this place. Be all right if we get goin'?" He cinches down his saddle and lays his head on its seat. "I can't get the smell of blood out of my nose. I've washed it out five times and…." He shakes the distress from his face as his thumb presses the owl claw into his wrist. "Rainy says we should ride north on the Chisholm Trail. It'll take us straight up to Fort Worth. From there we can cut across to wherever we want to go from there."

"Sounds good to me. Fort Worth's where I'd planned to go after this anyway."

"What's in Fort Worth?"

"My next bit of business."

"I'll go as far as Fort Worth with you. I'm not sure after that."

"I understand. Not a problem. I'll enjoy your company on the trail."

I'm pretty much a loner with a strong desire to do things my way, but having Uncle Lummy riding with me? He can be captain for a while, and then I'll be on my own again. I know he's just watching over me like he does everybody else. It actually feels pretty good to have a strong and decent man in my life, especially being family too. It helps me relax knowing he'll be watching our backs as will I. He's so much like Uncle Silas—height, build, hair, gentle though somewhat of a sad and weathered face. Cut from the same cloth, those two—Lummy and Rainy. Good men. But it's Lummy's hazel eyes that burrow into my soul I'm interested in getting behind. What's there? How deep is the soul of a man who has gone through so much? How has he survived and stayed sane in an insane world? I need to know. I don't believe I'll survive if I don't. I have a feeling I'll be finding out on this trip.

Lummy grabs the saddle horn, puts his left foot into a stirrup, and starts to heave himself up, but stops. "I'll be right back, Marion."

"Take your time, Uncle." But I'm as ready to get out of here as he is. Being stripped naked for all to see and my life threatened to save a boy's life was worth it. But, I know the scars of what happened here will show up when I least expect them. I'm already having dreams about that. They don't stop there. That incident conjures up demons of my past—wicked preachers, carpetbaggers, a voodoo witch, whorehouse owners, whorish men, and… I have to stop this. But I don't know how.

Lummy strides over to see his son Elzey one last time. Tears stream down Elzey's face. He's made it clear he wants his father in his life but knows all too well now that it cannot be. Not for a while. Lummy has to disappear in order to reappear mentally fit for such a time. They're within earshot, and I want to hear this.

Elzey dries his eyes with his sleeve. "I wish I'd known my mother."

Lummy hangs his head. "Susannah was the sweetest angel Creator ever sent to this earth. We'll all be together one day."

Elzey shakes his head. "I know, I just…."

Lummy takes Elzey by the shoulders. "Son, I'll do my best to come see you, and in time, send for you to come stay with me for a while. I just need some time alone. My head just ain't cleared up. I don't know if it ever will be. I just need some time and…."

I've never seen a man want something so badly but who knows he can't have it because of what he's done to make sure others have what he's always wanted. I look to the sky and study the clouds for a moment. "Thanks for giving me Uncle Lummy. You provide what I need even when I don't even know to ask, Lord."

Elzey wraps his arms around Lummy. "I know, Pop. I understand now why you did what you did. You wanted to protect me like you did when Tom Kimbrell wanted to kill me yesterday."

"Pop? How'd you know to call me that? Only my daughters Dell and Rosey call me that."

"They told me when I went to visit them. Hope it's okay."

"I like it." Lummy smiles. "You went to Choctaw County?"

"Cousin Tarle and I did. I wanted to find you. I had to know why you left me. I got to meet everybody and Uncle Jasper explained everything. I'd never been treated so good by people I'd just met."

"They are your people."

"Yes, sir, they are. I now have kinfolk in Choctaw County, Mississippi."

Lummy gathers his long hair and puts it back behind his ears. "Well, I'll be. How'd I not run into you two?"

Elzey shakes his head. "You did, Pop. I believe we saw each other when our ferry crossing the Mississippi passed yours going the other way."

Lummy puts his hands on his hips. "That's right… and you had Tarle right there with you. I thought I recognized him. It'd been so long since I'd seen him, I wasn't sure."

Elzey nods. "Pop, I know you did what you had to do then, and what you're doing now, I understand."

"We good, then?"

"Yes, we're good, and I look forward to spending more time with you one day. I need to know you. I want to know you, Pop."

Lummy tears up. "Thank you, son. Say hello to your folks back in Winn Parish. You, Tarle, and the rest, be careful goin' home. Make sure Wesley Wood gets back to Choctaw County. The Wood people have always been there for us, especially in the worst of times, 'cause they ain't scared." Lummy chuckles at his own comment. "Listen to Rainy. He's the wisest man I know." Lummy straightens his hat. "Now I gotta go."

Elzey hugs Lummy like he'll never let go. "I love you, Pop."

Lummy returns to his mount. He hesitates then hops up into the saddle probably like he did when he was in the war. "You ready?"

I smile. "Just waiting on you, Uncle."

Rainy squints and takes hold of the bridle on Lummy's mount. "Let me have a word before you go, if you don't mind."

LEAVING, A FOREGONE CONCLUSION

I can live anywhere because I don't belong anywhere.

Just Before Sunrise, August 24, 1886

IT'S JUST GETTING light when Lummy Tullos strolls away with Rainy, but waves me over. "Marion, come over here with us, please. We'll go in a minute."

I nod. "Be right there." I tie down my saddlebags, straighten my shirt, gird up my belt, and stride over to where Lummy and Rainy say their goodbyes. I notice my gait. I walk too much like a man. That's all right, because when I'm out here, it works. And when I need to sucker a man into telling me what I want to know, I can play the harlot. I shuck off the depressing thought that there's not much between the two in my life right now. Being a woman in a man's world ain't easy.

Lummy embraces his friend. "We've come a long way, you and me, Rainy Mills."

Rainy laughs. "Yeah, we surely have, you old rotten buzzard. From coyotes chasing your backside into my camp that night to us taking down Tom Ford, the West-Kimbrell Gang, and that pissant Tom Kimbrell and his wicked witch momma, it appears our association is all too well-founded upon a form of justice that leads to death."

"Yeah, well, hopefully not our own anytime soon."

Rainy poses like an actor in a stage play, and throws out his arm. "Oh, Lummy Tullos, we shall live forever, don't you know?"

Lummy chuckles. "Not in this lifetime."

I laugh as I step up. "You two ain't got a lick of sense." I can't help but wonder how they do it. Warring with some of the most detestable men God ever made from the clay whom Satan taught ever so well, and still joke with each other while Tom Kimbrell's body still lies warm. These two must've realized that they have to make each other laugh to keep from crying. Rainy and Lummy have been through hell together. For the sake of other people.

Rainy laughs. "Well, my dear niece, and you are my niece as much as you are Lummy's. Having reviewed your lively Lillie Langtry performance in recent events, I figure Lummy and I are in the best of company with folks who don't possess a lick of sense." He backhands Lummy on the chest. "We're in good company, huh, Lummy?"

"The best Creator has to offer, I'd say."

Rainy Mills winks and says, "Walk with us, Marion, if you will, please, ma'am." He puts his hand on Lummy's shoulder, and we stroll a few feet to the end of a dry gulch. They stare out into the vastness of the country but morning mist obscures their view of the plains stretching out before them. "The way may not be clear because of the fogginess of the future, but you both will always have a place in Winnfield, Louisiana." Rainy takes my hand. "You especially, Marion. You two walk the same path but there are times when you must lie down and rest. Make my home in Winnfield your home when you need just that, my dear niece."

Lummy shakes his head and turns to leave, but Rainy tugs on his jacket sleeve. "You remember that, too, my good friend. Come back with me now, if you like."

"I appreciate it. But you know I can't right now. But I do plan to visit. It'll just take a while to get there."

Rainy, a man who has been on the Devil's side of things yet reformed, pulls me and Lummy close for an embrace I've needed since Uncle Silas wrapped his arms around me the night he rescued me from the whorehouse in Natchez. A woman needs a soft, gentle, and safe embrace from a good man from time to time. I'm blessed to have these two men in my life.

Lummy wipes his eyes and nods at our horses. "Boots and saddles, Marion." He strides away with his long legs like he's off to a battle but stops. "Chisholm Trail, right?"

Rainy squints. "Yeah, it'll take you straight north to Fort Worth. Studied it on a map Kimbrell had on the wall in their ranch house. Should be an easy ride, I'm thinking."

"Then north it is. All right with you we take the Chisholm Trail, Marion?"

I hop on my horse with a gentle leap. "Yep, sounds good."

This time Lummy's joints pop, and he groans a little as he eases up into the saddle. He shifts around until comfortable, then nods and grins. "All right then, you lead."

Lummy Tullos, tall as a Mississippi pine and still stout as a broad oak, shakes his head like a kid who just heard his mother died. He looks to the heavens and speaks a few words—I wish I knew what they were. He stops in mid-sentence to stare into the brush and nods, speaks a few more words, and then turns to catch me staring at him. What I catch sight of next is a little old lady in the scrub brush giving Lummy a wave and disappears.

I ask, "Who was that?"

"Granny Thankful. She's been with me since I was a child. I only met her once when I was ten, but she's been my guide all these years. She passed not long after I met her. She shows up when I need her the most. She's been a faithful guide." Lummy looks back over his shoulder and nods at the bushes swaying in a gentle breeze. "Still is."

I need a guide like Granny Thankful.

Lummy's as kind and polite as a grandmother, smart as any school teacher I've ever had, closer to God than any preacher I've ever known, but possesses a ruthless and deadly unflinching determination when his family or friends are threatened and an unwavering willingness to do whatever it takes to make things equal, just, and right. Those are qualities I need, that I want, and from Lummy Tullos, I can learn. If I am to survive where I'm going, and who it is I'm after, I won't live without them.

We turn our horses away as a yellow sun rises in the east. I ponder the conversation Rainy and Uncle Lummy just had.

I can't help myself. "I've got just one question, boss."

"Yeah, what's that? And don't call me boss."

"What in the hell is a pissant?"

Rainy cups his hands on his cheeks and yells, "A rather vulgar, offensive description of a stupid and worthless, extremely unpleasant human being like, well, Tom Kimbrell there, if you can call him a human being."

Lummy grins. "There's your answer right there, straight from the professor's mouth. But there's more."

We turn the noses of our mounts north toward Fort Worth.

LUMMY SAYS NOTHING for a long time, so I try breaking the silence. "What was the toughest thing about what happened back there, Uncle Lummy?"

"Besides leaving my son?" He scratches the back of his neck and whispers, "Seems like leaving has always been a foregone conclusion in my life."

"I know that was hard and no small thing, but I'm really asking about what we did was the hardest thing?"

"I did the thing I said I'd never do again. I killed a man. I killed Tom Kimbrell." He drops his head. "And I had no mercy in me when I did it and have no remorse in me now that it's over."

I'm careful to say the right thing. I barely know this man, but I need his wisdom. "But you saved your son. You saved Elzey." I stop, and he stops with me. "You saved me, Uncle Lummy." We start off again.

"I know. Still, it's never easy."

"Would it be any easier if you were burying me or Elzey right now?"

"Of course not, Marion, what would you think of me?"

I take a chance. "Then cork that bottle of whine and let's get on with this."

"Get on with what?"

"Finding the people Kimbrell was meeting up with to sell Caroline."

"And do what when we find them?"

"Kill 'em all. There wouldn't be any sellers if there weren't any buyers."

I can see Lummy is pondering what I just said. "Marion, we done got the sellers—Tom Kimbrell, his gang, and Aunt Polly, and besides, I'm not sure I have it in me."

I stop dead still. "Uncle Lummy, I want the buyers, and I need you to go with me, do you understand?"

"I do. But heck, we don't even know who or where they are."

"I may not know who, except that he's called the Buyer, but yeah, I do know where. I got it out of the preacher just before I squeezed the life out of his guts back there."

CHISHOLM TRAIL

Old trails can lead to new paths.

Just after Sunrise, August 24, 1886

THE SKY TURNS light blue as darkness fades and warm sunrays make the bit of dew on the dry, dead grass glisten.

I remind Lummy, "We didn't finish our conversation back there about what a pissant is."

He laughs. "We didn't?"

"You said there was more. What do you mean?"

Lummy snickers. "You should've asked that question of your favorite sage who possesses a classical education from none other than a school I'm sure you're familiar with down in Natchez, Missip."

"Yeah, I'm familiar with the school run by the Catholics, and I went there for a bit, but never heard the word pissant tossed about. But you seem to know it."

"Yeah, when you've spent as much time with a man like Rainy, you can't help but learn a few things, most of it useless to most people, though." Lummy throws me a sarcastic grin. "Some you want to know and some you don't. Rainy don't give a man much choice. He never learned to keep his teeth together very well." Lummy lifts his chin up and snickers. "But I wouldn't have him any different. Still the wisest man I've ever known."

"Yeah, but still, tell me the rest."

"From what I understand, according to Professor Rainy Mills, some Virginia politician years ago, otherwise known as a high-paid bloodsuckin' leech, is said to have stolen the show when he took down a heckler during one of his stump speeches by saying, "I'm a big dog on a big hunt, and I don't have time for a pissant on a melon stalk.""

I laugh out loud. "Guess he put that heckler in his place."

"Would me, too, I reckon." Lummy leans over and smiles big enough to see his teeth for the first time I've seen today. "But probably not."

I shift my butt in the saddle. "I ain't one to heckle nobody, but I'm not for listening to fancy words from men who ain't got the smarts enough to know if they need to wind their asses or scratch their watches."

Lummy sits up straight. "Where'd you hear that?"

"I believe it was Tarle who said those words when he was complaining about something about somebody."

Lummy throws his head back and laughs. "Makes sense. My nephew learned that from his father, my big brother, Ben." He slouches to pat his horse's neck. "I do miss ole Ben."

We ride for some time without a word. I think we both need time to unhitch from the happenings of the past few days. And it was a wagonload of trouble. The Chisholm Trail is just the ticket—quiet, peaceful, and no people, at least not yet.

When I learned that Tarle's wife, Caroline, was snatched away from their home by the demon Tom Kimbrell as an act of revenge for Lummy killing John West back in Winn Parish, I knew I was a Tullos through and through. There was no way I was not going to help the people who have claimed me as kin. I had to help. I had to go. Tullos blood runs thick in my veins despite the fact that I wasn't born a Tullos. Being a Tullos doesn't depend on blood, but being family. And blood family ain't always the closest kin. Being a Tullos is a way of living, not just a name.

After Uncle Silas rescued me from that dreadful whorehouse in Natchez, and especially with the way he took care of my sister and me,

I'll always carry the name Tullos. I'm just now starting to understand what that really means.

"How far to Fort Worth, Uncle Lummy?"

"Rainy said about a hunnert eighty miles or so. I figure we can make it in five, six days at the most if we stay in the saddle." He backhands my shoulder. "What's this uncle thing?"

"I don't have any family. Uncle Silas died in the Marion Courthouse fire, and well, my sister died, God rest her soul, she—"

"I'm sorry to hear that. It ain't easy losing the people you love."

"Ain't that the truth?"

Lummy whispers, "What was her name?"

"Uh-uh. Nope, I don't repeat my dead sister's name. That's only for me."

"Can I ask what happened to her?"

"Fever got her, God rest her soul. She was a good'n. The best."

"She was if she's anything like you, niece. What was the best thing about her?"

Tears form, spill over onto my cheeks, and I cry. Hard. Lummy takes my reins, and we rest on our horses in the middle of the trail. I gather myself together, wipe the tears with my jacket sleeve, and take a deep breath.

"The best thing about my sister was she could always see the sunny side of things, no matter how bad they were."

"How bad?"

I shudder like it's wintertime though the temperature is rising. "It's hard to speak of, but I figure if anybody in this world would understand, it'd be you."

"Probably so, Marion."

"Sissy, that's what I called her, was always trying to help me with the inside stuff I could never conquer."

"Like what, if you don't mind me askin'?"

I look into the far-off distance, trying to decide which words to use. "She helped me to not take responsibility for things not mine." Now I slump a bit in the saddle. "Don't know if I can get this out."

"Take your time."

I draw in a deep breath and blow it all the way out. "She helped me... not blame myself for my parents' death."

"What happened?"

"They were murdered, right before my eyes. I couldn't move, I couldn't scream, I couldn't do anything." The weight the size of a huge boulder lands on my head and shoulders. I can hardly stay in the saddle.

Lummy reaches over to steady me. "How old were you?"

"Seven, but I should've been able to stop those robbers from killing the two most important people in my life besides Sissy. I should've been able...." I can say no more.

We sit on our mounts listening to the birds chirping, the rustle of the wind through the brush, and the steady breathing of our horses.

"It's all right, Marion. You were only seven years old. What could you have done?"

I scream, "Pulled a trigger! That's what I could've done!"

The world starts to turn dark, and I grow weak. Two big hands grasp my shoulders and shake me. Lummy hands me a canteen. I splash water on my face and take a drink.

I gather my thoughts. "I watched from under the bed as they butchered my father and then raped and killed my mother. The one-eyed leader laughed as they took turns raping her and then carved my mother up like a hawg. I couldn't do a thing."

Lummy whispers, "You had a pistol in your hands and—"

"Yes, yes, yes! I couldn't pull the trigger. I was so afraid. I was weak. I was stupid. I was...."

"That horror you will never get over, nor should you. It's part of what makes you who you are. But it cannot be what makes life worth living or what keeps you going. That will undo you one day, when you least expect it." Lummy sits back with the surprised expression on a man's face who just received a word from the Lord. "That's why you're here, ain't it?"

I know the look on my face is like that of a kid who got caught stealing candy from a jar in the mercantile. How could I know? I shake my head. How could he not?

"It's the same one-eyed man, isn't it? He's the man you're looking for, ain't he?"

I straighten up and take back my reins. "Yeah, except he had two eyes back then. I've been on his track for some time now. I got it out of the preacher I drowned back in Waterproof, Louisiana, where I killed him, the voodoo queen, and the carpetbagger. They had the preacher bringing stolen girls to sell back then too. I know that was years ago, but his mark is everywhere men are blind."

"Blind to what?"

"Blind to what's goin' on out here, you know, what happened to Caroline. Stealing and selling women for profit, pleasure, sport, and meanness."

"What do you mean by blind?"

"There's three kinds of blindness. One, the Lord allows you to have naturally if you're born that way. The second one is if somebody makes you blind." I ponder my next few words.

Lummy asks, "And the third?"

"Blindness by choice."

"You mean when someone has something right in front of them and they choose not to see it?"

"Exactly."

"So there's a bunch of people involved in this, is what you're sayin'?"

"A whole lot of people who choose to be blind, and to them, for good reason."

"Money?"

"What else?"

"Like our favorite professor told me once after I told him the story about taking down one-eyed Dawg Smith back in Winn Parish, 'In the land of the blind, the one-eyed man is king.'"

"Well, I'm here to kill the king and destroy his wicked kingdom, and I'll be needing you to tell me that story about Dawg Smith."

Lummy hands me a cold biscuit with salt pork from the sack tied to his saddle. "Eat this, it'll bring a bit of life back into you."

"Thank you."

Uncle Lummy, with the ease of a gentle mother, drew my pain out into the open and salved it with his healing words. I have the same warm feeling inside about him like I did the day Uncle Silas rescued me from that whorehouse and took me and my sister into his home. There is a reason we ride together, Lummy and me.

A whisper in the wind catches my ear. *"There is always a reason when Creator is involved. You will do well to listen to the one who has walked your path. From him you will learn to live life."*

I snatch my head around to see a flowing robe disappear into the brush. I look forward, back again to the brush, then to Lummy who is smiling.

He whispers, "She's with us. She's your Granny Thankful, too, now that you're family."

"I appreciate you saying that."

"Now about this uncle thing, just call me Lummy."

I just smile. We ride a ways lost in our own thoughts.

In time, Lummy starts looking around. "Let's start lookin' for a place to camp for the night. We both need rest."

"Away from people?"

Lummy smiles again. "A woman after my own heart."

"All right, *Un-n-ncle Lummy,*" I say with a grin.

FIRST STOP, ROUND ROCK

Late Afternoon, August 24, 1886

WE PASS A newly painted sign that teeters back and forth in the wispy dry wind. *Round Rock, Texas.* The population number has been scratched out a couple of times, always getting larger, so that now it shows five hundred souls who make their home in this place.

"How 'bout stoppin' here, Marion? Looks to be a growin' burg."

We enter the edge of town. "Yeah, out here in the middle of nowhere."

"Somethin's got it shootin' up like a cornstalk."

"Probably the railroad."

"Sounds 'bout right. Anyway, I ain't wantin' to go too far the first day, if it's all right with you."

"I'd rather camp outside of town."

"Yeah, let's get some supplies. Maybe a store clerk can point us in the right direction for a quiet place to lay our heads."

"Okay, I guess we're not looking for any excitement anyway."

Lummy holds up his hand. "Don't you think we've had enough for a while?"

I shift my butt in the saddle. "Fine by me. I know my behind could use a break. Besides, I'm sure your horse could use a day's rest."

"Yeah, I rode him pretty hard tryin' to keep up with y'all."

I wipe the sweat from my cheeks. "We could've taken the train up to Fort Worth."

"Nah, too many people and too much noise. 'Sides, I think we both needed time to settle down after the Tom Kimbrell fight, don't you think?"

"Yeah, you're right. Riding has become my church, if you know what I mean?"

"I do. Mine is the forest, hills, creeks, and rivers, especially the Mississippi, under a blue or starry sky, and even stormy if the mood hits me. Creator is everywhere, so why not find him everywhere."

"Outside of town will be fine, Uncle Lummy."

"Good, it's settled."

"When we stop at the mercantile, I'll pick out the food. I'll cook us something nice tonight."

"You can cook too?"

"Yeah, I learned how living at the orphanage. We all took a turn. I got pretty good at it. Kinda relaxes me."

"Good, 'cause there nothin' better'n than a woman busy in the kitchen cookin' up a good meal."

"Like I said, I took my turn. Yours is coming."

Round Rock is surprisingly modern to be so far away from any other town besides Austin. "I haven't seen this many stone buildings since I went through Vicksburg last, though a lot of them were made of bricks."

Lummy spies the various storefronts with their signs hoping to lure in customers. "Austin has some. This place looks to have anything you want and everything you don't need right here."

"Yeah, a broom company, meat markets, hardware and saddlery shops, drugstores, saloons, paint, dry goods, and grocery stores, and too many churches."

Lummy smiles sadly. "Always too many churches where preachers teach a soul about our Creator but rarely to know him as a friend."

I leave that conversation alone for another time.

We stop in front of a mercantile with Bernheim written over the door. Lummy laughs as we dismount and tie our reins to the hitching post. He leans over as we take the steps up to the porch. "I fixed a mighty mean rat for supper when I was in the Vicksburg trenches."

Not to be outdone, I laugh. "Good, I like mine well-done with fried taters on the side. And, oh, don't be forgetting the hot sauce them Cajuns make. Just soak mine in that before you roast it. Brings out the flavor." I almost wretch, but I dare not let him see it. I try to cough it off. But he sees.

Lummy belly-laughs, the first I've heard that coming from a man who looks to be an avenging angel of death with eyes that could burn a hole right through your soul.

The bells that clatter as we open the door make me shudder a bit. It's been too soon since I wore them around my neck to entice Tom Kimbrell into our trap back in Austin. That bout in the alley when he tried to rape me still lingers in my dreams. Today I caught myself thinking about it and didn't realize we'd traveled five miles before Uncle Lummy shook me back to the present. I've had that kind of waking dream before, but not like this. I cannot let my wits be caught off guard because of what happened, in the far past or a couple days ago.

An overly happy clerk asks, "What can I do fer ya?"

I speak up as Lummy wanders around the small establishment. "We need supplies. Beans, biscuit flour, bacon, a chunk of ham, papers if you got them, a sack of taters, and—"

"Glad to see y'all come in. We should have everything you need, and maybe more. Round Rock's growing even more now that the railroad hauls cattle north. I came here to open a mercantile when they still called this cattle-drive stop Brushy Creek. It took me a while, but I got into this building last year. My goodness, how things have changed since fifty-one."

The clerk drifts off into some memory. I clear my throat. He comes back to himself, and continues, "Used to be boom or bust in the cattle-drive days. Stores would sell out of most everything in a day or two when two or three big herds came through. Now we're lucky if we see ten drives in a year, and mostly smaller. But with the railroad coming in seventy-six, business has a steady flow and rhythm like a train steaming down the tracks. Things happened so fast, Austin was afraid Round Rock would take its place as the economic center of this part of Texas. We even have an opera house upstairs and—"

Lummy clears his throat. "We'll be wantin' some candy, and maybe a sweet cake or two of some sort."

The clerk trots down the side of the counter to the glass cases. "Got just what you're looking for right here. Any kind of sweet your heart desires."

Lummy follows the clerk down the counter. I check to see if there's anything else we need.

The clerk smiles at Lummy. "Got a sweet tooth, do ya now?"

Lummy doesn't look up from gazing at the various kinds of candy.

The clerk laughs. "Too much candy can make you sick, don't you know?"

Lummy looks up. "Well, my grandpa lived to be a hunnert years old."

The clerk puts his hands on his hips. "Eating a lot of candy?"

Lummy squints. "No, mindin' his own business. I'll eat as much candy as I please."

The clerk doesn't know what to say. "Well yes, of course, uh, I, uh—"

Lummy snickers. "Just pullin' your leg, mister. I'll take a sack of lemon drops and ten of them peppermint sticks, if it won't interrupt your jawin' none."

"Not all. I also have these—"

"Yeah, and two of those cakes there with the cinnamon swirl on them. I like those."

"Good choice. My wife made those this morning."

"Marion, get whatever you want." Lummy walks away without a word to look over the firearms displayed in the rack along the wall behind the counter.

The clerk starts walking to where Lummy is standing. "I'll make you a good deal on—"

I grab the clerk by the arm before he gets to Lummy. "If he needs anything, he'll let you know. Best leave him be. Got any books?"

"Yes, ma'am. I have a few left. What's your interest?"

"You got anything by Mark Twain?" The clerk trots into the back room where I hear him shuffling things around.

Lummy, without turning his head, says, "I met him once. He fished me out of the Mississippi River one time when I thought I was gonna drown. Interesting person, Mark Twain."

"I'll be wanting to hear more about that."

Lummy nods and takes a rifle from the rack. He inspects it like a soldier would, end to end, lastly throwing the rifle butt up into his shoulder and aims. He whispers, "It's got a good feel to it. But I'll keep my Henry just the same." He returns the rifle to the rack and eases toward me.

The clerk returns with a book in each hand. He holds up one. "I have *The Adventures of Tom Sawyer—*"

"I've read that one already. And the other?"

The clerk holds up a green, clothbound book that I can tell hasn't been read. He hands it to me like it's a newborn baby.

I wipe my hands on my shirt and take the book. "Is this brand new?"

"Just got it a month or so ago. Came in with a load of supplies. Been waiting on it for six months. Some items still move kinda slow, even with the railroad."

"May I open it?"

"Yes, but not very wide. It's not a new book anymore if the spine has been broken, you know, like a wild horse."

"I do." I feel the cover all over. "The green with gold lettering is just perfect. And the crown on the front...." I can only imagine how this story must go. I've got to know.

"That's a durable cloth binding that weathers well and the shiny gilt edges make it special, too, don't you think?"

"Yes, I do." I've always loved books. The stories in them have helped keep me sane when the dreams come. "May I?"

The clerk smiles and nods. "Be my guest."

I peek inside so carefully. "Franklin Press, published in eighteen eighty-two by James R. Osgood and Company in Boston. Right here in the United States. This is one of Mark Twain's latest, right?"

The clerk straightens up. "Yes, it is."

"What's it about?"

"Don't rightly know, but the newspaper review that came with it said it's about a prince and a poor boy switching places for a time. Something about Mark Twain bringing to light some kind of injustice in the world. I don't know much more than—"

"I'll take it."

Lummy scratches his head. "You handle that thing like it's precious. Why do you like books so much?"

"I can't live in the world I'm in so I read books to put me in a world I can."

"Makes sense." Lummy pulls out his leather purse and asks the clerk, "How much?"

I start to speak up, but he waves me off, giving me that burning stare. "I'm paying for the book. You get the supplies."

The clerk slumps a bit. "Five dollars?"

I reel back. "A bit steep, don't you think?"

"I'm sorry, ma'am, it takes a lot to get the finer things in life hauled to a place so far off the map nowadays like Round Rock. You understand."

Lummy clears his throat. *"I do,* and thank you."

I hold the book to my chest like a young girl clutches her dolly. "Thank you, Uncle Lummy."

It's clear he's as happy doing this for me as anything he's done in a long while, save rescuing Elzey. His eyes dance with joy at making me happy.

The clerk asks as he wraps my book in brown paper, tying it off with grass twine, "Could I also interest you in—"

"Nope, this is it. How much for the supplies?"

He figures the cost of our items with a pencil on a small pad. "Uh, that'll be four dollars. I threw the sweet cakes in for free."

I pay the man. "Thank you, kind sir."

The clerk smiles. "Enjoy the book."

I nod as Lummy takes the sack of supplies in hand.

Before we start for the door, Lummy asks, "Why Round Rock?"

The clerk jumps at the chance for more conversation. "It's named for the big round rock at the low-water crossing at Brushy Creek. Lotta horses, cattle, cowboys, and wagons trailed through that creek on their way north to Abilene, and south, too, I guess, when the trail drivers returned home. The railroad coming ended all of that. Now we're a water and fuel stop like so many places on the line, but it's been good for business and people moving in. We're starting to look like a real town."

I tip my hat, but he's not done talking.

"You'll like the creek and the rock, I'm betting. It's a quiet place now, though. Good place to camp too. Just look for the large round anvil-shaped rock. You can't miss it."

"All right to take a bath in the creek?"

"Don't see why not, if you're not too shy. There might be a few travelers there, but most likely not. Just keep watch. There's still some ruffians lurking about in these parts. I once knew—"

I'm ready to go. "Much obliged." But Lummy isn't.

"Ruffians, you say? Anybody in particular?"

The clerk shivers like a kid about to open a wrapped birthday present. "You better know it. Ever heard of Sam Bass, the famous train robber?"

"No," we both say, shaking our heads.

"Well, they tracked him all over hell's creation but caught up with him right here in Round Rock. His gang robbed the Fort Worth to Cleburne train back in seventy-eight. I was here. Texas Rangers Herold and Ware shot that ruffian July nineteenth that same year after being recognized and fleeing Koppel's store down the street there, but not before Bass shot and killed Deputy Sheriff A. W. Grimes. Bass died in a shack two days later without giving up the names of his guilty gang members. They call it the 'Sam Bass Shootout' now. People think of him as a hero, kinda like Jesse James. The gun battle put us on the map historywise, as they say."

"Musta been a heck of a fight." I lower my head to avoid where I hope this doesn't go. But it does.

The clerk props his elbows on the counter. "Yeah, sorta like what happened down in Austin a few days back. They say some vigilante group came in and took out a gang led by some fella named Kimbrell. Heard he was gutted like a fish. Must've been some devilish folks. Y'all know anything 'bout that?"

Lummy lies, "Didn't come from Austin. How'd you hear about it?"

"News travels fast on trains."

Lummy snickers. "Like good church lady gossip spreadin' through town like lightning, right?"

"Yeah, just like that. Some say part of the vigilante group might be headed this way."

I turn the knob on the door. "Like he said, we came from a different direction. Now, good day to you, and thank you."

The clerk grins like a mule eating briars. "Any time."

I tip my hat again and close the door behind us. Those damn bells. Now I'll think of Tom Kimbrell every time I walk in and out of a store.

When we get to our horses, Lummy whispers across his saddle, "We gotta get movin'. We ain't been gone two days and that news is followin' close as our own shadows."

I wring my hands a bit but grab the saddle horn and leap up on my mount. "Let's stay the night at the round rock and then get on up to Fort Worth quick as we can."

Lummy eases up into his saddle. "If that store owner already knows that we might be travelin' north, guess who else might know?"

"The Buyer."

We trot out of town like we're in no hurry. Suspicions are easily aroused in a town like this one.

CREEKSIDE CAMPING

A cool water bath can't take the heat out of bein' pursued.

Just as the Sun Sets, August 24, 1886

BRUSHY CREEK SWIRLS around the turtle-shaped round rock that marks the passing of thousands of cattle, horses, men, and wagon at this low-water crossing. It's everything the store owner said it would be—like a huge anvil-shaped boulder in the middle of the stream.

I start down the easy slope to cross. "The creek's so low a good-sized herd could drink it dry."

"Probably so."

I stop in the middle of the stream to touch the rock. Sometimes you need to touch something to make it real and a lasting memory. I reach to scoop a handful of the crystal clear water for a drink.

"Wouldn't do that if I was you. You don't know what's in it, especially with it being this low. I watched many a good man die because of bad water at Vicksburg."

I decide I'm not as thirsty as I thought I was.

We ease over to the other side where wagon wheels carved ruts in the limestone bedrock on the far bank.

Lummy stops. "Many a wagon made the crossing here to leave grooves in rock like that."

We find a secluded spot by a small stream a hundred yards or so away from the round rock. Just out of sight from any passersby.

I offer, "How about we camp here on these limestone slabs? Beats getting sand everywhere you don't want it."

Lummy nods and dismounts to care for our mounts as I lay out bedrolls in the grass between patches of bedrock and start supper. We need rest. And food.

And baths.

"Uncle Lummy, what are we going to do if the law catches up with us?"

"I guess we tell them the truth."

"That could land us in jail, you know."

"Maybe, maybe not."

"Guess you're right. We better get our stories straight if a badge or two happens along."

"We're only a good day's ride from the Kimbrell ranch, you know. I'd like to leave at dawn to get some distance betwixt us and them, if all right with you."

"I know, but there's only two of us. I think they'd be lookin' for a band of people, and probably not a lady traveling with 'em either."

"All right then. I think I gotta plan. Be back in a minute."

I grab my saddlebags and head into the bushes for a few minutes. I emerge wearing the patched up dress I used to trick Tom Kimbrell with in the saloon that night. Way too frilly for me, but it should do the trick. "What do ya think?"

Lummy's mouth drops. "Martha, you've come to see me." He shakes his head like he's got a bug in his ear. "Sorry about that, Marion. It happens sometimes. You look beautiful."

"You really loved Martha, didn't you?"

"With all my heart, just like I did Susannah. Martha gave me two beautiful daughters."

"Dell and Rosey?"

"Yeah, they each have qualities she carried, but they both got her beauty." Lummy squints to fight back a tear. "Miss them girls a lot. I'm looking forward to spending time at Rosey's house soon."

"That'll be good for you, Uncle."

"So what's your plan?"

"You're my uncle who took me in when my folks died. You're escorting me to Fort Worth where we plan to buy a small ranch, and find me a husband."

"A husband? Really?" He snickers. "Can you play that part?"

"As much as that idea is as foreign as to me as anything I could think of, me and Miss Lillie Langtry can take on any part a play requires. And besides, I think it makes for a good and easy lie to pull off. I bat these eyelashes at those boys, heck, they'll want to be marrying me and forget all about what happened in Austin."

"Guess you're right. So I play the part of the loving uncle who caters to your every whim?"

"Now you're getting the picture, U-u-uncle." I bat my eyelashes at him like a daughter who just asked her father to buy her the latest and fanciest new dress in the window of the ladies garment shop in town. "Think of Dell and Rosey if we have to get out of a jam with the law."

"I can do that." He studies me for a moment. "You *are* pretty, Marion. You remind me of my Martha. Sorry 'bout callin' you Martha."

"Not to worry. I take it as a compliment, Uncle."

"Good, let's get set up. I want to make the most of our time to rest and get an early start."

I nod. "Dawn it'll be."

Lummy finishes brushing down the horses and grabs his saddlebag. "Be back in a bit. I need to wash over a week's worth of stank off."

I wave him off, thinking the same thing now that I take notice of my armpits knowing other unmentionable places need a good washing. I slip out of the dress and get back into my trail clothes, but freshen up my hair to make me look at least a little girlish in case we have visitors wearing badges. I hang the dress on a bush like I'm trying to let the wrinkles fall out of it.

I get the biscuits going in the little cast iron oven, the ham sizzling in a small skillet, and beans bubbling in a pot that's just the right size for one can, all cooking utensils Lummy carries with him. The man's got stuff, but the stuff he carries reveals he's planning on being alone for a while.

I set out plates and forks trying to make the scene as homey as I can. I have everything just about set when two men slip out of the brush behind me quiet as a couple of rabbits. I catch them out the corner of my eye stalking slowly, thinking they are slipping up on me. I don't turn around, but I do lay my hand on Lummy's knife in my belt. The Derringer I have tied to a leather string dangles inside my shirt. They stop within six paces from where I'm squatted.

"Well, well, well, look what we have here. Just what I've been lookin' for and just what I've been needin'," a crackled old voice says.

The other man just snickers and takes a step forward. "And she's sure got the backside for it, Uncle." He walks a heavy step. From what I tell in his voice, he's big, young, and way too eager.

The older man slaps his hand across the young man's chest to stop him. "No, Clem, we better not. The Buyer'll have our hides if we soil this dove."

I bounce just a little, readying myself to spring like a cat. I turn my head slightly. "You men do not want to do this. Just leave me be, and we'll all be the better for it."

"No, little lady, we're gonna eat that fine meal you're fixin' for us. You're gonna serve us good and proper, like we deserve."

They both make smacking sounds like dogs licking their lips. My stomach sours from their smell. The older man's voice cackles like a crow. "My, my, the Buyer's gonna love this 'un. She's shapely and real pretty."

The younger one laughs. "To hell with that one-eyed bastard. Let's get our take and then bring her to him. When we're done, we'll dress her up in that purty dress hanging on that limb over there. The Buyer won't be the wiser."

They rush me, and I pivot on my heel like a child's toy top, throwing my right leg out to keep me from falling over. I yank Lummy's knife from my belt just as the young man reaches both arms out to grab me. I sink the knife into his thigh to the bone. He squeals like a stuck pig and bleeds like a sieve. The bloody knife slips from my hand, stuck deep in his leg. The older man pushes his partner away, but I'm up in a flash with the Derringer stuck in his eye before he can take a swing at me. He backs up, and I follow, keeping the pocket pistol jammed in his eye. He lifts his hand to slap the gun from my hand but stops when I push it deeper into his eye socket.

"Do it. Please do it. I'd like to see what this little ball would do to your rotten skull. It'll be bigger going out than going in, I can promise you that."

The older man freezes and Clem lays on the ground moaning. I push the old man back with the two shot Derringer barrel. He stumbles to the ground.

"I should sure as hell shoot the both of you. Throw your guns and knives over here to me. You even act like you're gonna put your finger near a trigger, I'll sink a ball in each one of your heads before you can say grits and ham."

I kick their pistols and knives behind me. I reach to where the knife is still stuck in Clem's thigh. I yank it hard so he won't forget it. I hold the Derringer on them as I wipe the blood from the knife on the boy's shirt and return it to its sheath. I back away a bit to get my six-shooter from the holster that's hanging from a log by the fire.

The older man whimpers, "We didn't mean no harm. Just wanted to have a little fun. That's all."

"No harm? Raping and molesting ain't any bit of fun. That's what's wrong with y'all. You're as blind as everyone else in this country, thinking you can do whatever you want to helpless women. Well, boys, I ain't helpless!" I rush over, six-shooter in one hand and Derringer in the other and press them against the two men's heads. "I ought'a... how can you sorry hound dogs even live with yourselves?" Sweat drips down the sides of my head, my hair soaked. "I should shoot you both right now." I cock the pistol and shove the older man's head back with the barrel.

Clem cries out, "Don't shoot him, please. He's all I got. My ma and pa died, and he took me in. He's my uncle, and well, uh, I ain't too smart."

"And you think him getting you into a spot like this is smart? You're both dumber than two sacks of hog crap and worth even less." I stare into the older man's eyes. "What's your name?" He says nothing. I kick him in the ribs. "I won't ask again."

He growls like a treed raccoon, "Josiah. My name is Josiah."

"Well, you best be finding out what that name means and get about living up to it."

Josiah wilts. "I don't know who no Josiah was, and I—"

"He was a good king in the Bible, you dumb-as-a-mule dern fool. Says he found the Good Book that'd been lost for a long time, dusted it off and started living by it. Changed his life. You best do the same, you ignert jackasses."

Josiah looks up. "I can't read."

Clem raises his hand like a kid in a classroom. "I can."

"Good, 'cause I just happen to have an extra copy of the Bible with me, and I'll even mark the spot about Josiah."

"So, you lettin' us go?"

"I don't know, but I'm lettin' you both live." Yeah, I do. Lummy took an oath not to kill another man if he didn't have to one time. I think I'll try starting right here with these two.

Josiah clasps his hands together like he's about to pray. Then quick as a copperhead grabs my ankle and pulls me to the ground. He's up before I can get up, but I shoot his kneecap. He hops around on one leg holding his knee like he's at a county fair square dance.

I get up and point the pistol at Josiah. He stops his dance and smiles. These two will never learn, and I'm not leaving him to do the same thing to someone else. I cock my weapon. I squeeze the trigger but a swift hand lifts the gun up as it fires.

"This ain't the way, Marion."

I turn with fevered eyes and fire in my cheeks as Josiah falls to the ground holding his knee, moaning. "And why not? They'll just do it again, to some other unsuspecting innocent woman. You know I'm right."

"I do." Lummy lowers my arms. "But you're better'n this… and I don't want you to lose your soul for these two wastrels, or how did you say it, two worthless sacks of hog crap?"

"So what do we do with them?"

"Take 'em into Round Rock and leave 'em with the law. Who knows, there may be a bounty on their heads. I'm sure this ain't the first time these miscreants have broken the law."

"Why would you want to do that?"

"We take in two ne'er-do-wells like these, that'll be the story that follows us. We'll take 'em to town first light and get out of here."

"All right, your call."

Lummy ties the two up to a couple of cedars twenty feet away, each facing a tree away from camp.

I want to puke. "Good, I don't want to even see their faces. It'd surely ruin my appetite."

"I got 'em cinched down pretty good, but do keep an eye on 'em. This kind can be pretty slippery. I'm goin' to take that bath I promised myself."

"You haven't bathed yet?"

"I spent a bit of time with Creator, you know, talking things over. Somethin' told me to come back to camp."

"I see, well, don't dally, it won't be long before supper will be ready."

"Sounds good." He trots off but stops and grins. "You handled yourself pretty good back there, Marion."

"That ain't my first dance."

"I know, but I'm still proud of you."

My heart softens, and I whimper a bit after he leaves. It's been way too long since somebody said anything like that to me. Somebody who meant something to me. It was Uncle Silas before he died in the courthouse fire. But why shouldn't I expect those words to come from Lummy? He is Uncle Silas's nephew, after all.

✶ ✶ ✶

I WALK TO the edge of camp to yell to Lummy that supper is ready when I see him walking my way with a small blanket tied around his waist, wet hair hanging limp. Dang, he's still quite the man. Broad shoulders, sinewy muscles, six feet six, and a mane like Samson. He's got to be over fifty but still has the look of a Greek god, at least like the statues I saw in a school picture book. He's dang sure good-looking and would make any woman a fine husband. I think he's done with marrying and all that goes with it. I can't blame him. How does love come after losing the one you loved the most? For him twice. I take a deep breath. Ain't for me to know. An old buck like Lummy just wants a quiet cane thicket to enjoy solitude, stillness, silence, and rest. What am I saying—I haven't even experienced my first real love yet.

Lummy looks up. "What?" He looks down and realizes he's half naked. He turns three shades of red. "I-I, I needed to wash my clothes. They smelled worse than I did." He makes sure his blanket is secure and hurries past me. "Give me a minute to get myself straight before you come back, if you don't mind."

I smile and laugh. "I don't mind, Uncle. But just be glad we're kin, otherwise...." I just let it go, but belly-laugh as he trots over to the fire and the blanket splits in the back to show his butt. I don't say anything. He's embarrassed enough. He ducks behind some bushes. It is funny, though.

I get to the fire just in time to find my biscuits brown, the ham cooked just right, and the beans good and tender. Lummy hangs his wet clothes near the fire. He's changed into another set of clothes. I wish I'd done that. Mine are pretty rancid too. I fix him a plate and hand it to him with a cup of cool water.

"Thank you, Marion. This is real nice. I'd about had enough of moldy biscuits, jerky, and water."

"You didn't even stop to eat?"

"Not after I went back to Winnfield and Aaron told me y'all went after Caroline. When I walked into Rainy's gun shop, Aaron said, 'I knew you'd come back. I've heard too much about you.' He told me what was what, and I grabbed a few things from the store next door and lit out like a fox after a cottontail. I figured it to be about four hundred miles, but decided I'd get there before you goin' cross-country."

"And you did, just in time. How'd you know where we went?"

"Aaron told me. So when I got to Austin, I went to that same saloon, and they were all up in arms about a ruckus that happened in town concerning a lady with bells on her breasts who took a piece of Tom Kimbrell's pride. People were laughin' all over town about it. It was pretty easy from there on in." Lummy squints. "I wasn't goin' to tell you this because I didn't know how you might take it, but I was there—"

"In that saloon when I played the harlot?"

Lummy grins and nods, then laughs out loud. "Maybe I shouldn't have said anythin'."

I huff like a deer snorting at a stranger in the forest. "You dirty rotten sack of snakes. Why didn't you tell me?"

"I just did. But I didn't know you then, Marion."

"Tom Kimbrell almost killed me in that alley. If it wasn't for—"

"I was there just in case. When I saw Wesley Wood with you, I knew."

"Just in case? And you just watched us battle Tom Kimbrell and his gang."

"You didn't need me."

I think about that for a moment. "You're right. We needed to do that ourselves, didn't we?"

"Exactly. I'm sure it was Rainy's plan all along."

"It was, if I know Rainy Mills… and I'm sure that I do now."

"Yes, you do." Lummy nods and settles in to eat his food.

I watch a man who eats his food slowly, savoring every bite. He needs rest. From the ride to Austin. From the battle with Tom Kimbrell. From once again having to do what's best for his son, Elzey, and not what he wants to do. Lummy needs rest from life. This man has seen the worst of what humans can do to each other. He's also done it. The way he ended Tom Kimbrell's life, with no remorse or concern, no… I shudder at that kind of hellish determination and willpower. I'm fortunate to have Lummy ride with me.

We enjoy our meal, Lummy takes care of the cookware and plates, and we chat just a little before he drops into deep sleep that bears a light snore. I have a hundred questions, but this man needs time.

About a half hour into his nap, Lummy wakes up snorting and snickers at himself. "You takin' a bath tonight?"

I was hoping he wouldn't ask. "I think I'll wait for the next opportunity up the trail."

Lummy nods. "Those two knotheads got you rattled?"

"Nah, not at all. Like you said, I handled myself pretty well back there. It's the thought that the law might be close behind us that makes me not want to be naked in a creek if they were to show up."

"It sure felt good, that cool clear water."

"Yeah, I bet it did. But a cool water bath can't take the heat out of being pursued."

"Suit yourself, but try to stay downwind of me, if you don't mind."

"Shut up, Uncle Lummy."

He rolls over and laughs as I snuggle up in my blanket to ward off the chilling night. I guess this'll mean we have to hurry along. I could use a bit more time on the trail to sort things out myself, but there's one thing that keeps plaguing my mind and won't stop. It's not the law. It's the Buyer.

FIND THE LAW, WHEN THE LAW IS LOOKING FOR YOU

7:30 a.m., August 25, 1886

WE LEAVE EARLY to drop the two miscreants off at the sheriff's office in Round Rock. I have to admit that I'm pretty nervous about facing the law. I'm not sure how I want to handle this. I've been in and out of sheriffs' and marshals' offices on and off since long before I started my quest to find the Buyer. But if we fit the description of any of those associated with killing Tom Kimbrell, we could be in a world of hurt. I lead the pack with Lummy trailing behind with the two men we caught in tow—bound and gagged on their horses. Onlookers give us much more attention than I like. It's a gamble being put on display like this, but I agree with Lummy, it's worth the risk.

We hitch our mounts to the post and Lummy leads the ne'er-do-wells' horses around to do the same. He steps between their horses, reaches up and grabs them by their jackets at the shoulders, and yanks them off like pulling corn head height.

I snicker as they hit the ground and moan. "Why'd you do that?"

He gives an ironic half grin. "For show. Now the good citizens will know if we're willin' to do that, these boys must be bad news, and we mean business."

He's right. As soon as he pulls them to their feet and marches them to the door of the sheriff's office, people just go on about their business like they've seen this many times before.

The sheriff sits back in his chair as we walk in, sipping his coffee. Lummy brings both men by their collars through the door and shoves them to the floor in front of his desk. The sheriff sets his coffee cup down. "Was that show of force necessary?"

I blurt out in the best aggravated tone I can master, "Sure the heck—"

Lummy pats the air to calm me, but I don't want to be calm. I want to yell, scream, and kick. He only has to say one word to tell me I need to be quiet. "Marion." It's the way he said it that makes me trust him, and do what he says.

The sheriff chuckles and leans forward. "I'm Sheriff Shad Griffin, Shad being short for Shadrach, one of the three Hebrew children. Who might you two be?"

"Nice to know you. I'm Marion, and that's my Uncle Lummy, that's short for Columbus."

Lummy grins at my sarcastic introduction. "My Uncle Silas served in the second war against the British with three men their commander called the Three Hebrew Children. One of them was called Shadrach too."

"Is that right? Where, might I ask?"

"Fighting in the Creek War and then in the Battle of New Orleans."

"Huh, that's interesting. I take it you were the one wronged in the matter regarding these two, given your state of mind, little darlin'." The sheriff stands and leans over his desk to get a better look at the two men lying on the floor.

"Dang right I was. And what do you mean, little darlin'? I'll have you know—"

"Simmer down, Marion, he's just bein' nice." Lummy takes my shoulder and squeezes it gently with his bear paw-sized hand. "You're upset, and rightfully so because of what you went through. So you best let me handle this, all right?"

I am upset, and at him. I've done this several times, but for some reason Lummy takes charge. But I do as my uncle says. Gentle as the lamb, the craftiness of a wolf—that's Lummy. I shut up. Really, I need to. I don't know what's gotten into me. I sound like a whiny child crying for her momma. I'm starting to sound more like a hurt little girl than a hunter of men. For some reason I feel the need to prove myself to Uncle Lummy. He's not expecting it or even promoting it. It's me. I think it's because he's becoming important to me, like Uncle Silas was.

Sheriff Griffin smacks the top of his desk with his palm. "I've been lookin' for these two wastrels for some time now, the slippery snakes that they are. Glad you brought 'em in. How'd you come across 'em? How'd you do it?"

"We were campin' down by the round rock when they slipped up behind my niece here whilst she was cookin' supper. They planned to have their way with her. I was off having a bath in the creek when I heard some commotion in our camp. Found these ruffians circling my niece like two wolves on a calf. So I took them down, and they stayed tied to a cedar tree all night."

The older man kicks at Lummy, and yells, "That ain't how it happened, and you know it."

Lummy slowly squashes the man's ankle with the heel of his boot. "You done?" The older man groans and stops talking.

Griffin scratches his ear and squints. "You do this by yourself?"

"I did. I learned a few things fightin' at Vicksburg that I ain't never forgot."

"Hand to hand?"

"Yes, sir. Stockade Redan on the Graveyard Road under General Shoup."

"Rebel?"

"Yes, sir. Twenty-Seventh Louisiana Volunteer Infantry."

"I was with the Forty-Seventh Ohio just across Mint Springs from you boys... oh, what did they call that fort? It escapes me now."

"The Twenty-Seventh Looseana Lunette."

He points his finger at Lummy. "That was it. Sherman thought you boys would run when we went up the hill in front of us on May nineteenth. He was wrong. You didn't. Must've been a thousand muskets laying down fire on us when you rose up as one man to stop us. Lord have mercy, that was awful." The sheriff hangs his head, shaking it slowly. "We lost some really good boys that day, and three days later in the second assault on the twenty-second." He takes a deep breath and sits up straight. "Haven't had to think about those days in a long time, Lummy. Hope I don't have to again for a long time."

"Yeah, me too. That was the day we fought with knives, pistols, short swords, bayonets, and rifle butts. I actually fell over into the pit in front of the lunette with a passel of bluebellies, excuse me, I mean Union soldiers and…." Lummy starts to sway a bit.

I steady him. "Sheriff, if you don't mind, could we please finish our business? You see, when he gets to talking about this for very long, he gets these—"

"War dreams, right?"

"Yes, sir."

"I understand. I have an occasional one myself. Terrible memories a man doesn't have much control over. They come as they please, do as they please, without much warning. My wife has had to splash water in my face some nights when I start reaching for my gun thinking the Rebs are charging us."

I'm saddened at what both these men have had to go through. "Yes, sir, I cannot imagine."

Griffin shakes his head. "She was a good woman to stay with me through all of that, thick and thin."

I soften my tone a little. "Any war hero deserves a good woman to go through life with, making it better for him… trying to bring a little joy into his heart again."

"I appreciate you sayin' that. She certainly did. Fever got her two years ago, God rest her soul." He stares out the window at a passing wagon. "I do miss her, but, back to the matter at hand."

"I'm sorry, Sheriff Griffin, I truly am."

"I appreciate you saying that. Until you've lost a love like I did when she stepped through the thin veil to the other side, I'm not sure a person really knows what love is. That make any sense?"

"Yes, sir, it does. I lost my sister a few years back. Don't think I'll ever get over that."

"Then you understand, at least in part."

"Yes, sir, I do."

Lummy presses the owl claw into his wrist. There's a bit of blood. He comes back from his war dream, grins, and says, "I'm all right, niece."

Sheriff Griffin smiles sadly. "Watch yourself, there's a bit of blood there on your wrist."

Lummy wipes the speck of blood with his shirtsleeve. "An old Choctaw friend gave me that to—"

"Bring you back when the war dreams try to take over? Yeah, my wife gave me this for the same reason." He holds out a piece of leather tied around his wrist with a small flint arrow point on it. "I do the same thing, my friend."

"They seem to come more often as I get older."

"That they do."

Lummy wipes his face with his sleeve. "Sheriff Griffin, you might want to feed and water these two slop-eatin' hawgs. We weren't in any mood to accommodate 'em in any way after what they did."

Griffin snickers. "Don't blame you, and call me Shad if you will, the both of you. You could've just killed 'em like those folks did with that Tom Kimbrell Gang down in Austin a couple days ago for all I would've cared. Talk about some wicked folks, those Kimbrells. They've done horrible things I heard, especially back in Louisiana somewhere."

"Wouldn't know anythin' 'bout that, Shad. We're just tryin' to mind our own business, but some folks don't like it when you try to go about life peaceable-like. They take it for weakness. Well, as you can see, we ain't weak." Lummy fans his hand in front of his nose and snickers. "The young one there, Shad, you might throw him in the water trough out front. He filled his britches on the way here. Smells to high heaven."

"Yeah, you're tellin' me. I get the drift over here." Shad shuffles a few papers. "I'll need you to write your statement of what happened and sign it for me, both of you. I'll carry it to court when these two go before the judge. It'll only take you a couple of minutes. Just give me the facts. Then you're free to go, and I appreciate you both."

Lummy nods to me. "You don't mind doin' it, Marion, do you? You know I don't write too well, and I'm startin' to feel a bit poor."

I write it short and sweet, and to the point. No elaboration. We need to get going before Shad asks more questions about us.

"I'll be happy to do it, Uncle. Maybe you should take a seat, rest yourself for a moment?"

Lummy sits in a chair and stares out the window. As I write a single paragraph, Shad pulls a couple of wanted posters from a stack on his desk. Lummy and I sign it, and I hand him the statement. He files it in a desk drawer.

"You folks are in luck. There's a reward posted for both of them. A hundred dollars for the old man and fifty for the kid. Besides their own rapin' and stealin', it seems they also were known to help young innocent women disappear into parts unknown, but not before they had their 'fun.'"

That catches my ear like a coyote hearing the step of a rabbit sneaking through the brush. I want to question them right here, right now. I lean in but Lummy stops me before I ask a question. I think I know what he's doing.

"That's a lot of money, Sheriff. Do we get it now?"

"Yeah, just let me write up this voucher. You can take it to the bank across the street when it opens at eight. Just sign right here."

We both hesitate, but Lummy quickly conjures up a fake last name. We can't be traced back to Winn Parish, and giving his real name, and possibly mine, would certainly do that. If he doesn't give any names, that'll look suspicious too.

"Just make it out to me, Columbus Ford."

"And where might you be from, Mister Ford?"

"I was born in Missip, but haven't been there in a long time. My wife died a few years ago, so I've been driftin' here and there, workin' where I could find it. Just ain't ever got over her passin'."

As Shad fills out the voucher, he offers, "Sorry to hear that, Mister Ford. Seems we have more than one thing in common, don't we? Fighting a damnable war and losing our wives."

Lummy stiffens. "Don't care to speak on either matter much more, if it's all the same to you, Shad. Meaning no disrespect, of course. I ain't rightly healed up about all that yet, losing my wife or the war."

He looks up and hands the voucher to Lummy. "None taken, Mister Ford. Just sign this form saying you received the voucher and our business is concluded."

Lummy hands the voucher to me. "My niece and I appreciate this. It'll go a long way to gettin' us on down the trail."

"Where you good folks headed?"

I can sense Lummy is getting a bit uneasy though he doesn't show it. I smile as pretty as I can. "He's escorting me back home to Red River Station. I was visiting my cousins in Austin and rode the stagecoach down, but I wanted to experience riding and camping on my way back home. So my uncle here was kind enough to come to Austin and take me home."

Before the sheriff can ask another question, Lummy pats the air. "Sorry, Sheriff, she'll keep us here until Sunday unless I make her stop."

I duck my chin into my chest, look up and smile, playing the innocent and clueless little girl that I sure as heck am not. I almost laugh, but I just give a schoolgirl giggle and say, "So sorry, Mister Shad, I know you must be a busy man. Thank you for calming me down and taking these men to get their due justice."

"My pleasure, young lady."

Lummy takes each of the criminals by the back collar and starts to pull them up on their feet. "Can I help you get these undesirables into their cells?"

"No, no need to do all that. You good folks have been a big help and the town of Round Rock thanks you." He stands and thrusts out his hand. Lummy takes it and Shad promptly sits back down. "Feel free to be on your way. Keep your eyes peeled out there. These aren't the only two ruffians traipsing around these parts."

As we leave, Lummy turns just before he closes the door, and asks, "Shad, just one more thing, if you don't mind?"

"Sure, anything, if I can."

"Anythin' I need to know about these people who steal young women and sell them off? That is, since where headin' north and all. You can see why I'm askin'." He points his thumb at me.

"I can. Give me a minute." He walks around his desk and leads the prisoners to the cells in the back.

Lummy and I step back in. He shrugs and waits until the sheriff is out of earshot. "Maybe we'll get a lead?"

The jingle of the keys opening and closing the cell door are too much like the bells above most business doors these days. I cringe and feel a sharp pain in my gut. I pull my pants belt away from my belly. It's a bit tight anyway.

Lummy whispers, "You all right?"

I lean over. "Yeah, I'm good. It's just those doggone little bells that flash memories into my head and make my stomach turn."

"I know exactly how you feel." He elbows me. "Shush, here he comes."

Shad shuts the door and turns the lock with the key. "Sorry about that, but too many wagging tongues and listening ears all around, especially out the back window of the jail late at night. Anyway, these bastards, excuse my language, Marion, who snatch girls and women have a system of communication better'n anything I've ever seen. So, what I tell you I don't want on the street out front in less than an hour. With those two involved in some way, I'm sure that would be the case. The one-eyed man has spies everywhere. That's why it's hard to catch him. Nobody's even come close to finding him. Heck, we don't even know his name. Slippery as a greased snake."

I offer, "When they were still behind me, Mister Shad, the older man, Josiah, said, 'The Buyer's gonna love this 'un. She's real pretty.'"

Shad rubs his chin. "Yeah, they really go for the pretty ones. It means more money."

I can't help myself. "Why isn't anyone doing anything about catching these outlaws?"

Shad sits and lays his palms flat on his desk. "I ain't sayin' I agree with this, but the truth is, everybody's afraid of him and his gang of devils. He's too well-connected, has dirt on just about everyone I know, and he's got spies scattered all through Texas and parts of Oklahoma. And besides that, he's made a wicked trade into a profitable business for a lot of people, if you know what I mean."

Lummy growls, "So everybody just turns a blind eye?"

I look up at Shad. "Didn't someone say once that in the land of the blind, the one-eyed man is king?"

"I'm afraid so, Marion."

I resist wringing my hands. This is going to be harder than I thought. I hope I can convince Lummy to come along. I need his wisdom, his experience, his quick wit, and fighting strength if I'm going to do this, and survive.

Lummy is crafty with his questions. "Any particular place we need to avoid between here and Fort Worth?"

"Just about anywhere there's saloons and eatin' establishments. Give Waco a wide berth. I've been told they run women in and out of there fairly regular. But the place you want to keep a sharp lookout for them is when you hit Fort Worth. Girls have been stolen and now work in the brothels there. Stay away from Hell's Half Acre. It's where the Buyer's men blow off steam and keep an eye out for new prospects to steal. Too many people goin' west through Fort Worth not to make it a good place to snatch women. Heck, they've even taken women in broad daylight and no one dares to do a damn thing about it. The law there is as corrupt as it gets. If it was me, I'd avoid that place like the plague."

"Good advice, Shad. We'll take it."

Shad follows us to the door. "One other thing. Keep your eyes peeled, even in Red River Station. Any place along the Chisholm Trail is subject to their outlawry, especially now that the railroad hauls cattle north. The trail ain't used like it once was which makes it a good place to hide out. And besides that, it's rumored that the Buyer's hideout is in the mountains, somewhere in Oklahoma not far from the Arkansas line. That's all I know. I'll let you go now. I need to get back to work. You take care now."

We tip our hats and Lummy says, "Thank you, kindly, sir. We will, indeed, be careful."

We walk across the street to the bank as the owner opens the door. "You did that pretty well, Uncle Lummy. Didn't know you had it in you to be an actor."

He smiles. "An actor who plies his craft on the stage of life, I would say."

"How poetic, my fellow thespian. Where'd you learn that?"

"Oh, man I used to know, Mister Gilmore. Before the war, he posed as a gambler for the sole reason of winning slaves in card games so he could set them free."

"Sounds like an interesting man with a good heart."

"Creator never made a better man from the clay. I learned a lot from that man. He died tryin' to save my Susannah...."

Lummy wipes a tear. I don't ask what else he was about to say.

"I'll be wanting to hear more about that Mister Gilmore, if that's all right."

"We'll see."

I know what that damns means. Most likely, "no." Lummy opens the door to let me into the bank first. The bells at the top of the door jingle. I shiver like in wintertime.

"Devilish things."

Lummy eases the door shut. "There'll always be reminders. Let those bells remind you how you helped save Caroline and my son, Elzey."

He's right. Lummy gets our cash, splits it with me, and we ride out of town in a gentle lope.

After we get a ways out of town, Lummy asks, "You all right with what I did back there?"

"I wasn't at first, but I figured out what you were doing. You took all of the focus off of me and onto yourself so that the sheriff wouldn't think twice to ask who I was and what I'm about."

"You've got somethin' you gotta do. Don't know if you want me along till it's done or not, but I'll go as far as you want me to."

"You mean that?"

"I do, or I wouldn't say it."

"How about going with me all the way on this one?"

"The Buyer?"

"The Buyer."

Lummy squints and scratches the back of his neck. He leans up on his saddle horn like he's scanning the trail up ahead.

"What? You see something up there."

"Yeah, I do."

"Well, what is it?"

"The future."

"The future?"

"You know your Scripture. I'm countin' the cost like Jesus talked about, whether we have enough with us to take them."

"We don't even know how many they are yet."

"I don't need to know that. I just need to know who I've got with me. Sometimes a small army can do what a big one can't."

"The story of Gideon, right?"

"Maybe so, but the story of the Tullos and Wood brothers with a few extra trusted friends—twelve to be exact—hidin' under a big rock and takin' on the worst bunch of miscreants Choctaw County ever saw, is the story I know and believe. I was there."

"So you'll do it?"

"I will. I'm not actually lookin' forward to takin' down another cyclops like Dawg Smith. Pretty hard on the soul."

"That's another story I want to hear, start to finish."

"In time." He stops. "But when our business is done, I'll be leavin' in another direction, understand?"

"I do, and will wish you well when you go, only if you promise I get to see you again."

"Done."

"I like you, Uncle Lummy."

"I like you, too, niece."

Nobody has really liked me since my sister died. I've been fine with it up until now. That just changed.

THINKING THINGS THROUGH

It's not always easy to slow things down to consider them.

Late Afternoon, August 27, 1886

WE RIDE ALL DAY, stopping only to water the horses a couple of times. Without talking. At all. Lummy must need the quiet. I know I do. Too many people, too much noise, too much....

We skirt Waco near day's end, stopping only at the edge of town to get a couple of items we failed to purchase at the mercantile in Round Rock.

As we mount up, I can't help but compliment Uncle Lummy, "Been thinking about the part you played back there in Round Rock with that sheriff."

He grins. "Wasn't exactly my first dance either, niece. I've done that several times."

"Lie about who you are?"

"Call it righteous deception. It's all through the Scriptures."

"Guess you're right. Abraham, Moses, Joseph, the spies Joshua and Caleb, heck it's full of that kind of lying, I mean, what did you call it, righteous deception?"

"Lying for a greater good, I say."

"Or, lying to save your backside."

Lummy winks. "That too."

As we trot our horses away from town, I get to thinking. It's not easy getting over having to play a part I once really had to live—a whore in a Natchez, Mississippi brothel. But we needed to know where Caroline was and getting close to Tom Kimbrell that night in the saloon was the only way to find out. And save her before she was sold to the Buyer. Having to dress like a two-dollar painted hussy, wearing bells on my breasts to get that demon's attention, I shudder. I have to laugh a little, though. It did work. Every time my breasts jiggled, it'd ring those little door bells I took from Rainy's gun shop before we left Winnfield. Kimbrell couldn't keep his eyes off them. But he learned the hard way. He got his last look as Uncle Lummy gutted him. I cringe just thinking about that man and him attacking me in that alley in Austin.

But I don't think I've ever been more humiliated than being tied up out in the open—butt naked—hanging from a tree for all to see when Tom Kimbrell was about to slash Elzey's throat. When Lummy ripped his shirt off to cover my body, I barely had the wits to know my name. I've got to stop thinking about it. I try to put it out of my mind. It's not working. We ride a little farther, and I can tell Lummy is starting to wonder about me. I'm too fidgety and need to stop squirming in my saddle. I sniffle a bit, but not so that Lummy can see.

Lummy whispers, "You did it to save my son, Marion, and for that, I owe you my life."

"What? How'd you know I was—"

"Because I've had to reconcile too many of the same kind of thoughts in my mind for way too long too, you know."

We plod along for what seems like an eternity, but it's only a minute or two.

"I know what I did was right, but because of what I had to do, I can't seem to—"

Lummy adjusts his hat to block the sun from his eyes. "Deal with the hurt and pain? You know why?"

"I'm trying to figure that out."

"It's not who you are and not the person Creator made you to be. He never intended for you to go through what you did as a young woman, nor with Tom Kimbrell. It goes against everything you thought you'd grow up to be, right?"

"So why did God allow *me* to have to go through it?"

"Why not you? Creator knew he could bet his entire reputation on you like a gambler going all in with his poker chips, property, possessions, and pride."

"And why would he do that?"

"Because Creator believes in you, that's why. He made you for a special purpose that only you can fulfill, but don't you know Satan is roaming around trying to undo every one of us?"

"Like Job in the Bible, right?"

"Exactly. Like Job in the Bible."

I nod at him comparing me to Job, with a lump the size of an apple in my throat. I choke out, "So how do I get there? Heck, I don't even know what I'm asking."

"You do know your Scripture, right?"

"I do, why?"

"Somewhere Jesus said you have to become like a little child all over again to get into his kingdom."

"Yeah, I read that. It means you must become obedient, good, trusting, and without question as to what God wants you to do."

Lummy barks, "No!" but catches himself. "Sorry for yellin'. It just irritates the hell out of me when preachers make a Scripture say what they want just so they can get more control over people dumb enough to believe that they speak for God."

"So what do you think it means?"

"Now that's the right question, on anything havin' to do with the Good Book. Read it for yourself and let no man say he has the last word on what God says in Scripture. What applies to him might not fit who you are. We all see the Scriptures from where we're standing, and rarely from any other vantage point. People only can speak to what they know and have experienced. Ain't no way a preacher with lily white palms could ever know where you've been or what you had to go through. But too often they have simple answers for some of life's most difficult questions. When a preacher, or whoever, tells you 'this is what God says,' or 'this is what God means,' you look 'em dead in the eye and say these four words. 'As you see it.'" Lummy huffs like an old bear that's been disturbed from his sleeping. "And if they keep at you about it, just tell 'em to add an extra s to that 'As' and tell 'em that's what they are, all right?"

"You get pretty riled up about it, don't you?"

He leans up on his saddle horn. "Creator has become too good a friend to let ignert men with no life experience tell me or anybody else how to live. It's like a preacher who once railed on about how every Christian, every elder, every Bible class teacher should spend five minutes in hell. Said it would make them better. I say the pastor ought to have to live the sermon he preached, and he should spend that five minutes in hell himself. I told him as much too."

"What'd he say?"

Lummy throws his head back and laughs. "Not to come back."

"So, Uncle, what does it mean, 'Except ye be converted, and become like little children, ye shall not enter into the kingdom of heaven?'"

"You quote it well. As I see it, it's simple. Take a good look at the path you're on, see what you find, and then return to become what Creator always wanted you to be."

"And what does it take?"

"Bein' reborn, like comin' out of the womb all over again so you can become your true self, as Creator made you in the first place. 'Can't be a true human being,' as my old Choctaw friend, Dan Creekwater, was fond of saying, 'until you become your true self.'"

"How do I do that?"

"Been baptized?"

"Yeah, did that in the Mississippi River after Sissy and I took care of the folks who killed Uncle Silas."

"Good. So, here's what I did, and still do. It's all I can tell you, but it might help." He rubs the back of his neck. "Stop everything. Be still. Look fear, hurt, anger, and pain straight in the face and not turn away until you control them, and not the other way around. Facing the true you will be the hardest thing you'll ever do, if you choose to do it. It's like peeling an onion. Lots of layers have to come off before you get to the sweet part in the center, which for you and me is the deepest part of our soul. Us bein' cooks and all, you know that the more layers of the onion you peel away, the more tears have to be shed."

I feel as though I'm sitting at the feet of an Old Testament prophet who knows my soul inside and out. Lummy speaks truth in a way I can understand it. In a way, I can receive it without somebody banging a Bible on the top of my head.

"Then take an even better look at what lies beneath all that. You will find the Marion you started off being. The Marion you were supposed to be. The Marion you can truly be and live with… and be tolerably happy with."

"I don't know if I can get back there with all that's happened—getting raped, the killings, the hating, the anger, the violence…."

"That's why I came with you. To help set you on a course of gettin' yourself back so you won't wander around lost and aimless. That is, if you want my help."

"Oh, yes, I desperately need your help."

"You're gonna do what you're doing, Marion, huntin' men for reward, and I'm not askin' you to give that up. You just need some anchors to hold you steady when the stormy floods come… and come they will."

"So, how'd you—" I can't go on. It's like I'm a little girl all over again, needing a daddy's shoulder to cry on. Lummy's will do. I stop my horse and cry like a baby. He gets down, walks around to my right side, pulls me off my saddle, and sets me on a log. He just holds me. Like Uncle Silas used to do. I feel safer now than I have in my whole life. I find it within my soul to whisper, "Thank you, Lord."

"That's right." Lummy's soft growl-like voice reminds me of a cat purring as he tells me it's going to be all right. A big cat, though—powerful and strong yet gentle and understanding. I melt into his arms and finally pull myself together. I pull back a little and dry my eyes. I can see he's been shedding tears too.

"I feel so weak right now, Uncle Lummy."

"I know, me, too, but the Good Book also says, 'When I am weak, I am strong.'"

"Because we're handing our life back to Creator, the one who made us?"

"Yes, to the one who knows us the best and loves us the most."

"How do you do it, Uncle Lummy?"

He snickers. "I don't. That's why I left Choctaw County. To be alone. To be with Creator. Take some time. As much as I need… to think and search my soul. To find once again the anchors that have held me steady in the storm." Lummy looks to the sky. "And there's been a whole lot of storms, Creator."

"So why'd you ride along with me, if you want to be alone?"

"You are Uncle Silas's niece, and mine now. How could I not offer to teach you how to get through life with at least a bit of sanity left in you? And make no mistake, I'm never alone, nor do I ever really get lonely. Creator is always with me, always true, can always be trusted, and never forsakes or abandons." Lummy wipes his brow and smiles. "But I do enjoy the company of my beautiful niece."

We stand and Lummy eases over to his mount. I follow. He lays his hand on my shoulder. "You're a good person, Marion, and don't let anyone tell you different. You're just gonna walk a different path than most because of that heart of yours."

"You mean a heart like yours?"

"I reckon so."

I can't talk. The lump in my throat is simply way too big. This man is wise beyond anyone I've ever experienced, and I need his wisdom and help.

Lummy walks our horses off the trail. "Let's camp here tonight. Looks to be a spring down in the gulch there, and we'll be out of sight. I'm hungry too. You cookin' tonight?"

"Sure, Uncle Lummy. I'm glad to… but you're washing the dishes."

He throws his hands up in surrender. "For your cookin'? You bet I will."

As I fix supper, he tends the horses. We relax by a warm fire and talk into the night. Around midnight, the night birds stop calling and coyotes call far off in the distance.

I stoke the fire and add a couple of pieces of wood. "I have to know, Uncle Lummy. What caused your war dreams? I mean, can you finger the thing that did it to you?"

"Why do you want to know?"

"I need to know how to deal with mine. The thing that causes my dreams that ain't so pleasant."

"You sure it's the same thing?"

"Well, I figure what was done to me and the things I do because of what was done to me tend to make me do things I don't want to do but have to. That make any sense?"

"It does, and then you have daytime dreams, visions, or whatever you want to call them?"

"Exactly." I wait a moment. "Granny Thankful any help?"

"When she wants to be, but I swear that woman—"

"What?"

"Expects me to get it right. But I had to."

"Get what right?"

"To learn to do things like she does. Granny Thankful rarely does what she wants to do either. She does what Creator needs her to do. Big difference."

"Guess you're right. Okay then, what Granny Thankful needs to do happens by the order of Creator?"

I wait for Lummy to start talking. He's probably lost somewhere back in Vicksburg during the siege, ducking a bullet or a cannon blast, from the looks of his movements. He finally stops and lies back. Soon he's snoring softly. Tonight's not the night. I'll wait for another time.

✴ ✴ ✴

LUMMY SITS UP quick as if shots ring out and draws his pistol. The morning sun blinds him. His hair is poking out in all directions and lines like on a map crisscross his head where he slept on a rumpled part of his blanket. He looks a mess, and I can't help but laugh.

He holsters his gun and shakes his head. "Why'd you let me sleep so long this morning?"

"You needed it, and so did I."

"I wanted to get a jump on daylight, but… heck, I don't know, guess I did need the extra rest. Thanks, Marion."

I hand him a hot cup of coffee. "And just where were you headed like your head's on fire and your ass is catching when you woke up?"

Lummy ducks his head, and grins. "Nowhere in particular, I reckon. Just want to get to my daughter Rosey's place sometime before Christmas."

"She ain't going nowhere. She'll be right there. You need to take your time, take it easy, and enjoy the ride. We'll get to Fort Worth soon enough, and I'll spring a room for us. We can get real baths and a sit-down meal in a restaurant."

"I ain't had real sit-down food since I left Annie Fanny's place back in Vicksburg. She did have some pretty good cooks. My Martha was one of 'em before we got married. First time I saw her there, she had flour on her nose from baking. Thought I'd seen an angel. Guess I did. Then there was Jenny who we rescued from some slaving rascals on the way to take down the West-Kimbrell Gang, and.…"

"You know she passed."

"What?" Lummy hangs his head. "No, not Annie." Lummy stares off into the distance. He whispers, "God bless her righteous soul. There'll never be another Annie Fanny."

"Yeah, I'm sorry, but I thought you knew. I heard Ise and Elzey talking about it. I guess Elzey and Tarle were there when it happened."

"I figured she wasn't long for this earth when I went through Vicksburg on the way to Winnfield, God rest her soul. She was a good'n. I will miss that woman. Crazy as… well, she's probably still a mess, stirrin' things up in heaven right now, I'm sure."

"You've had some really good friends."

"The best ever made from the clay. Most of 'em are gone now. Except for Rainy, my brother Jasper, Ise, and the Wood brothers who ain't scared, I've just about outlived all my friends." Lummy rubs the back of his neck. "That's a shame too."

"Yeah, it stinks I bet."

Lummy holds his finger under his nose. "Talkin' about stank, I noticed you didn't take a bath a few days ago at Round Rock."

I snicker. "I didn't want to hang my naked behind out for all to see again." I rub my hands together. "I want to take a soaking bath in a hotel proper-like, with all those sweet smelly soaps." I realize I'm talking like my little sister who enjoyed such things. Now I'm the red-faced one.

"So there is a real girl underneath those men's clothes and unbearable stank?" Lummy laughs at his own joke.

I change the subject. "Feel better, don't you?"

"That I do, and thanks. Good food and good rest'll do that for you every time. It makes the world look just a little brighter, and I need brighter."

WE GET A good fire going after a long day's ride. With our bellies full, Lummy takes out a smoke. He offers me one, but I decline. Never started, never wanted to.

Lummy lights the little half-smoked cigar and takes a deep draw and blows a smoke ring. He takes another and carefully snuffs it out then returns it to his pocket. "That's 'bout all I ever want these days. Just a taste to calm my nerves. Don't want the habit, so I limit myself to two good draws and let it go."

I take in the rich tobacco aroma. It reminds me of Uncle Silas. "Sounds reasonable to me."

A pack of coyotes strike up a chorus as an owl swoops in to perch on a lone oak overlooking our fire. She hoots once, ruffles her feathers, and settles in for a spell.

Lummy chuckles. "Two good reminders, coyotes and an owl." He touches the owl claw bracelet on his wrist and presses it into his skin. He whispers, "I've carried the wrongs I've done way too long. They haunt me on every turn."

That last part isn't for this conversation. "Oh, yeah? Tell me about the coyotes and the owl, I mean."

"The first time I met Rainy Mills was in Louisiana runnin' for my life with a pack of coyotes nipping at my backside. I didn't even know what a coyote was in those days, but I was determined not to become their evening meal."

Lummy pulls out a quart jar of liquid and offers to pour a splash into my tin cup. I wave him off. "Never took to the taste of liquor."

Lummy shrugs. "Your loss." He pours half a cup and seals the jar. He takes a sip, settles back against the log, stretches his long legs out with his feet to the fire, and lets out a big sigh. "I saw a fire up ahead as I ran with everything I had. I ran so hard I started puking. When I dove into his camp, Rainy fired off several shots, killing two coyotes, if I remember right, and scattered the rest in a hurry. The man saved my life, and we've been friends ever since." He takes another sip. "Then we found out we're kin, well, sort of. Granny Thankful was a Mills before marrying a Tullos, and Rainy's father was Thomas Mills who was Granny's cousin or something like that, I forget." Lummy drains his cup. "That was the first time he saved me, and there's been other times as well. I'm sure it won't be the last."

"They don't come any better'n Rainy Mills, do they?"

"You got that right. Glad he's settled in with a good wife, son, and his gun shop in Winnfield. Nobody deserves it more than Rainy Mills."

I ask, "And the owl?"

"Yeah, the owl." Lummy touches the bracelet on his right wrist. He stares at it for a few seconds. "Dan Creekwater was his name. Gave this to me to help deal with my war dreams." He holds out the bracelet for me to see. "He was an old Choctaw who hid out when the government sent those poor people on a trail that brought a lot of tears. I met him on the road when I first took off after Susannah, Elzey's momma, and my first love." He snickers. "Called me Crazy Deer Dancer."

"I'll want to know that story."

"In time. Dan was always there for me, when I left the farm, then hid me out when I had some bad men lookin' for me in Choctaw County, and was there for me several other times… and he died savin' my life when I left Choctaw County." Lummy stares off into the distance. The owl above us lets out a series of hoots, and those in the distance call back. He smiles and says, "Dan Creekwater is with us tonight. There's nothing to fear."

I want to ask about Susannah, but I think better of it. Nope, I go ahead and ask, "She was really something, wasn't she, Susannah, I mean?"

Without a blink, the words roll off Lummy's tongue like honey dripping from a fresh plucked comb. "Prettiest, sweetest angel to ever land on the earth." He stops.

I want more, but I don't ask. I will later. Lummy sits up and stares off into the distance again as if trying to find something he expects to be there but is disappointed that it's not. He must be looking for Susannah.

Lummy snaps back to himself with a start. "Dan was one of the wisest men I'd ever met, truly a son of the forest and hills, creeks and rivers, and all that live there. Like I said, he hid me out once in McCurtain Creek Swamp back in Choctaw County when I didn't need to be found by wicked men wanting to string me up or shoot me. He helped restore my soul and get a better sense of myself. He helped me with the war dreams."

"Kinda like you're doing with me?"

"Reckon so." Lummy nods. "Dan stood shoulder to shoulder by my side when I needed to protect my family and helped me make one of the biggest decisions of my life...." He drifts out into the distance again, and snaps back. "He died saving my life when I was leaving Choctaw County for the last time to come out here. I'll never forget that man."

Lummy is repeating himself. That's all right. He's earned the right, and I wish I knew where he goes when he stares off into the distance. What am I saying? I do the same thing, at times.

We sit in silence for a bit, and then I ask, "What was the big decision he helped you make, pray tell?"

"Deciding whether or not to join the Yankee Army to help end the war after having served with the Confederate Army through the entire Siege of Vicksburg."

"Did you, join up, I mean?"

"I did, right there in Vicksburg where I fought the Yankees for over a year. Kinda comical, ain't it?"

"Yeah, but I'm sure it takes an uncommon devotion to be willing to fight for what you believe and then change your mind when you feel you've been wrong."

"Yeah, that was it. I fought for home and family with the Rebs, but it hit my heart pretty hard when I realized I had been wrong, at least for me, that is. Understand me now. I fought with a good conscience for the Confederate Army, as did my brothers. But Dan helped me understand that I needed to return to my original oath to the flag my... our Uncle Silas fought under at the Battle of New Orleans. Too many fought and died to keep all the stars on the one flag. I wanted Mississippi back on the original flag, the Stars and Stripes. My great-grandfather Captain James Mills in North Carolina died so we could be free in the first place. I just needed to get my head back straight on what I believed deep down. Dan helped me do just that."

"Uncle Silas told me about the Battle of New Orleans. How he was only eighteen years old and ran around with some hero named Colonel Sam Dale."

Lummy leans over. "It's a good story, ain't it?"

"It is, but I want to hear what you did to help stop the war between the Rebs and Yankees."

Lummy rubs his eye. "Tom Poole, my best friend growin' up, and I led the Yankee cavalry to our hometown of Bankston where they burned the factories that were making supplies for General Hood's army near Atlanta at the time. Poole and me, we didn't do any of the burning, but we did agitate a few folks when we left a message on the Choctaw County courthouse in Greensborough."

"What'd it say?"

He smiles. "If I remember correctly, it went something like, 'The twentieth star for Mississippi is now returned to the right flag. May it fly proudly over Choctaw County forever.' Yeah, that was it, and we signed our initials."

"That was exactly what it said, right?"

"It was. It was that important to keep in my memory."

"I bet that was trouble when you went back home."

"I did go back home after the war, and yeah, there was a bushel basket full of troubles, but Dan, my brothers, the Wood boys who ain't never scared, Rainy, Old Bart, Tom Poole, J. A. Killingsworth, most all now dead now, though a few are still alive… they all gave so much, and oh… my dearest Martha…."

Lummy drops his head and cries. I've never seen so big a man, so strong and wise, break down like this. I don't know what to do, so I do nothing but just sit with him. He's been through so much. But, he carries on. And I need to learn how to do the same thing.

"Too many good men and women dead and gone for such worthless reasons." He wipes his tears on his shirtsleeve.

"All those people must've thought the world of you."

"Yeah, and me of them. Family like them ain't tied to no bloodline.

It's a soulful thing that connects us in this great big Universe. They all gave of themselves in the hopes I would someday have the life I always wanted, and by God, I did have it for a good fifteen years. When Martha died, there wasn't no reason to stay in Choctaw County. I decided to drift through Vicksburg and Winn Parish, say my goodbyes and go wherever the wind took me." He laughs. "You see where that red sky storm wind took me. To the very sort of thing I wanted to be shed of."

"Yeah, but for good reason, don't you think?"

"Without a doubt—for Elzey, for you, and the rest." Lummy pulls the jar from his bag again. "Maybe a little more now that the fire's just right and our food is settled."

"So would you have wanted it any other way?"

"Oh, heck no, wouldn't have changed a thing. I've accepted my life, just like you'll have to accept yours."

"Tell me about those men and women, your friends, I mean."

"Can't right now, but I will on the way to Fort Worth. There'll be time."

"I'd appreciate it."

I study Lummy pressing the owl claw into his wrist. He pours a bit more of the liquid from the jar. "Yes, I do believe the fire's just about right and the talk is about to get thick." He holds out the jar.

"I-I, I'm not too partial to the spirits, like I said. Afraid I might like it too much. 'Sides, I need to keep a sharp eye and—"

"I understand." Lummy holds the jar up in the firelight and enjoys the glow. "By the way, this is Wood brothers' moonshine. Best there is, and it's made from the sweet waters of Aaron Wood's Spring in Choctaw County. It'll burn the hair off your tongue, give you a swift kick in the butt, and put you into a sweet sleep when you lay your head down to dream."

"Sounds like a man with experience."

"Only on occasions like this."

I hold out my cup. "Then I believe I'll take a swig, Uncle Lummy."

We stare into the fire. Sip our moonshine. For quite some time.

THE TALK

Clear the soul and the heart, mind and body will follow.

Evening, August 27, 1886

THE NIGHTS OUT here are cool and sweet. The gentle breeze makes me want to let my blanket swallow me. The fire is just as anyone would want it to be, warm, but not so hot as to make a body move back from it. The flames crackle and flash orange, yellow, red, green, and even blue in rhythm like the sights and sounds of a county fair. One large branch we pulled from a dead tree lies across the front of the blaze. Ten tiny flames, each several inches tall like candles, dance like girls in a chorus line like I saw in Natchez once.

Lummy crosses his feet and puts his hands behind his head. "This is why I came out here."

I nod. The silence is healing. A shooting star races across the sky to burn out to the north in the direction we're going. A sign?

"Guess you saw that?"

"I did."

"Granny Thankful taught me to stay watchful to where a shooting star burns out. She said it points the way to your next destination, and will make the path clear. She said they are good luck. Guess we need that where we're goin'."

"We definitely need the path of a clear eye, don't we?"

"Reckon so. In more ways than one. Rainy told me once that the Greeks believed a shooting star was the soul of the dead rising or falling depending on which way it moves. I think they believed that the gods had their eyes on Earth the moment the star fell, and they listened to people's wishes and made them come true."

"I heard that before."

"Dan Creekwater believed they were a warning of a coming war."

"That sounds more like the truth for us, doesn't it?"

"It does. He also said to never point at one because it will reveal your hiding place."

I snicker. "Maybe we can get one of the Buyer's men to point at a shooting star so we can find his hiding place."

"Not sure it works that way, but sounds like a good idea."

"Yeah, we need all the good ideas we can get."

"Another thought I heard from the priest in Vicksburg whom I visited many times. He said the Jews had a saying when they saw a shooting star that goes something like this, 'Blessed are You, Lord our God, King of the Universe, whose strength and might fill the world.' I tend to believe that one is true and can expect to have the help of heaven with us like Saint Michael, the Protector of God's People."

"I know that to be true because the Good Book says so."

"That it does. I tend to believe all of it, the Bible, the Greeks, and Dan."

"The way the preachers tell it, if it ain't in the Bible, it ain't truth."

"There they go again. It's almost comical the way they declare God's truth with half-wit minds, usually sold out to Sunday collections."

"Dang, Uncle Lummy, you've got an interesting point of view."

"Well, here's my point of view. Follow me on this, and again, this is as I see it. Truth is truth, right?"

"Yes."

"God is truth, yes?"

"Yeah."

"All truth comes from God, correct?"

"Absolutely."

"Then what does it matter who says it? It all came from God."

"Guess you're right."

"Even Satan, the Father of Lies, can speak truth when it suits him. I know. I've heard him."

"That ain't good."

"That's why it's best to listen to God, form your own beliefs, and pay attention to whose voice you're hearin', even in church." Lummy's breathing hard. "Guess I got a little lathered up there, didn't I?"

"Well, if you're bucking for a full collection plate, that ain't happening in the church of the wild ole Chisholm Trail."

He holds out his hat. I dig in my pocket and throw in a one-cent piece. He fishes it out and slips it into his pocket, and laughs. "That's about what all that gassin' was worth."

"Yeah, but I could use a good shooting star to point me the right way, Uncle Lummy."

"Yeah, that'd be good." He studies the heavens like he's expecting a shooting star any moment. "So did you like the Wood brothers' moonshine made from the sweet waters of Aaron Wood's Spring?"

"It's smooth, and when I sipped it, I felt warm from the top of my head to the bottom of my feet."

Lummy grins.

"You gonna have your two puffs on that worn-out stub of a cigar?"

He snickers. "Maybe in a minute."

He's thinking really hard by the way his head is a bit wrinkled up. "Something on your mind, Uncle Lummy?"

"I was hopin' maybe you did, if you don't mind me askin'."

"Go ahead, shoot."

"So Marion," Lummy asks in a gentle voice like the cooing of a dove, "what's your next step?" He lights his half-smoked cigar and takes a long draw on it. "Guess I need to calm my nerves a bit." He twirls between his fingers the small lighter stick with a smoldering ember at the end. The stub of a cigar goes out with one good puff. Lummy looks at it. "Dang, I was lookin' forward to this." He tosses the butt into the fire. "Need to give it up anyway." He mumbles something about the once bright fires that have gone out in his life, the direction he's going, then his words trail off.

I don't ask what he's saying. I'm trying to come up with an answer to a question I don't want to answer right now, but this man is family, my uncle, and I need him in my life. He's traveled a road I'm just getting started on and his wisdom is what I need right now. That, and....

A voice whispers from the brush, faint, though clear, *"Now is the time to open your heart."* I turn sharply to see the flowing robes of who I know must be Granny Thankful.

"Right now? I just want to sit here for a minute or two."

Lummy doesn't even hear me. He must be lost in his thoughts a thousand miles away.

I don't want to talk, but I need to. I take a chance. "I guess before I do anything, Uncle Lummy, I need to get over being hung out naked for the whole world to see back there and what I helped do to those people, even as bad as they were. I know I joke about it, but don't think that I've ever played such a dramatic role like that scene in one of those stage plays."

I snicker at that God-awful sight. I shudder at a thought that sends me back to the orphanage in Natchez where the preacher running the place took advantage of a naïve young girl who had no choice but to run away and work in a whorehouse to keep her little sister from the devilish clutches of demon who called himself a man of God. He got his. I made sure of that, just like I did when I killed the preacher when we fought the Kimbrells in that red sky storm. I had no mercy then and no remorse now for doing either of those necessary deeds. I lift my head and take a deep breath.

"It's hard to kill people, even the bad ones. Still, it was good and right to end Tom Kimbrell's life, wasn't it? I mean, I don't know, what I'm saying is, I...."

Lummy whispers, "I understand the need to get over something as horrible as all of that."

I throw a rock into the fire and sparks fly up like so many lightning bugs. "And I need to rest a bit."

"We got all the time in the world, Marion. The Buyer ain't goin' nowhere, just like you told me about Rosey. We'll get him."

I shift my butt to a different position to keep my leg from going to sleep. "I need time to think."

"I told you I once took several months to make a decision about my next step. It was a big one."

"What'd you do?"

"I spent the better part of the winter of sixty-three with my old Choctaw friend, Dan Creekwater. I ended a bully named Lester's life and the Confederate Home Guard in Choctaw County wanted to nail my hide to the wall for it." Lummy scratches his arm. "Dan helped me get my soul back first so I could think straight to make a good decision."

"Dan did that for you?"

"Yeah, well there were few others who whispered in my ear from time to time. My pastor, my mother, and—"

"Granny Thankful?"

"I wouldn't have made it this far without Granny Thankful."

"What was the big decision again?" I know we've had this discussion already to a point. I say don't anything but just let him talk. I'm sure I'll pick up something new in this telling.

"Whether to join the Union Army or not. Actually, I enlisted in the First Mississippi Mounted Rifles there in, of all places, Vicksburg. I wanted to get to the source of the problem."

"Was that when you joined the Yankee Army?"

"Yes, in my small part of the world, that was the decision I wrestled with. Leading Yankee cavalry to my own hometown of Bankston so they could burn the manufactories was one of the toughest things I had to do. But, I wanted to end the war."

I jump in, "And I want to end this war the Buyer wages against innocent women. Did it help to do the thing you hated the most at the time?"

"I believed I had no other choice, and with Granny Thankful by my side, Saint Michael goin' before me, and my best friend to help steer me right, yeah, in my small part of the world, it meant doin' the thing I hated the most. But it set ablaze another fire, and I lost some of the best friends I ever had. Old Bart, and Tom Poole, not to mention a young runaway slave named Seth we took in and made part of the family."

"Really, you made a runaway slave family?"

"How could I not if I was gonna live who I am?"

"That's what I want to do."

"What? Join the army?" Lummy snickers.

I throw a rock at him. "No, you dern fool. Live who I am."

"I'm just kiddin', but no, you do it because you must do it. Wantin's got nothin' to do with it."

"All right then, I *must* do something to help my small part of the world."

"You just did, didn't you? Takin' down Kimbrell?"

"That was only the start." I pour us both a cup of coffee. I hand Lummy his and settle back against the log I'd been leaning against to sip mine. "I'd think of all people you'd understand what I'm saying, especially since you were going away to be alone and wound up saving your son's life."

"That's why I said we have no choice. We *do* what Creator gives us because of *who* we are."

"You know what I've got in mind, but it didn't really hit me until I realized that Tom Kimbrell and that old, wicked momma of his were only part of the problem." I hold my cup up to my lips but don't take a drink. "Just how bad were they back in Winn Parish?"

Lummy hangs his head. "Umph, worst stuff I've ever run up against, including what I faced in the war. Satan did too good a job teachin' them folks on how to become his demons. It was nothin' short of a storm of terror. I don't really like talkin' about what we did." Lummy swishes the remainder of his coffee around in his cup. "I don't even want to tell you about all the meanness the West-Kimbrell Gang dished out on poor innocent folks travelin' west." Lummy taps his foot pretty fast. "And, blowin' John West's head clean off with a shotgun wasn't somethin' I ever wanted to do either. Told myself that I'd never do anythin' like that again."

"But you trailed us all the way from Monroe where we caught the train and showed up just when—"

"My son was about to be murdered? Dang straight I did."

We sit for a moment, reliving the past few days. Talking it through. Getting it out of our souls. It helps. A little.

Lummy shakes his head. "Didn't think I still had it in me to gut Tom Kimbrell like a fish. I kinda lost my head there for a minute."

"Elzey's your son, Lummy. Anybody could lose his mind in a moment like that. Not a soul in this world has the right to judge you for doing that. You need to—"

"What? Be proud that I'm capable of doin' such things? All my life I've had to do the things no one else would, or could. Granny Thankful said it was me that had to do what I've done because I would walk away sane from it every time when others couldn't. Sometimes, I don't feel very sane." Lummy pats the air with his palms. "Sorry, there I go again. Gettin' riled up about somethin' I can't do anythin' about. Martha was always such a help when I got like this. Doggone it, I miss her."

"It's all right, Uncle Lummy, your heart's safe with me."

"I appreciate that. A woman I can trust has always been a comfort to me… Susannah, Annie Fanny, Granny Thankful, my ma, Martha…."

"What do you want to do?"

"Go see my daughter, Rosey. I'll go to Texarkana. She and her husband, William, live somewhere around there. They won't be hard to find. Said I can come and stay as long as I want. I just don't want to be a burden and—"

"Probably be good to spend some time with family for a while, don't you think?"

"I'm hopin'." Lummy tosses the last bit of his coffee into the fire. "I miss my Martha, my girls. Susannah. Especially Elzey. But I just need to be alone for a bit before I go see Rosey. I need to get my head on straight."

"I'll help make sure you get that time, Uncle Lummy. I promise you." I sip my coffee and change the subject back to the business at hand. "We know stealing Caroline from Tarle and taking her to Austin from Winn Parish was only worth doing if Kimbrell had somebody to pawn her off on."

"Yeah, we've established that, the one who Kimbrell planned on sellin' Caroline to, right?"

"Yeah, the one-eyed man Tom Kimbrell called the Buyer."

A CLEAR VOICE

*A voice from the past in the present can be
the shooting star to show the way.*

Dawn, August 28, 1886

I SLIP OUT of my blanket, and go find a place to relieve myself. Too much coffee and too much good conversation, I heard a lady say once. That's a truth no female can deny. I walk just far enough away and squat behind a bush but so I can still see the fire. As I take my morning constitutional, a slight slithering disturbs my thoughts. Coiled up under the bush I face is the biggest dang rattler I've ever seen. He's just lying there, tongue flicking in and out. I finish my business and throw the papers to the side. At that, the rattler starts to rise, tail twitching to give that unmistakable buzz, sensing a danger that I'm surely not. What to do? If I stand up, it could get my leg. If I roll over, it might bite my butt. If I can just... I lift my butt up and quickly push off with my feet as backward hard as I can as the rattler strikes, nailing my boot with what looks like at least one inch fangs. It coils back up as fast as it struck then slithers away.

"Whew, I made it through that. Guess a lady's got to pay attention where she squats out here." I sit for a moment, but a stinging eats on my butt like ants. I stand to find little rocks and dirt caked all over my butt cheeks. "Dang, ain't I the lucky one?" The spring is just a few feet away, so I hobble with my britches down to my knees to the water and wash myself. "Whew, my goodness, I surely do need a bath, Marion." I button up and ease on back to camp where I find Lummy making coffee and pulling the skillet out to fry some salt pork.

"Everything all right?"

"Yeah, except I almost got my behind bit by a huge rattlesnake."

"Down by the creek there?"

"Yeah, guess he was waiting on a rat or small rabbit."

"Rattlers need breakfast, too, you know."

"I don't want to think about that thing anymore. He had the meanest-looking eyes I ever seen, staring at me—like it could see into my soul or something."

"Maybe it could. Who knows what Creator uses to get our attention?"

"Well that snake certainly had mine. How about I make the biscuits?"

"I was hoping you would."

I get everything cooking and Lummy asks, "What's the worst scrape you've ever been in doin' your reward huntin' work?"

"Besides that rattler nearly nailing my backside? Oh, I don't know, most of the time it goes pretty easy. Maybe the time I had this bandit named Harry the Rat cornered in an old barn."

"Harry the Rat? Interesting name."

"Yeah, they said he was fond of cheese and never would be far from it. Actually that's how I finally found him, in a mercantile, buying a block cheese and some crackers."

"What happened?"

"He was squatting in an old man's run-down barn outside of town, so I followed him there. When I burst in on him and had the drop on him, I didn't know he had a partner. The partner had been sleeping in the loft and bailed off the ledge like a bobcat out of a tree on a squirrel."

"Dang, that must've hurt."

"My pride more than anything, but I was still pretty green to this kind of work. Anyway, when he leaped, I grabbed a pitchfork that was leaning fork up and shoved it in front of me. Let's just say he got skewered through the chest and that was the end of him. His body stayed propped up on that dern thing until the law came and took it away."

"What about the other one, what'd he do?"

"Stood and threw his hands in the air. Guess he figured if I could pull off killing his partner like I did, he wanted none of it."

"Dang, girl, you have had some tough adventures."

I grin. "A few."

The biscuits are brown, the salt pork is crisp, and Lummy made a bit of gravy out of the grease in the skillet. We sit back and enjoy our breakfast. I'm taking a sip of my coffee and Lummy is laying his plate on the ground when a rustling stirs in the bushes.

Out steps an old man holding the rattler that nearly bit me. Lummy is up on his feet quick as a cat with his pistol drawn. "Who are you, and what do you want?"

"Oh, I mean no harm. Just wonderin' if y'all wouldn't mind me borrowin' your fire to cook my breakfast here." He shakes the snake that's squirming and hissing.

I back up a little. "Just... just kill the thing, will you?"

"Oh, no, I keep 'em alive until I'm ready to roast 'em. Keeps the meat fresh." He takes a few steps toward our fire.

I pull my pistol. "I said, kill it."

"So I can use your fire?"

I look to Lummy who shrugs, and says, "Fine by us. Now kill it or be on your way."

Quick as the rattler struck at me the old man whips out his blade and takes the snake's head off with one slash. The snake head snaps, trying to bite anything it can grasp, but there's nothing to get ahold of. The old man lands a crushing blow on the snake's head and laughs.

"Works every time. Gotta be careful with a severed snake's head. It can still latch onto you several minutes after you cut it off."

Lummy reholsters his pistol. "Yeah, and they can still deliver the venom then, too, I've heard."

The old man starts skinning the snake like he's done it a hundred times. I'm sure he has.

Lummy grabs a pot from beside the fire. "How about some coffee?"

"Don't mind if I do, thank you. It's been a while."

I ask, "What're you doing way out here?"

"Oh, a little prospectin' but just listenin', mostly."

"Listening for what?"

He snickers. *"For what you can't hear in town."*

"What's that, old-timer?"

"Nothin'. I like to be where you can hear nothin'."

Lummy sits back down by the fire and pokes at it with a stick. "Sure as heck makes sense to me."

The old man washes the snake in the creek and returns, having rammed a stick through it. He hands me the snake on a stick and says, *"Hold this for me, will you?"* I extend it out as far from me as I can.

Lummy snickers.

The old man finds two sizable rocks and brings them to the fire. He takes the snake on a stick from me, carefully lays the snake over the fire on the bigger rock and then with his foot, he rolls the other rock on top of the stick to hold it in place. Pretty smart.

He stands back to admire his work. *"Now then, y'all got any salt? It'll taste much better if I put a little salt on it."*

I hand him a small bag. He carefully sprinkles just enough to cover it one end to the other. He smiles. *"I hate wastin' salt. Pretty precious in these parts, that is, if you don't get to town very often. Which I don't. Too noisy, too many people, too much goin' on."*

"Sounds familiar." Lummy asks, "How long has it been since you've been to town?"

The old man rubs his chin, pats his foot several times, and laughs. *"Can't remember, dang it. Does it matter?"*

Lummy hides a grin as he puts a bite of biscuit in his mouth. "No, no, just askin', that's all."

The old man looks in every direction. *"Ain't too smart to ask a body too many questions out here. You might get answers you don't want."*

Lummy leans in. "You got any answers I don't want?"

"I might." He studies Lummy like I read my books. *"You two are lookin' for somethin', ain't you?"*

"We might be. You got any idea what it might be?"

"Somethin' unholy... yep, I'm sure of that. I can smell it on you."

Lummy points at me with his thumb and snickers. "Sure you ain't smellin' somethin' unholy over there? She ain't had a bath... in how long now, Marion?"

I throw a rock at Lummy and ask the old man, "Smell it on us, how so?"

"I just do. Been too many places in too many situations not to recognize death when it's a-comin'. You two just got the look of men headed to battle... 'cept one of you ain't a man."

I ignore the comment about me not being a man. "What look?"

"The look of two people doin' the Lord's work of riddin' the earth of evil."

I look at Lummy, who stares intently into the old man's eyes. He asks, "What's your name?"

He shifts the snake on a stick to make sure it doesn't burn before it's done. *"Names mean nothin' out here."*

Lummy lays his hand on his pistol. "They do to me."

"It might rattle you a bit. Ha, get it? Rattle you a bit like this rattler unsettled that pretty girl there."

Lummy stands. "I've been rattled before. So has she, and I want your name. Give it."

The old-timer pats the air. *"All right, all right, don't get into such a fuss about it. Salis Sollut. There, you have it."*

I ask, "What is that, French? Sounds like French."

"Don't know, I never asked, though I did know a French girl once. It's what that lady in the white flowin' robes told me my name was when I came out here. Heck, I don't even remember how I got here, much less...." He tends to his roasting snake and hums "Amazing Grace" like we're not even here.

I turn to Lummy, and whisper, "He's clearly out of his mind."

Lummy doesn't take his eyes off the old man. "Maybe so. But you *do* recognize his name, don't you?"

"Not really."

"Spell it backwards."

"What?" I mouth *Silas Tullos* without making a sound.

"You think that's a coincidence, Marion?"

"Yeah, about like I do Granny Thankful showing up from time to time. Who knows what this Universe will throw at you."

"Exactly. Creator's got somethin' in mind. Let's just leave it alone and see where this goes. All right?"

I nod and sniff the air. "Smells like chicken baking in an oven."

The old man grins. *"Be glad to break you off a piece here in a bit when it gets done."*

The meat of a rattler looks good once it's cooked well-done. I guess if you're hungry, it's a fine meal. I taste it, but just thinking that thing was alive not long ago and tried to bite me, well, eating it just doesn't sit too well with me. I can say I tried it, though. I take another small bite. Not too bad if you don't think about what it is. It's tender, almost a little sweet, sort of like chicken. I guess I'd eat it again if I had to.

The old man smacks and chews like he hasn't eaten in days. There's something familiar about him besides his name. Something I recognize but just can't put my finger on just yet. Uncle Lummy says to leave it alone. I will. For now.

The old man finishes sucking the bones and throws them to the side. He chuckles. *"Ants'll get 'em."* He lets out a big sigh and folds his arms.

"You get it all, Mister Salis?" I ask.

"Every lip-smackin' part, bones clean as a whistle. Never know when you're gonna eat again, so eat all you can when you can, I say."

I throw a stick into the fire. "Guess you're right. I'll remember that."

He sits up. *"Lean times make for mean times, young lady, and don't you forget it."*

Is he trying to ruffle this hen's feathers? I shuck it off like water off a duck's back.

Lummy pulls the jar from his saddlebag. "How 'bout a taste, old-timer?"

He rubs his hands together. *"Don't mind if I do, thank you kindly."*

Lummy pours him a half cup and then the same for himself. He offers me the jar, but I wave him off. I want a clear head with this Salis person sitting here with us. I'm still not comfortable with him sharing our fire and where I'll be sleeping here in a bit.

Salis takes a loud sip. *"That's good stuff. It's been a while."* He stares into the fire for what seems like an eternity, then whispers, *"You know the man you're after is one of the wickedest walkin' the earth out here, don't you?"*

I'm getting a little nervous.

Lummy sits up. "Who might that be?"

"It ain't hard to figure out, son. You've dealt with such before."

"Then I know what I have to do, then don't I?"

"Not you, friend." He points at me. *"Her. She's the one to do it."*

His eyes turn blue like the hottest part of the flames for a fraction of a moment. I blink, thinking I didn't see what I thought I saw, but did.

Salis stands up, brushes himself off, and walks into the brush. *"I'll see you in Fort Worth, Marion."*

I get up to follow but Lummy shakes his head. "Let him go. He prob-ably wouldn't be out there anyway."

"I never told him my name."

"I know, but some things are best left to themselves when it comes to what we can see and what we can't see, and what we know for certain, and what we don't."

"What's that?"

"Didn't you recognize him?"

"What do you mean?"

"Tall as me, broad at the shoulders, like me, and talked like he was from Missip? *South* Missip, to be exact."

I think my eyes will pop out of my head. "Ain't no way it was him."

"How so? See any skewer stick lying about or any snake bones on the ground?"

I look around like I'm trying to keep a horsefly from landing on me. "No. Where'd they go?" I stand up and look all over the ground. "Where's his tracks?"

"Ain't none, Marion."

"What in the world is going on?"

Lummy whispers, "The bones, the stick, the tracks, the meat you tasted? They were never here... but *he* was."

I plop down on the ground confused.

Lummy looks into the night sky. "A good friend once told me, 'The boundaries which divide Life from Death are at best shadowy and vague. Who shall say where one ends and the other begins?'" Lummy leaves those words hanging in the air for me to breathe in, I figure.

"Rainy tell you that one?"

He squints. "He said it came from one of his favorite authors, a writer named Edgar Allen Poe. Said Poe wrote some pretty scary stuff."

"Can't be any scarier than the Kimbrells or the Buyer."

"And you would be right about that. We need to be keenly aware of what lurks under every bush of *the seen*... and behind patches of fog in *the unseen*."

The wind circles our camp and sends wispy campfire smoke in all directions. It stops like the door has been shut.

A voice calls from the distance, *"Your help has arrived. He will, your protector be."*

I snap my head around. "Did you hear it? What was that?"

"Better said, *who* was that?"

"Granny Thankful, I do believe."

I stare into the distance. The darkness is blinding but familiar. The silence is deafening but pleasant. "But who is the help that has arrived?"

"You mean you don't know?"

I ponder the thought for a moment. I look up to the sky and say,

"Thank you for sending Uncle Silas to me." It's like a thousand pound weight just fell from my shoulders.

And I sleep until light breaks over the rise.

FORT WORTH

Somebody once said "Hell is a city much like London."
He never visited Fort Worth.

Noon, August 31, 1886

FORT WORTH IS everything I don't want it to be—busy, noisy, too many people, and way too much going on. The constant *clip-clop* of horses and mules, the continuous chatter of merchants, farmers, out-of-towners, and townspeople bartering for food, supplies, housing, or whatever a heart desires makes me a bit nervy. The breeze carries along a mix of the latest Paris perfumes and hogpens, outhouse smells and baking bread, sweaty animals and humans, smoke from cook fires and trash burning, the aroma of leather and the scent of fresh cut hay. Street vendors ply their trade offering everything from the finest cookpots and dinnerware to the latest fashions, and of course, painted women. It's that last one I detest the most.

People dressed in all sorts of attire engage in all kinds of socializing in almost every way human beings can—getting their moment-by-moment news and whispering the latest gossips, starting fights and trying to stop them, listening to a stump preacher rail on about the evils of whiskey, tobacco, and whores on one corner with their pimps offering opium and ladies for hire across the street on the other. I want to throw a rock at them. But I don't. This place is nothing short of a living madhouse.

Mothers chase after children dashing to-and-fro like scattered rabbits between freight wagons and riders trying to get a glimpse of penny candies or a shipment of new toys. It's all very exciting but a bit too much for me. Uncle Lummy doesn't seem to be taking to it very well either. That means we'll be here only as long as we have to. I'm glad.

Still, this is where the hunt starts. I'm ready. And any fear I had vanished knowing Uncle Silas will be with me like Granny Thankful has been with Uncle Lummy all these years. Having the help of heaven soothes my irritated nerves. Knowing the angels who fight for us are greater than the demons who assault us gives me comfort.

I hold my nose as a band of mule skinners pass by on their way into a saloon. "How can a place be so muddy and dusty, sweet smelling and foul, and all at the same time?" I take a deep breath and blow it out. The sweet, buttery smells of cakes wafting from a bakery spark my taster and in the same breath I choke on the odor of a steamy dung wagon in this late August heat. "I hate towns."

Lummy laughs. "Yeah, me too. You should've been in the trenches of Vicksburg on day forty-six of the siege. There wasn't a sweet smell to be found, unless it was the relief of death."

"You got me there. I'll quit my whining."

We dismount and walk our horses into the nearest livery stable.

A crotchety old man whose pants are two sizes too big held up by suspenders looks up as he cleans the hooves of a pretty mare. "Curried and combed, watered and fed, rent a stall you can sleep in if you want to… all together will cost you a dollar each. Sound fair?"

I nod to Lummy. "I don't know, that sounds pretty good." Lummy shrugs, and I ask, "Where do the locals hang out and where might a good steak and potatoes be found."

Lummy kicks the dirt. "And a cold beer. I've got the taste for a good cold beer."

"Can't promise the beer'll be cold but take your pick. All them establishments down the row there have got their merits. But you can find everything you want and don't want in the White Elephant Saloon down yonder. That's where the action is, good and bad." He goes back to his scraping. "Just keep your eyes sharp and ears cleaned out good. Lots of rough characters rest their boots in Hell's Half Acre. You don't want to be there any longer than you have to, understand?"

I laugh. "Rough characters are who we're looking for." I flip the liveryman two silver dollars before Lummy can pull out his money purse. We start for the White Elephant. And Hell's Half Acre.

Lummy takes a deep breath and laughs. "Yep, here we go. Marion Tullos turned loose in Fort Worth. This will be interesting, to say the least."

"You know it. Just let me play the part I need to so we can get on about our business."

He holds up his hands in surrender. "Fine by me, I just want a good steak, potatoes with gravy, somethin' green, bread, a cold beer, and of course, somethin' sweet." He licks his lips a little. "But I will have my eye on you every moment we're in there."

"I'm counting on it, Uncle." I check my pistol and Lummy's knife in my belt, pat between my breasts for the Derringer that Uncle Lummy gave me when we went after Tom Kimbrell, straighten my hat, and walk too much like a man. It's a habit I've got when I start a path into possible danger.

The liveryman cups his hands and yells, "And remember, don't stay long in Hell's Half Acre unless you're rougher'n a cob and meaner'n a panther cat."

I wave at him and Lummy nods, laughing. "He just doesn't know who we are, now does he?"

I backhand Lummy's chest. "He surely doesn't. How could he?"

A foul-smelling cloud of spent tobacco smoke, sweat, and overcooked sizzling meat boils out of the White Elephant Saloon and Billiard Parlor like a riverboat smokestack. Laughter and cursing can be heard from down the street. We stand at the batwings scanning the room through air thick as Mississippi River fog, and twice as pungent.

I side-eye Lummy. "Now who do you think would want to spend any time in *this* hellhole?"

He snickers. "The kind of people we're lookin' for, I'm bettin'."

I push the batwings open. "I'm hoping we don't have to stay long."

Lummy snickers. "And here, we just got into Hell's Half Acre."

I stop. "Wait for me here. Let me see if my whorish charms will work on one of these degenerates."

Lummy moves to a corner. "I'll get us a table and order up some food."

I nod and ease through the crowd with my hat pulled down a little to avoid eye contact. I belly up to the bar at the end. The barkeep comes over polishing a glass with a towel. In the deepest, most manly voice I've ever tried using, I ask, "Got any—"

A man wearing nice, clean clothes, shiny boots, a fancy bowler hat, and sporting a gold chain obviously hooked to a watch hidden in the side pocket of his striped vest moves in beside me. A little too close for my taste, but that's why I'm here—to get close to somebody who will help us find the Buyer.

"The lady and I will have two shots of your best whiskey, barkeep, and put it on my bill."

I disregard him, and ask, "Could you bring me a sarsaparilla, please, cold as you got."

"Ain't nothin' cold in here but the wicked hearts that patronize the place. That'll be ten cents."

"Ten cents? What? Damn." I toss a quarter on the bar. He snatches it up and walks away with it. "And I'll be wanting the change back."

He turns and gives a growl, fetches a dime and a nickel from his pocket and flips them my way. The man who offered to buy my drink catches both with two shakes of one hand and lays them gently on the bar in front of me. I pick them up ever so gingerly to match his movements. Two points of a star peek out from just inside his jacket. That could mean only one thing. Lawman.

I give the most annoyed look I can muster, and ask, "What do you want? Shouldn't you be off polishing your star, or something else, for that matter?"

He stutters a little, being caught off guard at my blunt comments. "Well, uh, I-I—"

"Can't a lady drink in peace?"

He holds his palms up. "All right, all right, stop. Let's start over if it's all right with you. I'm Deputy Stedman Walker, but just call me Sted, please, ma'am. I do have a question or two if you don't mind? It's my job."

"And if I do mind, *Sted,* does it make any difference?"

"Not really, but I'd appreciate your cooperation."

"Your boss Ben Shipp still walking these streets, or is Longhair Jim Courtright running the show here in Fort Worth?"

"You keep up with the times, don't you?"

"I try."

"Oh, some call him Big Jim, and yeah, he's still around. When he came back home to Fort Worth, they all but threw him a parade. He's remaining a bit subdued for the moment. The law might just be about to catch up with ole Longhair Jim's racketeering and murdering. But that's another matter."

My ears perk up at that. Maybe this fellow can point me in the direction of the Buyer. He seems to know his business.

The barkeep sets my drink down carefully, and I flip him a nickel. He nods with a slight grin. "Thank you, ma'am. I appreciate it. Let me know if you want another."

I smile up at him and take a sip of my sweet drink. "Now, what do you want, Deputy?"

"Rumor has it there's a lady chasing bounties across Texas. They say she's gettin' pretty good at it. She's described as young, so, I'm guessing she hasn't been doin' that kind of work for very long. I also heard there was some trouble down Austin way she might have been mixed up in. Somethin' about a pretty, blonde-haired lady who wore bells, let's just say, close to her heart. Story goes, she and her *compadres* killed a few miscreants who'd kidnapped one of 'em's wife. They say the killers were from Louisiana, but I'm guessing they're long gone by now."

"Sounds like they did what the law is often incapable of doing, don't it?"

"Yeah, maybe so, but—"

"So what's that got to do with me?"

"The man's mother, Aunt Polly, as she likes to call herself, wants some kind of justice for what they did to her son, Tom Kimbrell. They gutted that man like a fish and then left his mother to the coyotes in the brush outside of Austin. She did survive, but just barely."

Dang, I hate to hear that. Aunt Polly, still alive? She could send word to the Buyer that we're coming if our presence is made known here. We've got to get on with this before we're found out.

Sted takes a sip of his whiskey. "The rest of Kimbrell's gang, well, seems they didn't fare much better. It was a real mess they say. Heard blondie took off with some old-timer and that they might be headed this way. You happen to know anything about that?"

"Should I?" I look neither right nor left, just straight ahead. "You pester every good-lookin' blonde-haired lady who stops for a drink before she's on her way?"

"Only if she fits the description of the one I might be lookin' for."

He lays his hand on my shoulder. I jerk away, not so much because it's him, but because of the past. "Touch me again, and I'll snatch you bald-headed."

"Sorry, didn't mean to upset you. Kinda touchy, ain't you?"

"I can be whatever I want." I shrug and take another sip of my sarsaparilla. It's good.

Deputy Walker leans in. "All right, I'll get right to it then. Who or rather, what, might you be looking for, little darlin'?"

I back up. "Keep your distance, you ruttin' buck." I set my glass down hard. "First of all, badge or no badge, I ain't your little darlin', and I got what it takes to back that up. If not, my uncle over there tending to his own business, like I'm trying to do right now, is pretty handy with a knife, Colt, and a Henry. So, let's just stick to the conversation, or you get away from me."

"That kind of talk could land you in jail."

I point my finger in his chest. "And your kind of talk could land you in the cemetery." I don't blink. He does.

"You're right. Sorry, ma'am, I shouldn't have said that."

"Well… I thank you for that. And please don't call me ma'am. I'm not an old woman, as you have obviously noticed."

"Yes, ma'am, I mean, well… you're certainly not an old woman… Miss—"

"No need for names." I move to a table in the back away from listening ears. Deputy Walker follows. "I'm here to help the law when and where it can't help itself."

"Really, and when is that?"

"When y'all don't have the men to chase down the ones who get away. I understand that's a sack full of 'em."

"So you're a reward hunter?"

"Shhh, keep your voice down." No one notices our conversation, and I don't want them to. I whisper, "I prefer outlaw hunter, and yeah, the reward is worth the chase. Keeps me in coffee, grub, and such."

Deputy Walker leans in. This time I don't back away. He has a completely different look in his eye. "I want to help."

I wipe the condensation from my sarsaparilla glass. "How do you figure on doin' that?"

"You goin' after just anybody on a wanted poster?"

I squint and study how I would disable this man if he was to come at me. But he seems genuine so I take the gamble and open up a little. "No, Sted, I only go after those who do to women what was done to me."

Deputy Walker looks around the room, watching for anyone turning an eavesdropping ear his way. He drops his head to clear his throat, and when he looks back up, his eyes burn like red-hot pokers ready to brand a steer. "If I'm readin' your meaning right, then I know who you might be lookin' for. And where you might find him."

THE WORD

When the right men show up....

12:45 p.m., August 31, 1886

I SIT BACK in my chair hard and give a slight nod to Lummy that I've found the man with the information we need. Our food arrives at our table, and I'm hungry. But I have to know more first. The food will have to wait. This is where I'll get the word of the Buyer's whereabouts or at least some helpful information. I can feel it.

The deputy scans the room without moving his head. "The Buyer has eyes and ears here." I start to get up, but he takes hold of my arm and whispers, "You need to listen. The Buyer's representatives were here just yesterday angry at what happened in Austin. They were countin' on a new shipment of ladies. Your bunch threw mud into their cook pot, and they ain't happy at all."

"What about the Buyer, was he here?"

"The Buyer never shows his face, heck, we don't even know his name or what he looks like."

I scratch my ear. "Sounds like he's as slippery as a greased snake on a hot summer day."

"And has the bite to back it up. They've killed many a man in their thieving of innocent women. This dangerous cutthroat would sell his own mother for a dollar. He never takes his victims. He gets in cahoots with those who will. Like your Tom Kimbrell. Then he squirrels them away at his hideout until he has a large enough selection from which his clients take their picks at an auction, like they were cattle."

"You think you got me and my uncle figured, don't you?" I hate being found out so easily, but this man seems to have a heart, and for good.

He lays his palms flat down on the table and then crumples his hands into tight fists. "I know you have to be the lady named Belle who helped take down Tom Kimbrell and his bunch back in Austin. Good for you, and your uncle over there. I ain't interested in that. That should've been done a long time ago, if you ask me. I want the man who they were going to meet to sell off your friend's wife."

This is getting more interesting by the moment.

"He's headed east to his old hideout in the Indian Territory until things cool down. That affair down in Austin got him a bit too much attention, and he don't like attention." He's shaking now, and I can see the man knows how to restrain himself. That's a good quality. Still, he's got something going on. Deep down.

I take a chance. "Deputy… may I call you Sted?"

He growls like an old boar raccoon caught in a hollow tree with the hounds baying. "Call me what you like, I just want to capture or kill the men who took my little sister and sold her south down Mexico way." His eyes drip a couple of tears, and he hangs his head. "I know she's gone. I'll never see her again." He pulls out a kerchief and feigns blowing his nose so he can wipe his eyes with no one else the wiser. "I tried to go after them and get her back, but I lost their trail. Nobody will help me, and I've asked. Many times. Everybody's too afraid of the one-eyed man. One man can't take down an organized bunch like the Buyer runs. There's too many of 'em."

Now I know he has a heart. "I'm sorry, Sted. I didn't—"

He sits up straight and leans his elbows on the table. "Nobody knows, but everyone is watching to see what you and I are up to. If they didn't have nothing to talk about, their lives would be even more worthless. We can't get all friendly like in here just because we have a common goal. We need to talk somewhere else. So let's make this look good."

"What do you mean?"

"You should go eat your meal, the food's good here, even though the place smells bad. We'll meet to talk, say in an hour?"

"All right."

"I'm about to insult you, and you're gonna slap me. Make it look good. Leave a mark. To hide my true intentions and abilities, I play a silly, incompetent deputy who can only get a girl if he pays her, and mind you, I ain't doin' that. But, I want to keep people thinkin' that way."

"Go ahead. I'll know when to slap you." I grin and the corner of his mouth turns up.

"Then, I guess we're partners in the crime of justice, Sted." I offer my hand, but he shakes his head almost unnoticeably.

He whispers, "Too many eyes on us."

I look around. "Meet us at the livery just down the street where the old man with the baggy britches and suspenders works."

He nods. "Now, slap my face and make a scene, like I tried to grab your butt, or somethin'."

I whisper in my sweetest voice, "You'd like to do that, wouldn't you, Sted?" Before he can respond, I slap his face hard enough to leave a red mark.

He reels back rubbing his face. "Dang, woman, I was just funnin' with you."

"Hurts, don't it, lawman? Well, I don't need your money."

Sted starts to get up but stops. "You don't look like you're doin' so well to make my money no good." He snickers, holding a finger under his nose.

"I do all right without you puttin' your paws on my butt, Deputy Walker."

"Do you make enough silver to buy a bar of soap?"

I can feel the heat in my face, not from anger but actual embarrassment. The saloon crowd is laughing at me now. It hurts my heart a little, but I keep my head. I see Uncle Silas sitting next to Lummy. My courage is renewed.

"I'm on my way, knothead, not that my bathing habits are any of your business."

"I'd like to make it my business, little darlin'."

I raise my hand to slap him again but hold it midair.

He snickers. "You must enjoy slappin' men, don't you?"

"Enough that I might just slap your ugly mule face twice."

"Oh, yeah? Try it." Sted smiles.

"Just say somethin' and find out."

The whole saloon crowd has grown silent and the bartender pops a club up and down in his palm. He winks at me.

Sted speaks in a loud voice like when he first approached me. "So, little darlin', might I assume that you're coming with me to my room so we can truly get acquainted?"

I push back the table with a jerk and for sure now have everyone's attention. I give Lummy a wink and a nod. He dangles his shaking head, trying not to allow his shoulders to bounce as he laughs. I almost burst out laughing at him laughing so hard.

"You should know well, Deputy, that the first three letters of the word assume pretty much describes the person doin' the assuming."

Sted stands up. "You callin' me an ass?"

I stand up. "Seems to fit right nicely." Laughter breaks out across the barroom.

"Well, the only man you could ever get would be ugly as a lop-eared, cross-eyed, slack-jawed, swayback mule with all its teeth gone."

"Cut your prattle, you loudmouth hawg's butt."

He steps forward. "A good beddin' and a bottle of whiskey would settle you down, little darlin'."

"You couldn't bed a dawg proper if you were given instructions with pictures, lawman."

Sted grabs my arm, but I jerk it away. He follows me but Uncle

Lummy steps in between us. He looks down at Sted from his towering six-foot-six frame. "Do we have a problem, lawman? 'Cause I know you ain't got one with my niece here."

Sted hides a grin and relaxes. "She sure has got a mouth on her, don't she?"

"If my uncle here doesn't whoop your behind all the way down the livery stable and back, I will." Sted winks to let me know he understands we'll meet there later.

Men and hostesses roar with laughter.

I put the icing on the cake. "Go on, now, git, before I—"

Sted tips his hat. "Yes, ma'am, I mean, little darlin'."

An old-timer with half of his teeth missing laughs loud and slaps his hand on the bar. "Looks like you lost again, Deputy Walker. You might consider givin' up the ladies."

I lightly kick Sted in the butt as he slips through the batwings. I flutter my eyelashes and plant my hands on my hips as I glance back over my shoulder with a grin at the crowd that sends up resounding hurrahs.

Lummy hands me a five-dollar gold piece. "Buy a round of beer for the house, then you'll surely have them all in your pocket."

I hold up the shiny half eagle and shout, "Beer all around, boys, I'm buying!"

Someone hands me a beer, but before I take a sip, I hold my mug up to hide my smile as Sted crosses the street. He is good-looking after all.

I turn to sit, and of course, Uncle Silas is gone. The bartender takes the covers off our plates he put there to keep our food warm, and it does look good.

Lummy chuckles and pushes my shoulder. "Eat your food, girl. And get those eyeballs put back in your head."

I can't help but smile. "Oh, shut up, Uncle Lummy."

THE SECOND BIG TALK

When difficult talk is good, it purges the soul. At least a little.

1:30 p.m., August 31, 1886

AS WE EASE through the batwings of the White Elephant Saloon with bellies satisfied, I pick my teeth with a small folding knife. It's not something I typically do, being a lady and all, but it casts an image for all to see. Lummy and I stand in the sunshine for a moment and take in the sights.

Lummy puts his arm around me. "Looks to me like somebody's got fire in her britches for a certain young lawman, I do believe."

I shrug his heavy arm off and elbow him in the ribs. He doubles over with a snicker. I give him a furrowed brow and frowned face. I can't hold it in. I burst out laughing.

"Guess you're right. I haven't had that kind of feeling in my heart or twixt my pants legs, well, I'm not sure, for any man now that I think about it."

"Ain't nothin' wrong with havin' natural feelings, in fact, I'd say it's a good and healthy thing if you ask me. Especially after what you've been through. Just take your time. Don't give yourself away too easily."

"How do you know so much about it?"

"I taught my Del and Rosey about good and bad men, and I saved my own fiery needs for my first love until after we were married. Yeah, I know."

"Susannah?"

"It was well worth it."

I hang my head and drip a tear. "But I'm already tainted, Uncle Lummy. Wicked men did a lotta bad things to me, some I chose to do because I had to make money to care for my sister. I just can't see how anyone would ever want fruit that's been bruised, and...."

I can't stop crying and Lummy half pulls me into an alley. He sits me down on a stack of boxes. I think he's fixing to yell at me. His hands are shaking, and he balls them up into fists. He relaxes them and sits down beside me, gently lays his hand on my shoulder and says in the sweetest, most caring voice I've ever heard coming out of a man's mouth, "Marion, you are as pure as fresh honey from the comb and true as an oak standing for a hundred years. It ain't never been about what was done to us in the past and what we've done because of it that makes us who we are. It is about who you are right now, who you want to be at this time, in this place. You can be anybody you want to be. Nothin's holding you back but you. You'll never have a life with a fine young man who loves you until you stare straight into the Devil's face without blinking and tell him he can't have you. He was the one who set you on the wrong course in the first place, not you."

I sniffle and snort. "I know, Uncle Lummy, but it's so hard. I killed the preacher who put his hands on me, and the carpetbagger, and the voodoo witch who killed Uncle Silas in the courthouse fire. Uncle Silas killed the whorehouse owner in Natchez who imprisoned me in the brothel. I played the part and Tom Kimbrell is dead, but I still can't get at what's eating on me."

"You're tryin' to sort it out."

I wipe my eyes. "Sort what out?"

"Whether what you're doin' is reckoning or revenge."

"How will I know which is which?"

"Reckoning is what must be done. Revenge is when you want to do it and too often enjoy it. It ain't always easy to tell them apart. Trust me, I know."

"So what do I do?"

"As long as you keep asking the question, you're probably all right. It's when you stop feelin' anything about it, well, that's when you're in trouble."

"Am I getting revenge or seeking reckoning?"

"Only you can know for sure, Marion."

"But how can I know for sure?"

"Walk around in your own soul."

"What is that and how do I do that?"

"That is for another day, but I promise, I will show you how. When you're ready, that is."

I contemplate that for a bit. "Walking around in my own soul. Hmmph, there must be something to it."

"There is, but right now, it's best to keep talking. Get it all out."

"Tom Kimbrell stealing Tarle's wife and the hurt I saw in his eyes, well, it shook me pretty hard when we first started out on the train to Austin. I wanted to get revenge on Kimbrell for what was done to me but wanted the love I saw in Caroline's and Tarle's eyes for each other when we rescued her. I want to catch and kill the Buyer, but I want so badly to have a good man to love. It ain't just about the fire between my legs that's driving me. It's what I've never had that I crave. A good man just to hold me, care for me, and who wants me for just me."

"Yeah, I understand."

"Then how can I do it?"

Lummy removes his hat and pulls back his hair. "I heard Pastor Silas Dobbs back in Choctaw County preach once that the Apostle Paul wrote somethin' like, 'I count not myself to have apprehended... but this one thing I do, forgettin'—'"

I break in, "Forgetting those things which are behind, and reaching forth unto those things which are before, I press toward the mark for the prize of the high calling of God in Christ...."

We sit still and quiet for a moment. Lummy takes in a deep breath and blows it all the way out. He bumps my shoulder with his. "Ain't as easy as it sounds though, is it?"

I smile up at him. "And if I remember my Scripture right, Paul tended to be a whiner too."

"So we're in good company. It's all right to whine on occasion, but not so's you start sounding like, what was it you called that deputy? A slack—"

"No, Sted said the only man I could ever get was a lop-eared, cross-eyed, slack-jawed, swayback mule with all its teeth gone."

Lummy doubles over laughing. I hold his bouncing shoulders to keep him from falling off the box he's sitting on. He straightens up. "Whew, that boy's got a mouth on him, wouldn't you say, *little darlin'.*"

I swat him on the back of his head. "Now don't you go to telling nobody about Sted, I mean…." Now he has me laughing.

"I'm gonna remember that one. Save it for when I see Rainy next and use it on him. And I promise I won't say anythin' about Sted, not even funnin'." He wipes his eyes. "You good?"

I lean against this giant of a man who's taken me in like I'm his own daughter. "Yeah, Uncle Lummy, I'm good."

He snickers. "Then, let's go see your boyfriend." He reels back like he knows he's going to get hit.

I slap his shoulder. "Dang you, Lummy Tullos!"

BACK ALLEY BLESSING

*You never know when the answer to the question you're
askin' comes runnin' around a corner right smack into you.*

1:45 p.m., August 31, 1886

WE STAND UP to head to the livery stable when a naked lady trying
to keep herself covered with a bedsheet dashes through a back alley. She
can't scream for lack of breath, but the look of terror on her face tells
me her pursuer won't be far behind. I reach out and yank her into the
boxes behind us as a scrawny, beanpole of a man with a long knife makes
the corner at a dead run. Lummy throws out a stiff arm. It catches the
man under the chin at Lummy's elbow. The man's feet fly up as high
as his head, and he crashes down hard on the alley floor like a sack of
potatoes, moaning.

Lummy jerks him up by the collar with his feet dangling underneath
his body. "Say a word, and I'll snap your neck, understand?"

I dive at the man who poises his knife to strike Lummy in the side.
"Lummy!" I make it to them just in time to grab the man's hand as he slices
through Lummy's jacket. I pull back the scrawny man's arm. There's a bit
of blood on the blade. I bend his wrist down hard, he hollers, but he drops
the knife into my other hand. Without a blink, I slash his cheek to the
bone. Lummy throws his attacker to the ground and puts his boot on the
man's neck. He checks his side as the man lies moaning and squirming.

Lummy pulls back bloody fingertips. "Sliced me pretty good, but he didn't do me any real damage, I reckon." He holds out his jacket and pokes his hand through the new hole created by the scrawny man's blade. "Dang it, I just bought this jacket in Bankston before leaving Choctaw County." Unaware, Lummy doesn't notice the growing spot of blood on his side.

I take a rag from my pocket and hold it against his flesh through the hole in his shirt, then wipe away the blood and look up. "You're going to need stitches."

The girl who was being chased whispers, "I can do it. I help Doc Sanderlin out sometimes. He showed me how. When too many cowboys get cut up or all shot to pieces at the same time, I help him with the sewing up. I can mend clothes pretty good, like your shirt and that coat there too."

Lummy looks at the wound. "Sounds good to me. What's your name?"

"I go by Delilah when I'm at work, but my real name is Josie. Josie Ray, from Natchitoches. That's in Looseana."

"Yeah, I know. I used to live in Winn Parish right next door. Got good friends there and—"

Josie rushes to Lummy. "Please take me with you. I'll do anything to get back home. They took me and killed my pa. Ma is all alone except for my little brother who ain't but nine, and that mean, one-eyed man who sold me to the whorehouse owner, and-and, when I kept runnin' away, the mean ole one-eyed man told me that if I didn't stop, he'd buy me back and sell me to somebody down in Mexico, and—"

I lift up my palms. "Hold on there, Josie, let's back it up a bit. You say a one-eyed man told you this?"

Josie cringes like she's about to get hit. "Meanest man I ever seen, or ever heard of. I watched him draw a knife across my father's throat like he was slaughtering a hawg and laughed as he did it. Said he'd learned it a long time ago from folks named Kimbrell and some man named John West." She shakes and shudders like she's freezing cold.

Lummy makes sure Josie is covered in the same gentlemanly manner he covered me after he killed Tom Kimbrell. What a world Lummy's had to live in. In one moment, he slaughters a man like a pig with the strength and determination of Saint Michael the Archangel and in the next cares for a broken lady like a shepherd boy dotes on a newborn lamb. From one extreme to another, how does he do it? What am I saying? Maybe not as long as he, but it's my life too. I just need to learn the lamb-doting part better.

I nod to Lummy. "I'm madder'n the Devil at a baptism." I kick the scrawny man again. "What's your name, boy?"

"John Smith, and that's all."

Lummy lets Smith sit up. He squats down and holds out his hand. I give him the knife his father made for him long ago. "Well, John Smith, if that's your real name, how 'bout I carve you up like a piece of ham if you don't answer my questions? What d'you say?"

Smith slinks back, holding his cheek that's trickling blood. "I-I, I'll answer your questions. Please don't cut me again. I'm touchin' my cheekbone right now." Lummy hands him a kerchief from his coat pocket. Smith presses it to his bloody face. "Once is enough." He hangs his head. "I'll talk. I'm dead anyway."

Lummy thumbs the knife and licks the thin line of blood that appears. "Maybe not."

I ask, "The one-eyed man, what's his name?"

Smith wraps his arms around his shoulders. He starts rocking back and forth, holding his private parts, wincing. "Don't know his name. Everybody I know, and that ain't many, calls him the Buyer. Lost his eye in a scrape in a whorehouse in Mississippi some years back and since then, besides killin' every lawman and reward hunter that crosses his path, he's been buying stolen women and sellin' them to the highest bidder. He's lookin' for a pretty, blonde-haired girl. Has been for several years. This girl Josie here just happened to have the good looks the whorehouse owner was lookin' for when we passed through here last year on our way with a load of women to sell down in Mexico. I was just gonna grab her and let the whorehouse owner think she ran away again with no one the wiser."

Without looking at her, I ask, "Is that true, Josie?"

She whimpers, "Yes, he's telling the truth."

Smith keeps holding on to his man parts and moaning a bit.

I ask, "What's wrong with you, boy?"

Smith looks from me to Josie. "You tell her. You did it."

Josie lowers her head with a grin and looks up. "When he dragged me into the alley, he stopped to make sure no one was following us. I kicked him in the place that makes him a boy. So I ran like a chicken escaping bein' plucked and fried for Sunday dinner."

Lummy squints. "Ummph, that had to hurt."

Smith groans. "Still does."

Lummy offers his hand that's not bloody to Josie. "Well, it looks like you take care of yourself pretty well. Josie, I'm glad to meet you. Where do we go to get me sewed up?"

I hold out my hand. "Hold on a minute, Uncle Lummy. We ain't done just yet." I kick the man on the ground. "What about this one?"

Lummy smiles. "Oh, he's goin' to see the deputy, just soon as Miss Josie gets me patched up."

I kick the man again. "Why were you chasing her?"

"Please don't take me to the law. My boss'll kill me for sure. Some of his men are deputies, don't you know?"

I kick him again, a little harder. "I done asked you twice now. Ain't asking you again." I grab his knife and bend down on one knee. The scrawny rat of a man starts screaming, but I slap his mouth. "Shut that cryin' up, boy, and start talking, or I'm gonna give you a matching cut on your other cheek." I lay the backside of the blade on his good cheek and start to draw it. He squirms like a night crawler thrown in a campfire.

Smith cries out, "All right, okay, I had to grab a girl for my boss since he lost out on that one down in Austin a few days ago. Said he'd kill me if I came back empty-handed since I didn't make the buy. Somebody killed all them fellers down in Austin before I got there. My contact there in town said it was some Looseana folks who came to get one of 'em's wife back. Can't say I blame 'em, 'cept it sure has left me in a bind. I figured stealin' this girl wouldn't cause too much ruckus, but I can sure as heck see I was dead wrong about that."

Josie wraps her arms around Lummy's waist. He winces from the pain of the cut she forgot he has. Josie eases off the tight hug. "Oh, I'm so sorry, Mister Lummy, but you gotta take me with you. Please, I'm beggin' you. I'll cook, wash, and do a bit of doctoring if needed. I won't be no trouble, I don't need much, I won't talk too much… please, take me with you."

DOC SANDERLIN

A bit of doctoring can heal a lot of things.

2:05 p.m., August 31, 1886

JOSIE TAKES US to Doc Sanderlin's place, and we sneak in the back door. Too many nosy eyes and ears to enter the front door. Fortunately for us, no one else is in his office. He's stretched out on a patient bed snoring like a hawg. I bet the man puts in more hours than he ever gets paid for. Josie kneels and shakes him gently.

"Hey, Doc, wake up. It's me, Josie."

Doc sits up like he's heard gunshots and asks, "Is that baby ready to pop on out? I'll get my bag, and I'll—" He stands up, stops, scratches his behind with both hands, and asks, "Who might they be, Josie?"

"Oh, my new good friends. The skinny little man there tried to kidnap me but these two saved me. Mister Lummy got a gash on his side in the mix."

Doc, a short man, shorter than me, with a gray mustache and silver hair washes his face in a dishpan and dries his face with a towel. "Getting too old for all of this. I was sleeping pretty dang good until y'all came in." He puts on his doctor's coat and points at Lummy. "Remove your shirt, please, sir."

I help Lummy ease the shirt off, careful not to bump his wound. We all notice Lummy's scars from his battles and skirmishes through life. I hand Doc the shirt.

"I can see this isn't your first fight. The war?"

Lummy squints at the coming pain. "Yeah, for a time. But I've had a few more conflicts, some before the war and some after."

Doc Sanderlin looks Lummy over as he lays down the bloodstained shirt with a hole in it. Josie grabs it and disappears into Doc's waiting parlor. His eyes trail behind her. "Poor girl. Heart of gold and sweet as a peach but having to live the way she does? Lord, it seems the Devil is in control of this world."

"Yeah, and he's got plenty of trained demons doin' his dirty work." Lummy winces when Doc probes the cut with his instrument. "You got anything to ease the pain?"

Doc steps back and places his hands on his hips. "Where'd you fight?"

"Vicksburg, and around."

"Gray or blue?"

I can see Lummy studying the physician to see if he can trust him. It's been quite some time since the war ended, but some folks still have deep feelings, and some still hold grudges, on both sides.

Lummy whispers. "Both."

Doc stops. "Really? I'll want to hear all about that sometime."

I chime in, "Yeah, me too."

Doc concentrates on his work. "I was at Shiloh when the Rebs almost ran us bluecoats straight into the Tennessee River. I was a surgeon in the Yankee Army then stationed on the boat with General Grant. Young and dumb, but willing to stand for what I believe, I set up a surgeon's tent in one of the camps. When General Albert Sidney Johnston sent his boys screaming that damned ole rebel yell, hell, all we could do was run like scared rabbits."

Lummy straightens up. "Glad I wasn't there. The Siege of Vicksburg was enough for me, that, and my hitch with the Mounted Rifles wearing the blue suit was plenty of war for anybody's lifetime."

I love hearing these seasoned men talk of old times, the war, and their lives. Somebody should write all of this down.

Doc washes the wound carefully and splashes a bit of alcohol on it. Lummy cringes like Doc just set him on fire. "I don't stand for much of anything anymore these days unless it's about saving people's lives. That's all that matters to me anymore. I've seen enough of what good and bad men can do to each other, and what some women can do, too."

I whisper, "Ain't that the truth?"

Lummy cuts his eyes at me. "Truth it is."

Doc stops. "I just wish we'd all just try and get along a little better."

Lummy braces for the needle and surgeon's thread he knows is coming. "Yeah, me too, Doc. I just want a bit of peace, and for what you're about to do to be over quick."

Doc snickers. "Shouldn't take more than eight or ten stitches, son." He shifts his feet as he pries open the knife wound. "Too many good men and families died in a contest that could've been settled with a good hand of poker, don't you think?"

"I always thought dominoes was the better game." Lummy cringes as Doc allows the wound to close and threads his needle. "Yeah, I wish it had been that easy… and I wish you could fix this cut that easy, too, Doc. You gonna sew me up or keep crawlin' in that hole in my side, walkin' around in it like you're doin'."

Doc snickers. "Yeah, son, let me get you some whiskey with a little laudanum mixed in. It's all I got for the pain. I'll give you a good dose. You let it give you the courage to let me sew you up. Be back in a minute." Doc returns and hands Lummy the bottle. "Take as much as you need. I got more."

Lummy holds the bottle up then drinks a good portion. He looks at me and grins. "Don't much like needles. Never did." He takes another swallow and sets the bottle down.

Smith whimpers like a small child. "What about me?"

I step up. "Yeah, and what about you? I should pour some of that alcohol on your face wound."

Covering his wound with his palm, Smith stands and eases beside Lummy. "Can't I get somethin' for pain too?"

I want to hurt him for cutting Lummy. "Like you really deserve it after what you've been doin'. You cut my friend here and I ought'a—" I raise my hand to slap him harder than the last time.

Lummy takes my arm and lowers it back to my side. "We do what we do because of who we are, not because of what they've done. We're not them. Let the boy have some whiskey and laudanum, Doc." Lummy nods. "We might just be able to save his life, and his soul with it."

Smith takes a quick swallow, careful not to let the fiery liquid enter his face wound.

Sted steps through the door and removes his hat. "Thought I was gonna have to send out a search party looking for you two but the livery man just told me he saw y'all come in here. Everything all right?"

I pat him on the shoulder. "We ran into a bit of trouble, but we got some more information, and Smith over there has it."

I pull Smith back and Sted takes him by the collar. "I know you. You were part of that bunch who went to Austin and came back empty-handed, weren't you?"

"Yeah-yes, sir. I was. But not no more, I ain't. I want to help, and I know where the Buyer stays, that is, where he's hidin' out."

I grab his ear. "You lead us wrong or into a trap I'll have your hide to make my next pair of boots, understand?"

Smith bristles at that comment. "All right, all right, you're makin' your point."

I get up in his face. "Look, boy, I'll skin you so quick it'll make your head spin. I'll have your hide tanning on the barn door before I have my morning coffee and enjoy watching you squirm in a vat of salt while I eat breakfast, you understand?"

Smith remains stoic, saying nothing.

Lummy takes my arm and whispers in my ear. "You're gonna need to lighten up on the boy. He said he's given up the life with the Buyer.

Let him. Let him change. If you don't, who's gonna let you change, that is, when you need to?"

He's right, and I know it. I turn to John. "Is that true, you're done with the Buyer and his devilish ways?"

"Oh, yes, ma'am, it's the straight'n narrow for me now all the way. I want a clean slate and will do any penance necessary to make up for my evil doin's."

"Okay, then. You can start by saddling our horses. The livery is just down the street. You got a horse?"

"Yes'um, I do."

"Tell the livery man who we are and that we need another horse and the rig to go with it, saddled and ready to go. We'll pay him when we get there."

Smith starts for the door smiling like a kid who's been told he gets to go to town for sweets on Saturday.

Lummy smiles and winks. "I knew you could do it."

I nod to Sted. "You mind goin' with him to make sure he doesn't run off?"

Sted's eyes melt looking at me. "I'll be happy to, Marion."

I do my best to resist smiling, but dang, he's good-looking. And he has an amiable spirit about him.

"And you, Smith," I cup my hands and yell, "stop calling me ma'am. I—"

Both Smith and Sted snicker with bowed heads like they just got caught farting in class at school. They say together, "Yes, Miss Marion," and elbow each other.

Lummy laughs. "They're just showin' you respect."

"I know," as I point my finger at one and then the other, "but you two call me Marion, got it?"

They both nod and smile at each other. Smith eases out the door with Sted behind him that rattles those little bells dangling above his head as he leaves. Those bells will haunt me the rest of my life. I see Tom Kimbrell's face every time they ring.

"Slap the Devil and throw those hell's bells out in the alley."

Lummy whispers. "Watch what you say, Marion. Even Michael the archangel didn't slander Satan when they were disputing over the body of Moses." I nod. He's right. Why anger the Evil One any more than he already is?

I turn to Josie. "Can you go get whatever belongings you've got and be at the livery in half an hour?"

She's like a butterfly dancing around not knowing which flower she's supposed to go to next. I take her by the shoulders and point her to the back door. "If you got pants and a shirt, pack them. Any money or personal stuff, stash it on your person somewhere."

Josie races to the door. "Yes, ma'am, and yes, ma'am, I'll do it."

"Hold on, Josie, I want you to go get food enough for four people for a week. Get salt pork, coffee, canned beans and peaches, flour for biscuits, and yeah, get some sweets. Pick up two more canteens and a bar of soap. Looks like I'll have to get my bath on the way to wherever the heck the Buyer is. Got it?" I reach for my money purse I keep inside my jacket.

Lummy tosses Josie a five-dollar gold piece. "Nope, I got this."

"Thanks, but I just—"

"We're in this together until we're not, understand?"

"Yes, sir."

"And there ain't no 'sirs' out here either, *ma'am*. Uncle Lummy works just fine."

I turn and place my hands on my hips. *"Ye-e-e-s,* sir, Uncle Lummy." I bat my eyes like a little girl wanting a piece of candy for her and her dolly.

Lummy laughs. "Oh, stop it."

I shake my head and call, "Josie? Humph." She's standing close behind and startles me.

"Yes'um? Right here."

"First of all, don't sneak up on me like that. I don't like anybody standing that close behind me, understand?"

"Yes, ma'am. Won't happen again."

"Just one more thing. Don't let anyone see you, especially the whorehouse owner. Slow down and go about your business like normal, understand?"

Josie stops at the door, takes a deep breath, and walks into the back alley at an easy gait looking both ways.

"I hope we're not making a big mistake taking on these two children."

Lummy laughs. "It's all your fault, niece. Your heart is as soft as butter and strong as iron. That's good."

"We'll see."

Lummy puts his shirt back. He tucks it in and straps his pistol belt around his waist. He cringes a little when he accidentally bumps his side. "How much, Doc?"

Doc squints, studying first me, then Lummy. "Fifty cents ought to take care of it."

Lummy hands him two dollars. "It's worth more than that to me, and this probably ain't nearly enough."

Doc laughs. "Don't you know nobody gets rich being a doctor? But thank you kindly."

Lummy snickers. "I've heard that, but now see it's all true." He shakes Doc's hand and turns to me. "I'm ready when you are."

I grab my hat. "Let's go out the back way."

"So nobody will see us?"

"No, so I don't have to hear the Devil's bells again."

THE BEGINNING
OF A PLAN

Just 'cause you got the particulars don't mean you got the whole plan.

2:30 p.m., August 31, 1886

WE STEP INTO the livery from the alley out back and wait to let our eyes adjust.

I whisper to Lummy, "Somebody's in here."

"Took you long enough to get here." Sted stands tall and lean, a Colt on his hip and a Winchester in the crook of his arm. He removes his hat to wipe the sweat and his short, cropped mane has waves like what follows a river steamer, rolling and gentle, and about the same color—soft brown. His dancing eyes break through the walls in my heart, and I can't stop it. This man is so perfectly formed and handsome, someone could use him as a model to carve a Greek marble statue like the ones I saw in picture books at school. We sure could use another hero like Achilles traveling with us on this odyssey. And one so easy on the eyes, like Sted.

Smith walks from one of the stalls leading a mare, saddled and ready to go.

Sted has the jitters. "I stopped by the sheriff's office on the way here to make sure no one knows about y'all. You won't believe this, but another girl was just taken from Red River Station." He's shaking like he's got the shivers.

Lummy goes to the stall where our horses are put up. "Where's that?"

Sted rubs the back of his neck. "Almost due north, just across the Red River, as you could imagine… in the Indian Territory." He slaps his hat on his leg. "I'm so mad, I could spit."

I stomp my foot. "Lummy, we need to head up to Red River Station and fast."

"Your call, Marion."

"So, Sted, what's the best way to get there from here?"

"Why the trail you came in on leads straight to Red River Station. It's a hundred miles, give or take a mile."

"Is there a faster way?"

"Sure, the railroad, but it'll cost you. It'll spare your horses, though."

I look to Lummy. "What do you think?"

"I'm good either way, your choice."

"The railroad it is then. We'll get to Red River Station and find out what to do from there."

Sted scratches his chin. "Surely somebody'll tell us what happened to that girl who just got snatched."

Did I just hear Sted say "us?" My heart flutters at the possibility he might join us.

"You'd think so. These men, if you can call them men, have everybody cowering like chickens when a hawk flies over." I look around the circle of people who are rapidly becoming my posse.

Lummy steps over to Smith. "Son, we're takin' a big chance on you. You could be joinin' us to be a spy or kill us in our sleep. But for some reason, I believe you're becoming a different man."

"Sir, I swear on the Bible I'm with y'all lock, stock, and barrel. I promise I—"

"Anybody can put his hand on a Bible and take a vow. The Devil does it all the time. Look me in the eye and tell me you're with us all the way."

Smith straightens up like he's taking the oath of allegiance to enlist in the army. "Mister Lummy, I promise to be faithful and true to you, Marion, Josie, and Sted at the cost of my life."

Lummy takes a step closer. "I'm holdin' you to it, young man, and pray that you succeed… because I will." Smith knows exactly what Lummy means. "One more thing, Smith. Tell us now where the Buyer's hideout is."

Smith shudders. "I'm afraid to even speak it, seein' how my life has been threatened so many times if I was to tell." Smith lightly touches the stitched up cut I gave him on his cheek. "It's about eighty miles this side of Fort Smith, Arkansas. A place called Robbers Cave. It's not far from Edwards Store near Red Oak."

Lummy takes Smith by the shoulders and shakes him a bit. "Good enough, John."

Smith lushes with embarrassment. "It feels real good doin' the right thing for a change."

"All right then, are we all good with that plan?"

Smith and Josie nod. Lummy purses his chin and nods. Sted stares at me like a boy who's falling in love with his schoolmarm.

I put my hands on my hips, waiting. "What's it gonna be, lawman? We're going after the Buyer and whoever else we might find."

Sted rubs his hands together. "I surely do want to go. It'd make me a marked man and the Buyer would send his men after me, and y'all for that matter."

"We'll all be fine. We need you to go."

Sted grins. "We?"

"We might luck up and find your sister, Sted."

"That's a good enough reason to go just in itself, but I have to know if you want me to go."

I lean over in my saddle and hold onto the saddle horn. "You're going to make me say it, aren't you?"

"Yes, I am. I'm goin' for my sister, but also I'm goin' to be with you, Marion."

"I want you to go, Sted." The burn in my eyes brings a tear. I dare not wipe it or be found out.

His stern face melts to that of a puppy dog. "Then, I'm goin' with you."

"We'll split any reward five ways, if good with all y'all?" Everyone nods in agreement.

I pay the liveryman fifty dollars for the extra horse and rigging for Josie. He threw the livery bill for our other horses in for free. We gather up, and I check our gang of justice seekers—Uncle Lummy, Sted, Smith, and Josie—all booted and in the saddle. An unlikely bunch to be my posse but the folks Creator sent to go with me.

"Let's go." We ease out of the stable, hats pulled down low, and make no sudden moves. There's so many people wandering these streets, I doubt anyone cares about… wait a minute. The old codger who we met in the desert and sat with Lummy in the saloon for a moment leans back against a storefront in a straight-back chair, chewing on a straw. He gives me a side nod at two men skulking behind a couple of posts down the street, trying not to be seen. I turn back to tip my hat to Uncle Silas, but he's gone. It figures. But I do appreciate the warning. The two men ease back into the shadows and wait. We amble down the street acting as though we don't see them, but I do keep my hand near my pistol.

After we pass them, Lummy leans over and whispers, "You get a good look at 'em? We're sure to see them again."

"Then let's go a few miles out of town, cover our tracks, and circle back for the train. We've got time before it leaves."

"Good plan. I like it."

OUR HORSES AND gear are loaded in one of the livestock railcars. We settle into our seats on the Fort Worth and Denver Railway car, and fortunately, we gave the two men stalking us the slip. We rode hard out of town, leaving an easy trail to follow. We peeled off the main road north like we were taking a piss break, then returned to the main road with so many tracks, the two following us wouldn't know which way we went. Those dern fools are probably still out there looking for us.

The conductor starts down the aisle taking tickets. "Sir?" I ask. "When will we arrive at Red River Station?"

He pulls out his watch. "This train will only take you as far as Henrietta. You'll have to ride back east, oh, maybe forty miles I'm guessing, to get to Red River Station located on Salt Creek."

"And if we want to get on a train headed east later, where should we do that?"

The conductor pulls out a small stack of schedules with maps from his inside jacket pocket. "Let me see here… now where was it you said you were going?"

"Back to the railroad, if that's the best way to go. Kinda in the Fort Smith direction, if that helps."

"It does. Let me see here now." He shuffles the papers and finally lands his finger on a spot on a map. "Here, ride east from Red River Station to Colbert, just across the river from Preston. You have to start there because the bridge washed out a few years ago. You should be able to go north to wherever you plan to disembark… Limestone Gap, I'm thinking, if you want to cut across country toward Fort Smith, Arkansas."

I nod. "Thank you, kind sir."

He checks his watch. "Humph, it's three o'clock. This train is usually on time, so we should be in Henrietta by seven straight up, barring no unforeseen problems."

"Such as?"

He holds up his finger and finishes taking tickets. He walks back and squats beside where Lummy and I sit. Sted leans over from his seat across the narrow aisle. "This train has been known to get boarded by outlaws on occasion. It's been a while, and frankly, they're overdue."

"What are they after?"

He grimaces. "Besides the occasional fleecing of passengers, why you, and"—he points at Josie—"her."

I squirm in my seat a bit. "And the railroad just lets them get away with it?"

"There's usually too many of them, and we never know when they… we tried keeping railroad marshals on board, but that didn't work either. So we just take our chances, and hopefully whoever is riding the train helps us deal with them."

"Where do they get on?"

"On any one of the nothing little stops where we have to get fuel and water for the engine."

"I see. Do you recognize them when you see them?"

"They wear a—"

Smith leans over and whispers, "A queen of hearts poker card in their hats." He pulls it from a bag and hands it to me.

The conductor's eyes light up. "That's it. It almost always has the top left corner snipped off."

"Why is that?"

Smith whispers, "Nobody dares bother a man wearing a queen of hearts in his hat. Not in these parts. It's like protection. You hurt one of 'em, you hurt 'em all, and all of 'em come after you. Left-hand snipped off means you're just a mule to haul ladies to the Buyer's clients. Right-hand corner snipped off means you snatch girls and women for the Buyer to sort out and sell. It's like a cattle auction where he hides out in the Indian Territory. I'm ashamed to even have this on me."

Lummy pats his shoulder. "You're not that person anymore, Smith. Don't worry about it."

"I'm just glad I'm on the right side of things again." He nods and sits back in his seat, tears dribbling down his cheeks.

Sted leans over to the boy. "You follow through with your new way of thinking, and we'll forget all about you chasing this girl and cuttin' Lummy, you hear what I'm sayin'?" Sted realizes he's made an offer involving two people who have the right to press charges. "Sorry, Josie and Lummy, I should've asked. Do you folks want to press charges against Smith here?"

Josie looks to Lummy who shrugs. Lummy smiles and answers, "As long as he stays on the straight and narrow, I'm good. Josie?"

She grins. "Me too."

She stares at Smith for a moment longer than he's comfortable with. He turns red and ducks his head with a grin. Did I just see a spark?

Then Lummy's face gets rigid and stern, like a rock face on a mountain. He peers through eyes slits narrowed by the sun and pronounces, "You get off the straight and narrow, Smith, it won't be the pearly gates you'll be waltzing through. No, I'll personally send you through the gates of hell and won't feel nothin' about doin' it, understand?"

"Yes, sir, I do. You can count on me."

Lummy collects himself. "Sorry, John, it's hittin' me pretty hard right now what we're about to face, and I'm tryin' to trust you, son."

Smith leans up. "I will not let you down."

Lummy purses his lips and nods. "All right, then."

I squeeze the conductor's shoulder. "Thank you, kind sir, we'll be ready if there's any trouble on the way."

"Don't mention it. Glad I can count on you good folks."

The steady rocking and rolling of our car on the tracks lulls me into a sleep I've needed all day. A bit of peace on the trail in the land of the blind where the one-eyed man is king. At least for now.

A MAN APPROACHES while I rest, my hat pulled low to shade my eyes from the red western sun streaming through the window I'm leaning against. He sits down beside me and reaches to hug me and rub his hands all over me. I start to fight him off, kicking and screaming for Uncle Lummy to help me when—

Someone shakes my shoulders. I draw Lummy's old knife—now mine—

and start to stab someone, anyone, when a strong arm catches my thrust and a voice whispers, "Marion, it's me, Uncle Lummy. Everything's all right."

I stare into his eyes for what seems like an hour but only a moment. I catch my breath. "Sorry, Uncle Lummy, I must've been dreaming."

Sted hands me a kerchief doused with water the conductor brings. The cool, damp cloth feels good on my face. Smith and Josie both have their mouths open. I must've frightened everyone in the train car.

Lummy nods to Smith and Josie. "She'll be all right. Just a bad dream, that's all." Other onlookers still stare. Lummy snaps his fingers. "Nothing to see here, folks. She just had a bad dream, that's all. Be on about your own business. Thank you."

I'm shaking a bit. "Thinking about those men maybe boarding our train sent me back to Natchez in the whorehouse. I was...."

Sted puts his arm around me but not so tight as to be uncomfortable. "It's all right, Marion, you don't have to say any more."

He offers me a sip of water, and I smile in thanks. I watch the landscape roll by without trying to think about anything.

The train comes to a stop as the late afternoon sun blinds my best efforts to look outside. We stand to stretch. The conductor quicksteps down the aisle to us. He leans over to whisper in my ear, "They're here. Two men with queen of hearts cards in their hats. What do we do?"

I end my stretch. "What can we do, or better said, what are we allowed to do?"

"Anybody here got a badge?"

Sted opens his vest to show his shiny star. "I do. I'm a deputy sheriff from Fort Worth. Will that do?"

The conductor straightens up. "Dang straight it will. We need to make a show of force, if you're willing."

I grin. "Just the excitement we've been looking for, sir."

Sted says, "Lummy, Marion, raise your right hands. Do you swear to uphold the law under the authority given me by the sheriff of Tarrant County?"

Lummy and I answer together, "I do."

Sted grins. "Sorry, I don't have any extra badges for you."

I check my holster. "My badge is strapped to my hip and in this sheath on my belt."

Sted squints. "Good 'nough."

I lean down. "Josie, you and Smith stay here and watch our stuff. Smith, I don't want them to see you. If they do, they'll for sure know what we're up to. So hide your face."

"Thank you, ma'am, I'll watch after Josie and—"

"Stop calling me ma'am, and from what I've seen, she'll be watching over your boney little butt."

We all laugh. Even Smith takes it well.

By the time we reach the end of our car, a commotion has already broken out between the conductor and the two men who have been tracking us.

Sted pulls Lummy and I both back to take the lead as we stop outside and turn toward the boarding platform. The two men shove the conductor. He trips and falls back on the railcar boarding steps.

The tall one asks, "And who might you be?"

"Sted Walker, Deputy Sheriff of Tarrant County from Fort Worth, and these are my sworn deputies."

He laughs and elbows the younger man who has his hand on his pistol. "Well looky here, a sawed-off lawman, an old worn-out trail tramp, and a girl. You think you can keep us off this train? See these cards in our hats? We've got business on that car, and we're gonna—"

"Do what?" I bark as I draw Lummy's knife from its sheath and point the blade at his neck. The clicking of Lummy's Colt .44 lets me know he's ready. "And as far as this old trail tramp goes, he's rough as a cob and has twice the grit scattered across a Mississippi River sandbar."

"Is that right, little lady," the taller one says as he undresses me with his eyes. "Yeah, the boss would be pleased to have you come along with us. He might want to keep you all for himself and—"

Sted slaps the man so hard he falls to his knees, shaking his head and holding his face.

The tall man yells, "You nearly broke my jaw, you worthless lawdog." He starts to stand but Sted puts the heel of his boot on the man's chest and shoves him back on his backside. The younger man reaches to pull his pistol but Lummy yanks his .44 quick as a rattler strike and has it pointed at the man's head.

"Do it, and I'll part your hair just below the scalp line, understand?"

The younger man reholsters his gun. I put the knife under the younger man's chin. "Uh-uh. You'll be giving that pistol to me, and get your partners there while I'm askin' nicely." Both hand their weapons over without a fuss. I hand them both to Sted who gives them to the conductor.

Sted holsters his pistol. "I ought'a take you to the local sheriff, but figure there ain't one here. I ain't takin' you with us, so you best find somewhere else to go, 'cause if I see you again, I'm gonna shoot you and take what's left to the sheriff in Fort Worth, got it?" They nod and leave.

"Wait." I place my hands on my hips. "Not before you boys do two things. First, you apologize to the conductor. He's only doing his job."

They remove their hats and apologize. The tall one asks, "And the second thing?"

"I want the queen of hearts cards from your hats, both of you."

"We can't, that'll signal a lot of folks that we're not under the Buyer's protection no more, and...."

"You should've thought about that when you joined up with that sorry sack of snakes."

They hang their heads and walk away. The younger cries, "We're dead, aren't we?"

The taller one whispers, "Deader'n a doornail."

RED RIVER STATION

Sometimes a nothing little town can offer the best hospitality.

7:15 a.m., September 1, 1886

WE RIDE TO the end of the line at Henrietta, and deboard the train. The conductor wishes us well. "You folks go with God, and if I'm thinking right, when you get off at Limestone Gap, go to Riddle's Station, which used to be a stop for Butterfield Overland Mail stagecoach. Once you pass through The Narrows, you'll want to take the trail to the right toward Red Oak. Edwards Store is not far from there, another stop on the stagecoach trail before the war. You'll probably find what you're looking for there."

I turn to Smith, who nods in agreement. "That's the place, Miss Marion. I heard 'em talkin' about Edwards Store. It ain't too far to their hideout from there. I've been to Red Oak once before, but not to the hideout. Don't imagine it'd be too hard to find, if the right question is asked of the right person in the right way."

"You mean the local Choctaws?"

He nods. "That'd be your best bet, ma'am."

I let the "ma'am" reference go this time. I tap my chin with my index finger. "You might be a big help after all, Smith, if you're brave enough."

Lummy whispers, "What're you talkin' about, Marion. He's just a kid. You want his blood on your hands too?"

"The way I got it figured, we'll all have each other's blood on our hands, but more so the Buyer's and his henchmen. I don't have it all worked out, but we've got to start making some kind of plan. Let me think on it a bit. Then we'll talk, all right?"

Lummy throws his hands up in surrender. "Your call, like I always say."

Smith straightens up as if called to attention by a sergeant in the army. "I'm ready to do anythin' I can to help."

Josie steps up beside him. "Me too. I'm ready."

My mind is working alive like a beehive in springtime. Smith and Josie might just get us inside the hideout. A plan is forming in my brain. I just need a little time to sort it out. Mostly sort how we can do this and me not get us all killed.

"Let's get on up to Red River Station and see if we can pick up any information there we can use."

WE ARRIVE AT the edge of the sleepy little one-street town of Red River Station at dawn the next day. We're tired and hungry, but at least where I hope we can find out which way to head next. I know we'll go east, but if we can pick up the trail where the Buyer's men left from here, we might have a good chance of catching them, and getting to the hideout.

Red River Station looks like it would've been a booming center of attention back in cattle-drive days. Not now. We stop at the only place open—a run-down mercantile that happens to have some sort of café inside. An old dog lifts his head to howl half-heartedly and rolls over to go back to his napping. The owner of the place walks out onto the porch and greets us with open arms.

"Glad to see you folks. You must've been traveling all night, I 'spect."

I dismount and wrap the reins around the hitching post. "And you would be correct. Can we get breakfast?"

"How does ham and eggs, fried taters, biscuits and gravy, a side of baked apples, and all the hot coffee and cold milk you can drink?"

Lummy licks his lips. "I don't know, sounds pretty good to me."

"Malachi White's my name. Just call me Mal. Come on in, please. All are welcome."

We sit at the table in the back of the room, and being the only patrons, it's nice to have a quiet place all to ourselves. Mal brings out five big stoneware mugs and a pot of fresh coffee.

"Cream and sugar are there on the table. I'll have your food out in a bit. My wife, Christine, is a fine cook." He sets us each a cup and pours the steaming dark brown liquid. He turns to leave but asks, "You folks just passing through? What am I saying? Nobody stays in Red River Station. Everyone passes through these days. Ain't much for business around here anymore. Not since the cattle started being hauled on trains."

I study this man to see if he's someone I can trust.

Lummy stirs sugar into his coffee. "We're just passin' through, but we heard about a young woman snatched from around here somewhere. Wonder if you might know anythin' about that?"

Mal staggers for a moment, then breaks down and cries with his shoulders slumping in despair. He wipes his tears as his wife brings out hot biscuits. "The rest of your food will be ready—" She sets the basket of biscuits on the table. "Mal, what's wrong, dear?"

He sobs a bit and blows his nose into his kerchief. "Oh, these folks asked about our daughter who was taken two days ago by those rascals with the queen of hearts cards in their hats."

I ask, "May I know what happened, if it's not too hard on you?"

He straightens up and steadies himself. He starts but Christine takes over when he starts to sniffle again. "You have to excuse my husband, he's just all broken up about our daughter. Me, too, but I have high hopes we will get her back."

I sip my coffee and set the mug back down. "Yes'um, we're sorry about you losing your daughter. How old is she?"

"Sixteen looking like she's twenty-one, if you know what I mean. They came in all friendly like, had supper with us, and...." Christine starts weeping.

I get up to console her, and she stiffens up. "Nope, I told myself I was gonna stay strong through all of this. And I will."

I admire this woman. "Mind if we ask you a few questions?"

Mal brightens up. "You folks lookin' for these bandits? Yes, please, ask us anything."

Lummy leans back in his chair with his coffee cup in hand. "We're gonna be here for a bit, to eat, rest, and such. Why don't you bring our food, Missus Christine, and we'll try to figure this thing out. And yes, we are on their trail. That's why we're here."

Christine lays out a fine breakfast table with more food than we can eat. She and Mal pull up chairs as we gorge on the best food we've had since Fort Worth.

Lummy nods for me to do the talking. I'm sure he'll chime in if I miss something. "Mal, Christine, go on, tell us exactly what happened and don't leave out a detail."

Christine starts in, "There were three of them. I noticed they were traveling light, like they came in from a camp somewhere else. We've seen a lot of drifters and cowhands lookin' for work pass through here. They ate good, paid us well, and asked to sleep in our barn out back for the night. We had no objections, but around midnight we heard some scuffling and then saw them riding off with our daughter Carol Ann draped across one of 'em's saddles. She was kicking and screaming somethin' fierce, and...." She can hold it no longer. She bawls like a calf lost from its mother.

I whisper, "So she's a fighter, that's good."

Mal wraps his arms around his wife and looks each of us in the eyes. "Can you help us? Will you help us get our daughter back?"

Lummy asks, "Can you tell us what they looked like, anything that'll help us know who to look for?"

"Yes, now that you mention it, one had a riverboat gambler's hat, black I believe it was, and who went by the name Michael. The second one was scarred all down his neck like somebody threw a pan of grease on him. But that other one, the one-eyed man, he never said a word. He just hummed the same song over and over. What was it, that tune he kept on hummin', Christine?"

Without blinking, she says, "'Camptown Races.' You know it?"

Lummy looks at me, and answers, "Yes, we know it."

Christine rubs her forehead. "The reason I know it so well was as he and his demons rode away, the one-eyed man kept singing at the top of his lungs, 'doo dah, doo dah.' It was the only words of the song he sang. If I'd had a gun, I would'a shot him dead off his horse."

Mal comforts his wife. "Now, now, dear, you know we can't…."

I ask, "What are you thinking, Uncle Lummy?" Lummy takes a deep draw from his coffee mug.

Smith clears his throat. "I know them, two of 'em at least."

I grow impatient. "Well, spit it out, Smith."

"Never seen the one-eyed man before, though I know who he is, but them other two, I know their names, well, the names they go by. Michael Angel and Little Dave Greasefire, as you can understand why he's called that. Michael makes you call him Saint Michael, like in the Bible. He's the meanest of all the Buyer's men. He carries a double-edged sword and is fond of slicing up people who get in his way, or if the Buyer tells him to do it. Little Dave likes to burn people alive, pouring tar or bacon grease on 'em, and then he lights them up. Neither one of them has a heart." Smith shivers like a blast of cold air hit him between the shoulder blades.

I rake the table with my fingernails. "I could take that sword from the devil's angel, carve them both up like a Sunday ham, and burn them piece by piece. Why I'd—"

Lummy takes my arm and holds it. "Save it for later, Marion. We'll catch up with them, watch and see."

"You're right, Uncle." He removes his hand and pokes his wrist with the owl claw his Choctaw friend gave him. He's struggling with this just like I am.

I ask, "Mal, Christine, anything else?"

Christine refills our coffee cups with the pot on the table. "Carol Ann was wearing a white nightgown wrapped in a blue patchwork quilt I made her not long ago. She's about your size, ma'am, and has dark brown hair shoulder length, kinda curly."

"That's a big help, thank you."

Josie leans over and whispers, "They've already redressed her by now to look like a boy. Keeps down the suspicions. But, they won't throw that quilt away."

"Anything else?" I scan our group, most of whom hang their heads. "Uncle Lummy, would you say grace and ask God to help us in our search?"

He nods, we bow our heads, and he says the prettiest prayer I've heard in a long time. He prays like God is sitting right here with us. He finishes, and we eat our fill. In silence. God is sitting right here with us. I feel him.

WE REST ALL day in the barn, catching enough sleep to make it until the next stop, which might be in a couple of days. We enjoy a fine supper around four o'clock and pack up. Mal and Christine load us up with food and won't let us pay for the meals we had. Lummy lays a double eagle on the counter when they aren't looking. That man's heart is bigger than his tall, well-built frame.

Sted and Smith bring the horses from the barn where they have been fed, watered, and combed. Smith is a farrier at heart, loving horses and caring for them like they are his children. I think he's a good boy at heart. Probably just got mixed up with the wrong people at the right time—meaning, a young impressionable boy with nowhere else to go until somebody showed him some attention and gave him a place to belong. He's with us now, though. I pray that he changes. I have faith that he will.

WIRING A FRIEND

Going to war means calling your best warrior to battle.

3:00 p.m., September 2, 1886

THE LITTLE-UNDER-a-hundred-mile trek across Choctaw land was pretty uneventful. We rode four hours, rested one, rode four, rested one, and so on. We ease into Colbert, just north of Preston and across the Red River. The rail line starts up again here since the bridge across the Red River is washed out. We ride into the small town and spot the depot.

Lummy whispers, "Come with me."

I look back. "Sted, would you and Smith take the horses just out to the edge of town, and watch after Josie? Lummy and I will figure out where we'll eat and stay for the night, and if it's safe to do so."

Lummy and I dismount, and as we hand our reins over to Sted, he tips his hat and winks at me. I can't help but smile. I lean over to Lummy. "I believe I'll be gettin' that bath here."

Lummy laughs out loud. "That sure will be fine by me. I believe the horse I'm ridin' smells better'n—"

I pop his shoulder. "Why you, I ought'a slap the—" I hold my hands and surrender to my better judgment.

Lummy whispers, "Seriously, though, that young man sure has got a sweet tooth for you, niece. Better watch him."

I backhand his shoulder. "You better watch it, with that big mouth of yours. I don't want him thinking I got eyes for him."

Lummy snickers. "You don't think he already knows you do?"

"And what if he does?"

"You're in a good spot, Marion. Havin' a bit of love for someone else is part of the healing. It means your heart isn't sealed up like a stone rolled over a cave."

"Hmmm, hadn't thought of it like that." I change the subject. "Where we going?"

"To call on our best warrior." Lummy picks up his pace, and I struggle to keep up. I have to trot to keep up with that long-legged rascal.

"You don't mean?"

"I do mean."

"You know he's probably just now getting home good, and you want him to come help us with this?"

Lummy stops in the middle of the one-street town. "Let's just say I won't do this without him." He starts walking again to the train depot, and faster.

We enter the telegraph office, where the little bells irritate the fire out of me again. I want to shoot them off the top of the dang door. But I don't. I've got to learn to deal with them and not let them deal with me.

Lummy gives me that look of *let me take care of this.* He walks over to a fairly recent map posted on the wall. He studies it without placing a finger on it, ever watchful of the telegraph clerk who seems to be a bit nosy. He steps over to the small window where the clerk looks over his spectacles that have slid down his nose and asks, "What can I do for you?"

"I want to send a telegram, please, sir."

"All right, what would you like to say?"

"Come now to the town of your father's grave."

The clerk looks up. "That's it, no town, no name."

Lummy leans in. "Is there a problem?"

The clerk is a bit nervy. "It's just that we like to have a better sense of where our customers are headed and who they are to better serve them. You know, in case they run into trouble."

"Should I be expectin' trouble?"

"No, no, I didn't mean… I apologize, sir. Now who would you like to send this to and where?"

"Rainy Mills in Winnfield, Looseana."

"Fine, I'll get this done in a few minutes."

"You'll do it now, and I want a return message sayin' it's been received, understand?"

The clerk lets out a sigh. "Yes, sir, Mister?"

"Coyote."

"Coyote?"

I want to burst out laughing but manage to hold it in.

"Is there a problem with that too?"

"Oh, no, no, sir, I'll send it right now. Your return message verifying it is received should follow in a couple of minutes. Amazing and wonderful world in which we live, isn't it?"

Lummy and I seat ourselves on a bench and wait without saying anything else to the clerk or to each other. It's clear he's the type to have loose lips if the price is right, or if his life is on the line. Lummy certainly knows how to play the cloak-and-dagger game.

The clerk announces after a few minutes, "Done, and here's your receipt. That'll be fifty cents."

Lummy slaps two silver dollars and a half-dollar on the counter. "Fifty cents for sending the message, a dollar for your silence, and a dollar for your name written on that receipt. I want first and last name."

"What? I'm not sure why…."

"I said, the money is for your silence, and I want your name in case I find out your loose lips happen to spout off the right information to the wrong people, understand?"

"I do."

"So say it… you were never here."

The clerk starts to hang his head.

Lummy barks, "No, sir, you look me in the eye so I won't forget you, nor you me. Say it."

The clerk fidgets and wrings his hands. "I could get in serious trouble for this."

"You could get dead because of this, and besides, you would lose your job at the very least. Now you wouldn't want that, would you?"

"No… no, sir, I wouldn't."

"Say it and look me in the eye."

The clerk sits up straight on his barstool. "You were never here."

"All right, then, who was never here?"

"You were never here. None of you."

"See, that wasn't so hard, was it?"

"I'm confident that I don't know the answer to that just yet. He has eyes and ears everywhere, don't you know?"

"We do. But don't you feel much better about yourself?"

"I don't because if *he* finds out I saw you and didn't tell him, well then, I'm dead. Dead if I tell, dead if I don't."

I ask, "Who has eyes and ears everywhere? He who?"

The clerk looks out the front and back windows, and whispers, "You know I know who you're looking for. The Buyer, that's who. He and two of his men came through here with a couple of girls he snatched somewhere west of here down around the Texas border and—"

I step forward. "Did one have a blue-and-white patchwork quilt wrapped around her?"

The clerk furrows his brow. "Why yes… matter of fact, yes, she did. How would you know that?"

"Never mind that. You just keep your trap shut like my rather large friend here has instructed you, understand?"

"Yes, ma'am. Just so you know, his men come through here often checking for any news about anybody I deem suspicious. If somebody saw y'all come in here, they will be asking who you are. What should I tell them?"

"Do we look suspicious?" I ask.

"That telegram says you are, but I'm no friend to the Buyer. A couple of his men rode in not long before y'all did. I'm sure they're still hanging around. Probably eating a meal in the café a few doors down. Won't be long after you walk out of here they'll descend on me like a couple of buzzards on a dead dog."

"At least you're not a dead dawg. Not yet, anyway." Lummy laughs but the clerk doesn't.

I notice on the schedule posted on the wall that the next train north will leave in an hour. I elbow Lummy and wink. "Sir, if you don't mind me asking, does the ferry cross the river regularly?"

He smiles and stands up. "Oh, yes, ma'am, as soon as a fair load is ready to cross."

"How much?"

"Ten cents a person, fifteen apiece for animals."

"Thank you." I look to Lummy. "I believe that would be the best way to go to Fort Worth, cross the river and catch the train on the other side, don't you?"

"Sounds good."

The clerk waves. "You come back now, anytime."

We step out of the telegraph office. "Good thinkin', Marion, throwing that clerk off our track. He's gonna talk, especially if a knife is put to his throat."

"Yeah, I know it, Lummy. And we've got to get that Smith kid out of sight. If the Buyer's men are here, they might recognize him, and Josie, too, for that matter."

"What's after that?"

"I have a plan."

We find Sted, Smith, and Josie resting in the shade of a scrub oak at the edge of town. That's good. Hopefully no one saw them.

I ask, "Sted, did y'all stop anywhere, by chance? See anyone suspicious, talk to anyone?"

Sted gets up from where he's been leaning against the tree. "No, why? What's goin' on?"

"Tell you about it on the way. Let's get going." I look at Lummy. "Guess I'll be foregoing that bath again."

We mount up and slip out of town the best way we know to not be seen. We circle around and hide down by the river where the willows grow thick. We can still see the town but no one can see us.

"When the train blows the whistle to board, we'll ride around the back side of the depot." I hand Sted money. "Go to the ticket office and get us boarding for somewhere past Limestone Gap. That'll throw the Buyer's men off if they're following us. Hopefully we can get on board without making too much noise or being seen."

Lummy offers, "Sted, why don't you stay there and watch. You're a lawman. Anybody asks, you can tell 'em you're goin' to pick up a prisoner or some story like that."

Sted grins. "I can do that." He walks his horse up the riverbank and back to town.

It's not long before the whistle blows. We trot our mounts to the train depot and up on the loading dock straight into a livestock car. Sted is already inside waiting for us.

"I told the clerk in the ticket office that I was on a secret mission for the government and that my posse needed to board without being noticed. Anyway, I worked it out that a few miles down the track the train will stop so we can enter the passenger car."

I smile. "You did good, Sted, thank you."

Lummy asks, "Did you see anybody we might need to be aware of?"

"Yeah, a couple of yahoos stepped out of the telegraph office talking about us crossing the ferry and catching the train to Fort Worth."

I breathe a heavy sigh. "Good then, we can rest our minds about that. At least for a little while anyway."

We dismount, remove our mounts' saddles, and settle for the train ride northeast and to what's waiting ahead.

Lummy and I stand off to one side. I ask, "Are we crazy for doing this? I mean, this is a lot."

"It is, but the reward is worth the risk. And I'm not talkin' about the money."

"Then what?"

"You're healing. Let this, what we're doin' bring you closer to puttin' some things behind you. It has to happen. That young man Sted has eyes for you, and you for him, and that's good. Even if it goes nowhere, it's been good for you to have that kind of interest again, or maybe for the first time, I don't know."

I hang my head. "You're right, Uncle Lummy. I've had a few men that crossed my mind and touched my heart a couple of times when I was with them, but nothing like this. Sted is a good man, isn't he?"

"Yeah… yeah, he is."

LIMESTONE GAP

Getting clean helps a body sleep better.

2:20 a.m., September 3, 1886

THE RIDE NORTH is pretty easy. The first stop of any size is Caddo. While the train takes on water and more fuel, we step over to a small café and wolf down ham biscuits and coffee before the whistle blows to reboard. We settle into our seats and into a much needed rest. I was hoping for a bath back there in Colbert, but there was no time. And I stink.

I'm a bit embarrassed by my own smell, especially with Sted around. They say the one person who can put up with your own bad body odor is you, and even get used to it after a while. Not me. I grab my saddlebag and canteen and head to the toilet closet to wash. The little room with the one-seater toilet is hardly big enough to turn around in, but I make do. I look down into the toilet to find the ground going by underneath us. I guess the railroad tracks are well-fertilized. I laugh at my own bad joke.

I wash off with soap and a rag I have in my bag and water from my canteen as best I can. It feels good to be clean, at least the worst-smelling parts. I need to do something about my dirty, oily hair, but can't until we get somewhere. Maybe Limestone Gap will have a place to bathe, even if it's just a creek.

I return to my seat to find my bunch stretched out as best they can and snoozing. I snuggle up against Uncle Lummy's shoulder who must've fell immediately into dreamland. I wake thinking I'd only been asleep for a few minutes but the conductor is announcing, "Limestone Gap Station, and it's seven o'clock sharp."

I feel as tired as I did when I sat down. We're all moving slowly when the train whistle blows, the first signal that it will be pulling away soon.

I tell my gang, "Let's go."

We retrieve our mounts and saddle them for the next leg of our ride. But I'm hungry and need a bath. We walk our horses over to the mercantile that doubles as a café and hitch them. We start to make the steps when a tall, dark man sporting a large hat and twin pistols steps out the door, the little bells ringing behind him.

"And who might you good folks be?" He gently opens his jacket to reveal a badge inside attached to his vest.

I side-eye Lummy to give him the lead. "Oh, nobody in particular, really. Why do you ask?"

"I'm Captain Charles Leflore with the Choctaw Lighthorse police and this here is my partner, Sam Sixkiller. We keep a sharp eye out for any outlaws. Been way too much killin' and train robbin' lately, and we aim to end it."

I take a step up to shake his hand when Sted thrusts out his hand. "Pleased to meet you gentlemen. I'm Sted Walker, Deputy Sheriff from Fort Worth, Texas, and if you have a moment, we'll be happy to tell you our business."

"All right, we were just about to get breakfast before we head out to Muskogee, if you'd like to join us."

Sted looks to me, and I wave for him to follow behind Leflore and Sixkiller. We trail inside to a large round table and about the time we get seated good, a squatty dark-skinned lady with the sweetest smile brings over coffee and the fixings.

"We have salt pork, eggs, corn pone, and gravy. Sorry no biscuits. Supply train is runnin' late. Will that do?" We all nod.

Leflore holds up his index finger. "Put it on my bill, Missus Blue Sky, please, ma'am." She smiles and nods.

I start to say, "Now, Captain, you don't have to—"

"It's the least I can do with what you're here tryin' to do."

"How's that?"

"I know exactly why you're here. The clerk in Red River Station sent word that you'd be coming and the conductor verified it was you. The Buyer, right?" He takes a long sip of his coffee and watches my eyes. There's no fooling this man.

"Yes, sir, we want to take him down and get back a girl he and his gang took from a good family in Red River Station. Sted also lost a sister in one of the Buyer's raids."

"Yeah. Sorry, Sted." He hangs his head. "I just hope she's still alive. Lots of women and girls the Buyer snatches either don't make the trip or even kill themselves when they realize they'll be sold like cattle and abused in every unholy way imaginable."

I shudder at his words.

Leflore gently takes my arm. "You must understand what I'm talkin' about, don't you?"

"All too well, Captain."

"I could tell that about the time we sat down here together."

"Will you help us?"

"Wish I could, but we got so many problems there just ain't enough of us to go 'round. We cut off one snake's head and four grow up and out of the stub, like the Hydra. I just wish I knew how Hercules killed that monster."

Lummy swishes his coffee around in his cup. "One snakehead at a time, I'm thinking."

Leflore elbows Sixkiller, who looks straight ahead and says nothing. "I like this man. Heck, you must be, what, six four, maybe five?"

"Six foot six, and still growin' if I keep eatin' the good food I believe we're about to receive." Everyone laughs.

I lay my palms flat on the table. "But seriously, will you help us?"

Leflore squints. "I would if I could, but Sixkiller and me, we leave for Muskogee after breakfast to find a couple ne'er-do-wells we've been chasin' for some time now."

I chance it. "Can I ask who?"

Sam Sixkiller growls, "Sure you can. A half-breed who goes by Black Hoyt and a white man named Jesse Nicholson. They've been kickin' up their heels and causin' a ruckus up that way. We aim to stop 'em." Sixkiller buries himself back into his chair with his coffee mug pressed against his lips.

Leflore waves his hand. "So you can see, we're happy you're here. We need all the help we can get. Judge Parker is willin' to bless and reward anybody willin' to put on a badge, honor it, and rid the Indian Territory of rat filth like the Buyer. We've been after him for a couple of years now."

Blue Sky brings our food and sets a nice table. We thank her, and she mumbles something about mud all over her floor, and I check my boots. Yep, I drug in part of the street with me when I came in like the rest of my companions.

Leflore samples a piece of salt pork and asks, "How'd y'all get involved with the Buyer?"

I tell him our story about Tarle's wife, Caroline, being taken by Tom Kimbrell, how we rescued her, and after that, we decided to go after the source of the problem, the Buyer.

Leflore finishes his last bite and washes it down with coffee. "So you're the bunch who came from Looseana and took out those outlaws in Austin."

I'm surprised. "Yes, well, part of us are. How'd you know that?"

"Oh, word travels fast when there's telegraph lines and railroads pushing information along."

Sted leans in. "He's right, Marion, and it's a good and bad thing."

Captain Leflore stands and wipes his mouth with a napkin. "We need to hit the trail, and you good folks have your work cut out for you. I usually do my prayin' before I eat, but this time, I'd like us to pray before we all scatter to do the Lord's work. Y'all okay with that?"

We all nod as we finish what we're chewing on. Leflore holds out his hands palms up and prays that we defeat our enemies with the help of the Army of the Almighty. He thanks God for the food, says his amen, and plants his wide-brimmed hat on his head.

Sixkiller stands, and grins just a little. "Get 'em. Show 'em no mercy, 'cause the Buyer will show you none."

Leflore nods for me to follow him out the door. I turn to my posse. "Be back in a minute."

Leflore leans against a post, picking his teeth with a splinter. "You know what you're gettin' into, lady?"

"I believe I do, and there's no stoppin' us, Captain."

"No, I wouldn't think so. So, ride toward Fort Smith to Riddle's Station just before you get to the mountains. You'll see 'em in the distance. Travel through The Narrows and take a sharp right along the hills and find Edwards Store which is not far from Red Oak. They will receive you well. Ask for Andrew, a cousin of mine. He will steer you straight."

"Straight where?"

"Robbers Cave. That's where the Buyer will be, I'm sure of it if he just snatched some new girls. He's probably gettin' ready for another auction, which means he'll be movin' those girls to another location soon. So don't dally. Get on up there and get about your business before he disappears."

"Tell me about Robbers Cave?"

Leflore scratches his ear. "A formidable fortress nearly impregnable. Judge Parker has been tryin' to clean it out for years. Jesse James and even Belle Starr hid out there on occasion. It's a maze of rocky wickedness that'll get you killed if you don't know which trail leads up to it or what path to take through the rocks. Take this." He hands me a double eagle gold piece. "My cousin is a good man, but he won't do this unless I pay him. Can't blame him. It's a helluva risk, and he has a family."

"I thank you, Captain."

"Don't thank me yet. Do that when I come that way after Sixkiller and I take care of this Black Hoyt business. I'll meet you in Red Oak when you're done and take any prisoners you might have. Don't think you'll have any, but it is wishful thinkin'." He snickers. "Now, get your people out here, I want to deputize y'all."

I yell through the batwings, "Lummy, Smith, and the rest, y'all come on out. Sted Walker is already a lawman. You won't need to deputize him." Everyone eases out on the porch.

"You're right."

Lummy, Smith, and I stand up straight and repeat the oath to uphold the law in the Indian Territory and receive badges by the authority of Captain Charles Leflore in the jurisdiction of Judge Isaac C. Parker.

"That'll keep things legal but won't keep you from cashing in on any reward."

Josie claps her hands and Leflore gives her and Smith honorary badges as well.

Being deputized makes me feel better about all of this. "Good, we'll be needing the reward money to get back home."

"You'll be able to get it in Skullyville when you're done. I'll have the voucher ready for you when I see you next." He takes my arm and says, "And make sure I see you good folks again, you hear? Be careful."

"Yes, sir, we will."

He leans in and whispers, "I have a ranch not far from here. It's a good place to rest and hole up for a while, or if you ever need my help."

"Thank you kindly, Captain. I'm sure I'll be taking advantage of your generosity."

"Good, my wife is almost always there. And she's a fine cook and good woman."

I nod, tip my hat, and smile. "Good luck, Captain."

He winks. "Same to you, lady reward hunter."

I never thought of myself as a lawman…law-woman, better said. But, if it gets the job done and the help we need, then so be it.

FINDING ANDREW

The first thing Andrew did was to find his brother Peter
and take him to Jesus. We're looking for Andrew.

Midmorning, September 4, 1886

AROUND MIDNIGHT, WE cross the bridge spanning the Fourche Maline River to reach Riddle's Station, once a stop on the Butterfield Overland Mail route. We rest a moment but move on through The Narrows to find Edwards Store near Red Oak. The store sits fifty yards down the hill from the dogtrot house that looks to have been built some time before the war. We stand in the brush for a moment, getting the lay of the land. The midmorning sun breaks through the trees, and it feels good.

I ask, "Lummy, would you ease up to the store and see if this Andrew character is around. I don't think we should ride up in force. Might signal the wrong person to run tell the Buyer we're here."

He tips his hat. "Good idea. Be back in a bit."

It's not long before Lummy walks his horse back down the hill from the house with a tall, lanky Choctaw alongside him who looks like he could take down any man placed before him with ease. He and Lummy laugh, bantering back and forth. That Lummy hardly meets a stranger anywhere.

Lummy leads the man into our group. "Folks, this is Andrew Flying Hawk. He actually came from Missip, not far from where I grew up. He knew a good friend of mine's family who once lived there. Anyway, he's here to help."

I hand him the double eagle gold piece. "Your cousin, Captain Leflore, said give this to you for your trouble."

"Thank you kindly. I'll take it when I earn it, or you can give it to my family if I'm dead. Either way will be good. I'm glad you people are here. The man you seek is of the Devil, and he must be killed. I will help you."

I pat him on the shoulder. "We're counting on it."

Lummy laughs. "Just like in the Bible, the first thing Andrew did was to find his brother and take him to Jesus. Well, now that Andrew has found us, he won't be takin' us to Jesus, that's for sure."

WE CAMP NOT far from the store off the trail that leads to Red Oak. A small, rocky creek offers water and a meadow with somewhat dry but adequate grass for our animals. After about an hour's rest, Lummy leads his horse to the edge of camp.

He clicks his tongue and side-nods, signaling me to walk with him. "Marion, I'm leaving for Skullyville. Rainy should be there by now, if not, he's close. If I start now, I might be back by noon tomorrow with a bit of rest figured in."

"How far is it?"

"Not quite fifty miles. I'm sure Rainy will have done the same thing. If I can get there by suppertime tonight, let the horses rest until an hour before dawn, I'm thinking we should be able to get here not long after noon."

"I should go with you."

"No, I'll be fine. You need to make a posse out of this bunch."

"I've never done that before."

"From what I can tell, you have done most of the hard work already. Just get them going in the same direction. They already know you can do the gee-hawin'."

"All right, Uncle Lummy, but you be careful. There's ruffians about and surely someone will have seen us coming this way."

"I will, Marion, be careful that is."

He trots away to go get the man who saved his hide on several occasions, and he his. It must be something to have a friend like either Rainy or Lummy. Sted's face pops into my head. Can't think on that now. But he is becoming just that.

The sun is nearing high noon. "All right, let's get camp set up. Josie, you and Smith get the campfire going. I'm hungry and want something good for supper. Sted, let's you and me go see what they've got up at that store." I stop before walking away. "Andrew, would you join us for supper?"

"Yes, ma'am, I would like that."

Smith and Josie snicker.

"What's so funny?"

"He called you ma'am, but we believe you're too scared to say somethin' about it, fearin' you might get scalped."

Andrew belly-laughs. "Choctaws rarely scalp their enemies, but I might just take it up."

They both roll with laughter and Andrew starts dancing around singing songs that must be in Choctaw. I swat the air at them and leave.

"C'mon, Sted, let's go, at least you might be good company for a moment." He bursts out laughing, and I can't help myself. I do too.

THE CAMPFIRE IS a nice bed of coals. We feasted on a supper of fry bread, brown beans with a chunk of ham in them, fried potatoes, and cool clear water. Sted bought a sack full of sweets to share all around. Smith and Josie went after them like two little kids. Those two don't seem to have had much of a pleasant growing up by any stretch. It's a small thing, but it's good to see them happy, talking, and playful. They must be about the same age.

I lean back against a log Andrew pulled up for us to enjoy. "Ain't it something, Sted? Just a few days ago he was chasing her with a knife and now it looks like he's sweet on her."

Sted throws a stick into the fire. "Yeah, and she was forced to tend to men like a grown woman. And her eyes say she's sweet right back at him."

Sted grows quiet, and I grow uncomfortable. I can feel this man. What he's feeling. What he's thinking. He scoots over closer.

"Marion, I—"

I put my finger to his lips. "Not now, Sted. Later. Let's get through this and see where we are, all right?"

He shies away like a boy who was hoping for his first kiss out behind a tree in the schoolyard.

I pull him close by his jacket. I kiss him on the lips. Hard, but just for a moment. "Will that carry you?" He nods, and I laugh. "You look like a mule eatin' briars, you're grinning so big."

He stops smiling. "That's because I've got somethin' to grin about, Marion. Somethin' deep down inside. I want to tell you that—"

I put my finger on his lips again. "That will have to wait until this is over, Sted. We must stay clearheaded, or we'll be weak when we go to take these ruffians down."

He hangs his head, but he is not dejected. He looks up from under his brow and smiles. I swear I could drag this man down beside the creek and wear his fine body out. He sees it and smiles even bigger.

"Not now, Marion, not now." He gets up to go check the horses. I have to fan myself like I've seen fancy ladies do.

When Sted returns, I ask, "Everybody good? Had enough to eat?"

Everyone nods.

"Well, fill your cups with whatever you're drinking and gather 'round. We need to start making a plan. Andrew, how far is it to Robbers Cave from here?"

"Less than twenty miles, by the way the crow flies."

"Good, good, that means we can ride in and take care of business, ride out, and have horses waiting here so we can just keep going in case we're being followed. Make sense?"

Everybody nods. Andrew speaks up. "My brother, him and me used to hunt up around that big pile of rocks. I could probably draw you a map of the place. I ain't no artist, but you'll know which way to go when we get there."

"When we get there? You're coming with us?"

"They took my little girl when she was but ten years old. My brother's girl too. They were about the same age. They've been gone now for several years. I couldn't get them back. We still mourn for them."

"I'm so sorry, Andrew."

"And besides, you will need a guide, and it will be dark when you attack." He looks into the sky like he's searching. A lot like the way Uncle Lummy does when he goes somewhere else in his head. "I just want one thing when this is all over."

I ask, "What's that?"

"I want his head. I want the Buyer's head."

My stomach turns. "Why?"

"I will mount his skull on a pole by my house as a warning." Andrew looks off into the distance. "I believe that's all I will say on the matter, Miss Marion."

I draw in a deep breath. "All right, then. Anybody got any objections?"

Sted shakes his head, as do the others.

Andrew gets up to go wherever it is he stays at night. "I will have your map at first light. We will want to travel to Robbers Cave in plenty of time before dark." He disappears into the darkness making no sound.

Sted leans over. "What're you thinking, Marion? We've got to get into that cave somehow without their guards knowing it."

"I know, I know, it just ain't come to me clearly just yet. Let me think on it a bit more. Let's get some sleep. We'll leave as soon as Lummy and Rainy arrive tomorrow."

Sted sits back. "Who's Rainy?"

"Rainy Mills, Uncle Lummy's longtime friend. Said he wouldn't do what needs doing here without Rainy by his side."

"That's how I feel, Marion."

"Whatever do you mean, Sted Walker?"

"I don't want to do anything without you by my side ever again, Marion."

"Oh, Sted, you're just infatuated with me."

He stands up and dusts himself off. "Marion, I love you, and I ain't kiddin', neither." He walks away like a man ready to fight for what's his. I've never had a man feel this way about me, ever. I look to the sky and ask Creator, "Will you let us survive this so I can know what it's like to be loved by a good man?"

The breeze stops. The clouds gather to cover the stars. The air becomes humid and an owl sweeps in to perch above my head in a tall pine. I peer into the darkness and a dim light wanders through the trees. I start to back up but the log is behind me. I can go nowhere. I'm frozen, not by fear but by curiosity.

The light pauses at an old cedar tree not twenty yards in front of me. I ask, "Is anybody else seeing this?" All are asleep.

The old man Salis Sollut—Lummy and I know as Uncle Silas—eases into camp and squats by the fire. *"How goes it, my niece?"*

"How'd you find me?"

"How do I find anybody or anythin'? Heck, I don't know. I just show up."

"Like Granny Thankful?"

"Yeah, like Granny Thankful. She is a sweet one, but has a fiery heart when it's needed."

"Will you be with me like Granny Thankful's been with Uncle Lummy?"

"As much as I am needed and allowed."

"What do you mean, allowed?"

"Creator has his ways, Marion, and Creator knows best, but you must have the will to survive, to defeat the one called Satan in this place."

"You mean the Buyer, don't you?"

"Yes, and him too."

"What do you mean, and him too? Is there someone else I need to know about?"

"You mean you don't already know, my dear niece?"

"I'm sure I don't."

"By the words of the man who knows his own soul all too well."

"Uncle Lummy, right?"

"Only if you accept his wisdom."

"I do."

"Then you know who the first devil who must be conquered is?"

"Yes, I do."

"Then say it."

"Why, if I already know it?"

"So Michael, the Protector of God's People will hear it. He cannot come until you speak the words of awareness."

"What are those words?"

"The words I just asked you to speak."

"That the first devil who must be conquered is me?"

"Well-spoken, my niece. That being must be spewed out of your soul like foul water. Now rest."

I wake to Sted gently shaking my shoulder and handing me a cup of coffee. "Here, Marion, thought you might like this." He sits down across the fire from me. "Must'a been a helluva dream."

"If you could only imagine." I sip my coffee and wait for my head to clear. The only thing clear at the moment is what I must do. I must do what needs doing but not let it do to me the thing that will destroy my soul. I'll speak to Uncle Lummy about it when he returns. And with Uncle Rainy. too.

I look to the beautiful dark, cloudless sky. "Lord, keep us all in the palm of your mighty hand."

"You look tired, Marion."

"I am. How long is it till daylight, Sted?"

"A couple of hours."

"Good." I set my cup down and pull my blanket up around me.

The night bugs sing a chorus that sends me into the deepest sleep I've had in weeks.

A LIKELY PLAN FROM AN UNLIKELY MAN

The best plans come from the least likeliest person sometimes.

I'M STILL GROGGY from sleeping so dang hard. "Why'd you let me sleep so long, Sted?"

"You've been runnin' pretty hard since you left Austin, I'm guessin'. You needed it."

I don't want him taking care of me, and I want him to take care of me. Am I that messed up? Though I live in a man's world, I am a woman. Can't think on this now. Later.

"You're right, Sted. Thanks for watching out for me."

He tips his hat and leaves. I need time to think, and he knows it. I take my tin cup of steaming coffee down by the creek. I wash my face and find a log to sit on. It's peaceful here.

I think about the Buyer, but more so about how people can allow themselves to become so blind in a world of hate that's so obvious. I guess when power and money is involved, the one-eyed man is king in the land of the blind. There has to be more to it than that. There's lots of ways to get power and money. But to sell human flesh like it is livestock and for purposes only demons could conjure up, there's got to be something else driving this kind of wickedness.

"There is, Miss Marion, it's true, the part about the land of the blind. The Buyer is king 'round these parts."

I turn and Smith is standing ten paces to my rear. "Come out in front of me, Smith, if you got something to say. I don't like anyone standing behind me."

"Yes, ma'am, I mean, Miss Marion." He walks out of the bushes with his hat in his hands.

"Just Marion, Smith, if you don't mind. We're all friends here."

"Yes… Marion." He looks up and then down the creek like he believes someone might be watching, listening. He whispers, "I've just been thinking about what we can do to get at the Buyer and save that young lady he took from Red River Station. They were some good folks back there in Red River Station and—"

"They are good folks, but what's on your mind, Smith? I really need this time to think."

"Yes, yes, I was thinking about the one-eyed man, the Buyer, and the tale of 'Odysseus and the Cyclops.' It was my favorite story that our teacher read to us from Homer in school back home. You remember it?"

"I do, and it seems like Odysseus and his men got trapped in the cave when the giant rolled a stone across the door."

"They did get trapped, but that brought out the best of what Odysseus was known for."

"What was that?"

"Trickery."

"You have been to school, haven't you?"

"I have. I just play a bit dumb so folks will leave me be. I don't like gettin' much attention, you know. I just like watching and learning, then figurin' stuff out like Odysseus did."

"So what are you thinking, Odysseus, I mean, Smith? I'm all ears."

He snickers. "You probably won't like it, but here goes. Let Mister Andrew, who is well-known in these parts, bring me and Josie to the Robbers Cave like we have been wandering around out here lost."

"Why would he think you should show up at the cave?"

"Remember what I was doin' when you found me? I was trying to catch Josie and bring her here to make up for the lady we didn't capture in Austin because of what y'all did to Tom Kimbrell." He grins. "Don't you see? It makes perfect sense. That would put three of us inside the cave with the Buyer's men. Mister Andrew can get his reward for bringing me and Josie to the cave and then he can report back to you what he sees, you know, the number of men, how many weapons, and all."

My mind is a beehive working alive with Smith's plan. "You're smarter than you look, or act, Smith."

"And that's the way I want it. I want people to think I'm slow. It's a good cover."

"So what happens once you're inside the cave?"

"Well, you know Odysseus tricked the cyclops by gettin' him drunk. I figure if I bring a barrel or two of moonshine with me as a peace offering, I might do the same thing and work out some way to signal you and the others when to attack. This time I'll be the one to make sure the stone is rolled away from the entrance, so to speak."

"Have you ever been to the cave?"

"I didn't want to say earlier, I don't know why, but yes, only once, in the dark, and blindfolded. So I'm not much help there, Marion. But Andrew told me that he can come get you, Lummy, Sted, and the other fellow after he leaves the cave and lead y'all close enough to attack when I give the signal. With his map, we should be able to do what needs doin'."

"That's right. Andrew did promise me a map of a sort when he gets here this morning."

"That should help."

"Thank you, Smith, you're doing good."

"No, thank you, Marion. Where would I be if y'all hadn't showed up when you did? Most likely I'd be dead. This is my way of makin' amends and at the same time become the man I know God wants me to be. Thank you for giving me the chance to redeem myself and do somethin' good in this world, especially 'to one of the least of these,' like Jesus says in the Bible."

"So you know your Scripture?"

"Yes'um. My daddy was a preacher. He was a good man, that is, until some bad men shot and killed him and my momma one day whilst I was down by the creek fishin'."

"So he was a good man?"

"The best. He talked a lot about grace, mercy, and forgiveness... gentlest man I've ever met. He was good to me, Marion."

"So how did you get mixed up with the Buyer?"

"He came along while I was sittin' on the porch of our dogtrot cabin after the funeral for my momma and daddy. He said he was goin' after the men who killed them. What he was really doin' was chasin' after men who had robbed him, you know, men who called themselves the Buyer's men, but weren't. You don't cross the Buyer like that. Anyway, he put his arm around me, consoled me, and said I could come with them. Next thing I know, I'm caught up in somethin' I can't get out of, except by dyin' or runnin', and I tried runnin' once."

"What'd he do?"

Smith raises up his shirt and there are at least twenty scars on his chest made by a red-hot poker pressed into his flesh. "Don't worry, they don't hurt no more. But they sure remind me about runnin' away. So you can see why I was so determined to—"

"Catch Josie and bring her to the Buyer."

Smith hangs his head. "Yes, ma'am, and I'm as sorry as I can be about that." His head pops around like somebody whistled at him. "But you know what? Josie has forgiven me. Yep, told me so. I really like Josie. She said we're friends on a mission for the Good Lord. What do you think, Marion?"

"I think that when you find a friend as good as Josie, you do whatever it takes to keep her."

He scratches his ear. "Yes, and I will." He stares down the creek as the water trickles and bubbles, sounds soothing to a weary soul. He snaps back from wherever his daydream took him. "Thanks for listenin' to me, Marion, to my plan, and my heart."

"You are very welcome, Smith. One question before you go."

Smith scratches his head. "What's that?"

"Why didn't you tell us your story before now?"

"I didn't think you'd believe me. Nobody has believed me about anything since my parents were murdered. I don't know why." He bobs his head thinking. "Thank you and Mister Lummy for believing in me."

"I see. Makes sense. Mind if I have some time to think?"

"Oh, no, ma'am, I mean, Marion. You go right ahead. Want me to send Andrew over when he comes with your map?"

"That'd be perfect. Thank you."

He backs away like he's leaving the throne room of a queen. He bows and turns to go back to camp. It's good to see people change. It gives me a bit of hope for myself.

A wisp of a breeze blows by from a grove of cedars just up the creek. The smell is nothing short of heavenly. *It'll be good to witness you change, too, Marion.*

A shadow slips through the dark and shadowy cedars that bring that sweet aroma in the wispy wind. "Thank you, Uncle Silas. Just don't leave me to myself."

"You are never alone, my dear niece. I leave you with a reminder."

He disappears. A stick cracks behind me and a small red cedar cross is dropped into my lap. I jump up and there stands Andrew grinning. "They say it's always been easy for a red man to sneak up on a white man, well, a white woman in this case." He touches his arms and then stares at me, and snickers. "You know, it's funny. I'm no more red than you are white. I'm dark brown, and you're light brown, and that's because we've been out in the sun. Nothing more. I guess some folks need to have different colored stripes for human beings so they can judge 'em the way they want to. Don't make sense except to those who need such things."

"I think it's because they don't like who they are so to feel better about themselves they gotta make somebody else look like they don't matter as much."

"I may make a good Choctaw out of you yet, Marion."

"I appreciate it, and this cross."

"Smell it."

I hold the small cross carved from the heartwood of a cedar. "I like the sweet, thick odor it gives off. You make this?"

"I did."

"Why?"

"A long haired old man came to me last night and told me to, that's why."

"Uncle Silas."

"He didn't tell me his name, but he said when your mind gets cloudy like early morning fog on a river, just smell the cedar, and it will not only clear your mind, it will keep it alert and give you a bit of comfort."

I take a deep whiff of the fragrance and feel better already. "But why a cross?"

He shrugs. "I don't know. I just did what the old man asked me to do. Maybe because it has special meaning for you?"

"It does, and in the best way possible."

"Good, let it help you."

"And the map? Did you get a chance to draw it?"

"I have it in camp. I remembered more than I thought I would."

"Thank you, Andrew. I'll be there in a minute."

He nods and walks back to camp. I roll the little cross around in my fingers. The leather string goes through a hole from one side to the other at the top rather than front to back. That means it'll always face the front. I put it around my neck and smell the beautiful wood.

I whisper as I hold the little cross up to the sun, "This does have much meaning to me. It means I have to be willing to sacrifice all of who I am so I can become everything I am to become."

I drop the cross inside my shirt. It hangs just above the Derringer.

"So that's what it looks like to be an avenging angel—the cross of Jesus and a weapon of Saint Michael."

A gust of wind blows my hair, and it wraps around my head. I pull it away, and a voice chuckles, *"Now you see a bit more clearly, my niece."*

TWO RETURN

And I thought I was an avenging angel until
two veterans returned to the war.

Just Before Noon, September 5, 1886

JOSIE HAS JUST filled our plates when Uncle Lummy and Uncle Rainy ride up. I am so glad to see them. They dismount, and I rush to hug them both. They're a little startled and look at each other like, *Is this the same Marion?* Both lightly pat me on my shoulders. I want to cry, but I can't, not now. My posse needs me strong.

I step back and look Rainy up and down. "So what's this, Uncle Rainy? You going to a funeral or something?"

His face says gentle and relaxed. His eyes seethe anger. He has the look of a man who's been to hell and back, and ready to go again. "I rarely attend funerals. Black is my friend when death follows close behind."

Lummy nods, and says, "Let's get on with it, Marion. We both hoped Tom Kimbrell would've been the last battle for us."

"It means everything that you two are with me. Y'all come on in, we were just about to eat dinner, and Josie is a fine cook."

Josie brings Lummy and Rainy each a heaping plate of fine-smelling food and a cup of steaming coffee, beaming like the brightest star in the night sky. I'm learning, I do believe.

To be a better person, that is.

I sit between Rainy and Lummy, and motion for everyone else to gather around. "Any trouble on the trail?"

Rainy squints. "Not that we know of, but there's a lot of suspicious-looking people around."

Lummy finishes chewing a bite. "Yeah, especially in Skullyville. That place just breathes evil. Glad we were only there a little while."

Rainy ducks his head and concentrates on his food. "Skullyville is not one of my favorite places on this Earth."

I have to ask. "Maybe this isn't the time, but what really happened in Skullyville?"

He lifts his head and sighs. "You're right, Marion, this isn't the time. Maybe later, if you don't mind?"

"Oh, no, sorry, I shouldn't have asked."

"Not a problem, niece. We'll talk after we do what we came for." Rainy looks to Lummy. "But I would like for us to go back there when we're done here. There's something I don't want to do, but I need to do."

Lummy takes a bite of biscuit and washes it down with coffee. "Sure, Rainy, whatever you need, brother. I'm with you."

I can't help but feel that I sit in the safest place in the world. Between two of the best men to ever walk it. Oh, they've done their bad things, and they've got their secrets, but I would imagine they would've been two warriors easily chosen to be part of King David's Mighty Men like in the Bible, his personal guard. I look around the fire and then ask to say a prayer. Everyone stops eating.

I look to the sky. "Lord, you know I ain't much for praying. I figure you already know what's in the hearts of women and men before we even think to ask. But I'm asking tonight. I want you, O Lord, to go before us. I want the angels to go before us, surround us to guard our hearts, and fight for us. I want Saint Michael, the Protector of God's People to lead us as we bring these demons of Satan to justice and set 'the least of these' free." I look at my friends. Their heads are bowed.

"For Josie, Smith, Andrew, Sted, Rainy, and Lummy, be at their front and at their back, on both sides and all around, above their heads and under their feet. Leave no part of them unguarded and give them the strength of Samson and the trickery of Delilah." Josie snickers just a little, as does Smith. "Forgive our wrongs, oh merciful God, but forgive us when we show no mercy to those who do not deserve it. Hold up our arms when they tire of battle as Aaron and Hur did for Moses as we fight our own Amalekites. Defeat the power of the Buyer. Let the cyclops lose his other eye that he might forever be blind in the land of the blind where he no longer rules as king." I sit up straighter. "Thank you, my friends. You have restored my hope in human beings, and I give myself to them as you, O Lord, gave yourself for us. In Jesus's holy name, let us all say together, amen."

All around the fire just sit, lost in their thoughts. Finally, one amen, two, then three until all agree that it should be so.

Lummy clears his throat. "Rainy, remind you of anybody?"

"Yeah, Old Bart when we fought the fire that calmed the storm back in Choctaw County. Old Bart. Helluva man, and the praying-est man I've ever known."

Lummy puts his arm around me. "I believe Old Bart's spirit is with us because we just heard his words through a helluva leader the Lord has risen up to defeat the one-eyed man." Lummy looks off into the sky, and I wait for his words to come. "You know, Rainy, Old Bart prayed a very similar prayer before he and I, J. A., and others took down another cyclops when the battle involved white and black, back during the war."

I have to ask, "I bet you could almost see Saint Michael slashing that great sword of fire across the sky as he defeated that demon and his horde."

Lummy whispers, "No bettin' that I almost did, my dear niece. I did."

Everyone thanks me for the prayer and goes back to eating. I'm with friends. Good friends. The best I've ever had. And I'm happy as I have been for a long time. And will be, until we have to discuss the plan. Then happiness must be put aside for what needs doing. But for now, we need to relax and enjoy each other's company.

We eat and talk, laugh and tell funny stories. Rainy is a talker but his tales are good. He tells us about the time Uncle Lummy came running into his camp like his head was on fire and his ass was catching with a pack of coyotes hard on his heels. Lummy just laughs, enjoying being the center of attention in a good way. I figure Uncle Lummy has had to be the center of attention in many ways he never wanted in life. Uncle Rainy too. But for now, it's a good thing.

I start a speech that maybe didn't need saying, but I give it anyway. "Y'all all know this'll be dangerous and some of us might not make it. I do appreciate everyone here, and I'll do my best to get everyone back here safe and sound. Y'all mean much to me and, well…."

Rainy elbows Lummy who fakes wiping a tear. "Well, I believe I'll just start bawlin' like a lost calf lookin' for his momma's teat."

Lummy covers his face and acts like he's crying and sobbing. "Me, too, oh dear, what am I to do? I just love all of y'all so very much."

"All right, all right, I get it, you knotheads." I backhand Lummy and Rainy both across the chest. "But I thank you all for being my friends and for doing what you don't have to."

Lummy nods, as do the others. "We all feel the same, Marion."

"We all do, Marion, but before we go any further and…." Rainy laughs and stands to strike the pose of an actor. "Speaking of doing what you want to do, or not, listen to this. You'll like it. An old woman walked up and tied her mule to the hitching post. As she stood there, brushing the dust from her face and clothes, a young gunslinger stepped out of the saloon wobbling with a gun in one hand and a bottle of whiskey in the other. The young man, obviously drunk, looked at the old woman and laughed. 'Hey old woman, have you ever danced?'

"The old woman looked up at the gunman and said, 'No, I never did dance, and I guess I never wanted to, now that I think of it.' A crowd had gathered by this time, as you can imagine, and the gunslinger looked around, pleased with the attention he was getting from his audience.

"'Well, you old bag, you're gonna dance now,' and started shooting at the old woman's feet. The old woman prospector, not wanting to get her toes blown off, started waltzing around and leaping at every bullet fired. Everyone laughed and jeered at the old woman. When he fired his last shot, the young gunman, still laughing, holstered his gun, and turned around to go back into the saloon.

"The old woman quietly pulled a double-barreled shotgun from her pack mule and cocked both hammers. The loud clicks carried a distinct sound through the dry and dusty street breeze. The crowd stopped their guffawing. The young man turned slowly. The silence between the old woman and the young gunman was deafening. The young man stared down the two barrels like they were twin howitzers aimed for his head. The shotgun never shook nor wavered in the old woman's hands. She quietly asked, 'Son, have you ever kissed a mule's ass?' The young—and dumb, I might add—boy of a man swallowed his spit hard and said, 'No, ma'am, but I've always wanted to.'"

I thought we'd never stop laughing. Smith rolls around on the ground while Josie tries to pick him up. Andrew falls off his log on his back with his feet high up in the air, shaking with laughter but making no sound. Sted wipes tears from the corners of his eyes, and grins, saying, "Dang, I ain't never heard anythin' like that before."

I spill my coffee all down the front of my shirt bouncing so hard as Lummy shakes his head, saying, "That Rainy sure can tell a good story."

I needed that. We all did. But now the laughing is over. We've got business to attend to.

After everyone collects themselves, I hold up my hand. "It's time we make a plan."

Rainy takes a sip of coffee. "You have one?"

I point to Smith with my thumb. "He does, and Uncle Rainy, with the wonderful classical education of yours, I do believe you're gonna like it." I hold out my hand. "Andrew, how about that map?"

THE PLAN

If you're gonna enter the Devil's lair, you best have a way out.

Just Before Noon, September 5, 1886

WE POUR OVER a crude, hand-drawn but adequate map that will lead us to the Buyer.

Rainy leans over the map. He squints and points. "What's this?"

Andrew replies, "That's Robbers Cave. That's where the Buyer will be. You will find him there."

I add, "Captain Leflore of the Choctaw Lighthorse said it was a fortress with all kinds of twists and turns." Andrew nods in agreement.

"So they're hidden up in the rocks?"

Andrew rubs his nose. "That's it. The entrance to the cave sits high above the forest floor but there's ways to get inside."

Rainy scratches his chin and looks at Lummy. "So they'll be in the rocks like we were back in Choctaw County hiding at Big Sand Rock."

Lummy grins. "Yeah, when we took down Tom Ford and his bunch."

Rainy smiles. "And had a steady supply of Wood brothers' moonshine."

"Indeed." Lummy snickers. "Made from the sweet waters of Aaron Wood's Spring."

Rainy laughs out loud. "Yeah, the Wood brothers, they ain't scared."

"You got that right." Lummy holds up his hand. "But there's a little more to that story. You know the James-Chaney Gang hid out there not too long before Jesse was murdered, right?"

I'm getting a little impatient but these men need to have their time and there's always wisdom to be found in one of their well-told stories. I settle back for a few moments.

Lummy's eyes dance as he tells the story. "Yeah, it seems they robbed a bank in Corinth, Missip, then rode hard to Wood family land. How they knew to go to the Big Sand Rock is beyond me, but they did. Young Wesley Wood told me about it before I left home for good not long ago. Besides not bein' scared, the Wood boys can keep a secret. Seems one of the Chaney men took up with one of the Wood girls. He stayed in Choctaw County, and they later tied the knot. They had a couple of young'uns but when Chaney found out that Jesse was murdered, he became so distraught with the thought of the law finding out where he was and coming to take him away, he ended his life."

I ask, "So, Jesse James and his gang was close to where you lived, and you never knew it?"

"Not until that Wood boy told me."

I break in to get us back to business. "Humph, well, I guess if you knew how to defend a rock fortress then, you can help show us how to attack one now."

Rainy leans in, studying the map. "The place is like a maze. This story is shaking out to be more like Theseus and the Minotaur in that Labyrinth than Odysseus and the cyclops."

Lummy looks at the map. "Yeah, lots of twists and turns, but we can use them to our advantage just like the Buyer and his men do."

Rainy hands me a small ball of twine and says, "For good luck, Marion. You may need this to find your way back out."

I wink. "Yeah, but with one big difference. We know the Buyer's weakness and Josie is that weakness. Me, too, I'd imagine. Smith here was on the hook for making up for losing Caroline back in Austin. He was supposed to bring her to Fort Worth—"

Smith cuts in, "Actually, to Red River Station, and when I didn't show with a girl in tow, they took the storekeeper's daughter. I'm sure she'll be in the cave waiting to be sold."

"Right, thanks Smith for that point of clarity." I draw in a deep breath. "So, Smith proposes that he takes Josie in like she's been captured to make up for what he lost in Austin and that gets us inside. Andrew will do the leading since he knows the hills and will act half drunk and appear to be no threat. He'll size up the number of men and how well they're heeled. He'll report back to us and then help us navigate the rocks to get at the Buyer and his men before they know what hit 'em." I sit back, still studying the map. "What do y'all think?"

Rainy nods to Lummy in agreement, but asks, "What happens if the Buyer isn't happy with Smith's offering for having botched things the first time?"

Smith breaks in, "I'm willing to risk it, and I...." He turns to Josie. "But I can't speak for Josie here."

"You're right, I can speak for myself. They won't harm me as long as I'm of some value to them, and I can help keep Smith alive, if things go sour before you get to us."

I ask, "Andrew, Smith said we could sweeten the deal by taking in a load of moonshine. You got anybody who could supply us with a couple of kegs?"

Andrew slowly grins, revealing a couple of missing front teeth. "I sure do, and he'll give it to us for what we're tryin' to do. They took his niece a couple of years ago. Heard she died on the way to Mexico." He sniffles a bit. "Always loved that little girl like my own." He pushes back his shoulders and squints. "I'll do anythin' I can to send them rascals to hell." Andrew straightens up. "I've been to Robbers Cave one time, on a moonless night, and I'm pretty good in the woods. I can get us there."

I turn to the veterans of such wars. "Lummy, Rainy, when should we start on this road?"

Lummy shifts around. "I think you... if this is what we're really gonna do... you should have Andrew lead Smith and Josie to the—"

"And me, Uncle Lummy."

Rainy stands up. "Oh, no, sir, that's not going to happen. They'll kill you right off."

"They don't know me, Uncle Rainy, and besides, who better to play the harlot one more time than Miss Lillie Langtry of Natchez one more time? I can do this."

Rainy and Lummy both sigh in either resignation that I'm doing the right thing or that they know they can't stop me once my mind is made up. Doesn't matter, they'll come along no matter their conclusion.

I ask again, "So when should we begin?"

Lummy looks to Rainy, who then looks at Andrew. "You'll know best, Andrew."

"From what I understand, they'll probably be gettin' over a bad drunk, so those in the cave won't be suspectin' this. If I lead you, Smith, and Josie up to the cave around daylight, and bring more moonshine, they'll be a lot easier to deal with."

"How far to Robbers Cave?"

"'Bout twenty miles, I'd say."

"About a four hour ride then?"

"Yes, if we do not travel like turtles."

Smith and Josie snicker. Dang, they're just kids, but kids with experience.

I calculate in my head. "So we need to leave at midnight just to make sure we have extra time to get situated. The sun gets up pretty early these days."

Andrew nods. "That'd be 'bout right."

Rainy asks, "What about guards?"

Lummy chuckles. "There's always guards."

Andrew points to three places on his map. "The ones we need to deal with are the guards at the entrance of the Stone Corral, the Devil's Slide, and the entrance of Robbers Cave itself. There'll be one leading up to the rocks. I'll get him to take us up to the cave. So that's one. There might be one or two more scattered about, but it's a chance we'll have to take."

Sted chimes in, "Agreed. I'll wander the rocks and take the ones unaccounted for. Be watchful, I may be followin' you behind someone followin' you."

"That's good, Sted." Rainy scratches his ear and studies the map. "Lummy, can you take the Stone Corral? I'll get the one at the Devil's Slide then we meet at the mouth of Robbers Cave to take care of the third guard?"

Lummy nods. "Yes."

Andrew snickers. "No need, I'll take him down on my way out of the Devil's den like a rabbit still in his bed on a frosty morning about the time you get to the mouth of the cave."

I nod. "Good enough. Sounds like we got it all covered."

Sted snickers. "Yeah, except us gettin' killed."

I wince, knowing any one of us could lose our lives in this quest of mine. But, in my heart I believe not a one would be here if they didn't want to be. Bringers of justice don't have to be lily white clean and sparkle to do what Creator needs to have done. Lord knows I'm as dirty as the next person in life and in living. Still, I do believe we're on Creator's side in all of this. If I wasn't sure that was true, I would've come by myself and taken my chances with the Buyer alone. Then Creator could deal with whether I was right or wrong for doing it.

I clear my throat. "If y'all can do that, Smith, Josie, and I will be ready when we take down the Buyer."

IT'S THE SNEAKIN' PART I LIKE

*The best part is sneakin' up on those who think
they're the only ones doin' the sneakin'.*

Nearing Midnight, September 5, 1886

WE LAZE AROUND the campfire, sleeping off our last supper. We need all the rest we can get. When we start this thing, we won't stop until we reach Skullyville. The Buyer surely has many people around who profit from him being king in the land of the blind. They don't need to know anything has happened until we're long gone. I don't worry so much for me but for the youngsters, Smith and Josie, I do. Heck, I'm not really worried at all. In fact, save any one of our people getting hurt, I think this'll be a bit of entertainment, and at the very least, a honing of my skills as a tracker and reward hunter. Besides, what's better than sneaking up on the ones who think they're the only ones doing the sneaking?

Looking around as I think about sneaking, I ask, "Where's Andrew?"

Lummy pulls back a cedar branch and out steps Andrew Flying Hawk, dressed as a traditional Choctaw warrior—breechcloth, deer head mask with two cow horn spike antlers, paint on his face and body, pouch slung across his shoulder, bow in hand with a quiver on his back, but even more menacing, a glaring fire in his eyes that says he comes to kill.

He notices the shock on our faces. None of us probably ever have seen anything like this or likely ever will again. "You go in your way, I go in mine."

Lummy leans over and whispers to Rainy, "Dan Creekwater did the same thing when my brother Elihu wanted to hunt deer in the old Choctaw way when I stayed in McCurtain Creek Swamp back home and enjoyed a bit of peace before the second storm. It worked too."

Rainy points to Andrew's behind. "Was he dressed like that?"

Lummy snickers. "Almost naked as a jaybird."

Andrew chuckles. "Just don't be lookin' at my behind. I know my backside's hangin' out, but for tonight, I'm a warrior."

I ask, "What about showin' up drunk?"

"Oh, I'll show up drunk but won't be drunk. I'll do that after I get my reward for these two." His grin resembles the Devil's. "I'll splash moonshine all over me, and they'll think I'm drunk. This is one Choctaw who can hold his liquor."

"And, what about the moonshine?"

Andrew straightens his headdress. "Tied down on my mule. Smith, you will carry the two small kegs once we start up to the cave. It's a steep climb. I will follow behind you and Josie with an arrow nocked in my bow in case this goes bad, understand?"

Josie and Smith nod and giggle. I'm sure it eases the fear to laugh in the face of evil, no matter how scared a person might be.

Andrew whispers as we check and recheck our weapons and rehearse our parts in this dangerous charade, "Time to go. Make sure your eyes watch one way and your ears listen to the other. You cover more ground that way."

Heck if I know what all that means, but all right. I ask, "Everybody ready? Once we light out on this trail, there'll be no turning back." I turn to Smith and Josie. "You do understand that, right?"

Smith offers a shy grin, but musters up his strength. "Miss Marion, you got to know that Josie and me both been in this predicament more than once. We know what's ahead, and we've put both feet in the circle with you. We're good, if you are."

I'm a little taken back, but he's right. I must keep my own head. I've been the victim of a whorehouse, of a murdered uncle I dearly loved, playing the part of Belle with Tom Kimbrell, but I've never willingly, knowingly danced my way straight into hell and asked the Devil to put up his fists. I will need to conquer any fears and anything else that may take my mind from me and go wild on these ruffians like a raccoon surrounded by a pack of hounds. And that, I am very capable of doing.

We strike out at midnight straight up and wander through The Narrows to circle back around and come in from behind and above Robbers Cave. We can't take the risk of slipping and disturbing the rocks. So we ease our mounts in a wide arc away from the fortress and settle them into a cedar grove down by a creek at the base of the hill.

Andrew whispers, "This is good. We leave 'em here. No moon tonight so if I get lost, all paths lead downhill to this creek. One way or another, you find horses." He grins. "Just be quiet as a Choctaw and use your night eyes." Lummy presses the owl claw into his wrist, a gift from Dan Creekwater, another Choctaw warrior who undertook many a battle just like this and now has gone up into the sky. He's with us. I know it. In the far distance, an owl hoots one time. That makes me feel better.

Andrew waves for us to trail behind him. We follow, trying to step in his exact steps. He'll take the safest way to keep us from stumbling on rocks or breaking sticks as we move like a small herd of deer through the woods. We circle around to the east so daylight will be behind us if it catches up with us before we get where we need to be. The ground is littered with fallen sticks and pinecones. Not much brush for cover, so we move from tree to tree, hoping the guards are dozing.

Andrew stops short and raises his hand. He stares into the blackness that shields our approach and turns with hands cupped over his mouth. "Cigar smoke. A guard I did not expect."

I strain but can see the faint red ember at the end of the guard's smoke thirty yards ahead. I mouth, "What do we do?"

Andrew throws up a hand for us to wait. He eases down the gentle slope covered with pine needles, his deerhide moccasins making no sound. In fact, there is no sound to break the silence of this strangely comforting place inhabited by demons.

Lummy whispers, "The once haunts of demons often become the strongholds of saints."

His words shake my heart. I lean into his ear. "You're not talking about Robbers Cave, are you?"

"You guessed it, niece."

I watch through a few small pines as Andrew stalks his unsuspecting prey. Though the night is dark, the stars shed enough light to make his shape and movements easy to follow. Guess I have night eyes after all. The small light of the cigar disappears and the muffled gasp of the fallen guard sends a night bird chirping away. We all tense for a moment. Andrew is back to us before we see him having circled around wide to make sure that was the only guard. He has a grin on his face and blood on his hands. I don't ask.

We sneak into the rocks and find the opening to the Stone Corral. Six horses stand near the entrance. One saunters over to us and Andrew offers it a small apple from his pouch. He gives a double click with his tongue and the others ease over to us. Before he's done, all six are munching, and he has become their new best friend.

We slip into the Stone Corral through a narrow spot where we spy another guard whose head bobs like a fishing cork. Lummy starts for him, but I lay my hand on his arm and shake my head. He shrugs and steps back.

I pull my knife, sneak up behind the man who has no idea his last breaths are being taken. His broad hat might be a problem, so I wait a moment. An owl hoots and the guard snorts and sniffs himself awake. He removes his hat to reshape it. I slit his throat like I would a hog. He falls back on top of me, gasping and kicking, but unable to make a sound.

I'm exhausted. I feel the weight of the man's body being lifted off of me. Lummy and Rainy lift the man up and throw his body behind some rocks. Andrew starts toward the corpse, and I whisper, "No."

"Not for you to say, Marion. This was one of the men who took my niece. I take his hair and soul to my brother's family."

"Do what you must." I hang my head and whisper, "I did when I killed a preacher, carpetbagger, and a voodoo witch. It wasn't a pretty sight."

Rainy rubs his shoulder against mine and whispers, "And I did when I killed the man who murdered my father and raped my mother, and the judge who let him get away with it."

Lummy wraps his arm around my shoulder. "And so did I when I, well, did the same thing on too many occasions." He and Rainy follow behind Andrew who begins his stalk again.

I squint into the fading darkness as dawn steps into the forest for the first time this morning. Andrew throws his arms into the air with the scalp in one hand and his knife in the other. He gives a shout that has no sound. I know the feeling of the reckoning, of making things right and equal again. Funny thing, though, killing those who killed Uncle Silas didn't bring the relief I'd hoped. It only makes me more determined to get the Buyer.

I admit, "Guess we're all down in the outhouse hole covered in crap."

Sted comes up from behind me and gently touches my neck. It feels good, but I brush it away. "Not yet, Sted, We must keep ourselves sharp."

"You're right, on both counts."

"What do you mean?"

"We're all guilty and there ain't much way of digging ourselves out of it except by one way."

"Oh, yeah, and what's that?"

Sted kisses me lightly on the lips. "When the 'not yet' finally happens for us." I want to melt. That man could take me right now, and I couldn't stop him. He grins. "Let's go. There'll be time."

ENTERING THE LAIR
OF THE CYCLOPS

Satan's lair is always open to the righteous.

Just Before Daylight, September 6, 1886

WE SNEAK THROUGH a narrow spot deeper into the Buyer's lair. Andrew throws up his hand, and we circle around close. "This is where we split up."

"Tell us what to do."

He says, "No turning back from here. Time to play our game with the Buyer. Anybody want out, now is the time."

No one says a word and no one even shifts their stance.

"All right then. Lummy, turn south and there will be a guard at the bottom of Devil's Slide. He most likely will be seated on a rock overlooking the forest floor in front of him. Will you take care of him?"

Lummy nods and holds out his hand to me. I know what he wants, and I give it to him. The knife his father made for him when he was just a boy. The knife he used to take care of another cyclops long ago. I place the razor-edged weapon in his right hand. His eyes are hard as steel with no emotion, no remorse about what he's got to do, and no words. He waits for Andrew's signal.

Andrew turns to Rainy. "Rainy, you must continue straight across through a slit in the rocks. There will be a guard just on the other side.

"Sted, once Rainy takes his man, you go straight on from there and the last guard should be twenty good paces farther. That should only leave two men in Robbers Cave, if the number of horses match the number of men." Andrew clasps his hands together. "Sted, Lummy, Rainy, these men are the worst of the worst. Show no mercy."

Rainy and Lummy say nothing, but I do. "These men know what to do. Just give the word."

Andrew sighs. "Rainy, Lummy, and Sted, when you are done, follow us and wait near the entrance of the cave. You will know when to rush the cave. I will give a Choctaw war whoop. Count the number I give so you will know how many men are in the cave. Some may not have a horse here."

I ask, "Everyone ready?"

Andrew turns to me. "You still good with this?"

"Yes, why?"

"I must treat you badly as Smith will do with Miss Josie."

"What do you mean?"

"I must make it look real."

"I get it. Do what you must. I'm a big girl."

"Good, first, we must make it look so before we get to the cave mouth. Strip off all your weapons and valuables." I already had handed Lummy the knife his father made him. He slips it into his belt. Andrew places the rest of my things behind a rock, while Smith does the same with Josie's. I keep the small ball of twine Rainy gave me in my pants pocket.

Andrew looks me over. He says, "I'm sorry to do this." He backhands me just hard enough to bring blood to the corner of my mouth. He tears my shirt but leaves me covered. He messes up my hair and rubs dirt on my face and arms. Smith follows his lead and does the same with Josie.

"You must look, how do you say it, haggard? But you are still very pretty, Marion."

I look at Josie who's smiling like she's having the time of her life. I snicker. "You boys sure know how to dress down two ladies."

They tie our hands and pull tight on a lead rope for each of us, then stop.

Andrew, who has a tear glistening in his eye, looks to Smith. "I take no pleasure in it."

Smith drops his head. "Me neither, ladies. Not at all."

I pop them both on the shoulders. "And that's why you're the right men for this holy war. Let's go get us a cyclops."

ROBBERS CAVE

The best place to fight Satan is on his own ground.
Defeat him there, and he has nowhere else to run.

Daylight, September 6, 1886

AS WE SCALE the steep incline that forms a huge V halfway up to the mouth of Robbers Cave, Lummy, Rainy, and Sted sneak along through the rocks to our left and right. I've never seen men who carry themselves so gently at their age move with such ease and stealth like foxes seeking rabbits in a pine thicket. Sted slips and a small rock goes tumbling down the rock face, bouncing and finally splattering against a pile of boulders below. Everyone stops still as ice in wintertime. Guess I spoke too soon. At least about Sted, that is. Still, that man—he gets my heart beating harder than this climb is doing.

The guard at the top, eating a plate of food, sets it down, and draws a fine bead on Andrew who leads the three of us. Smith makes a smart play and jerks Josie's lead rope hard enough to take her to her knees. Andrew grabs me by the hair and holds up his other hand in surrender. It was all planned in whispers on the way up.

Andrew throws his right hand up higher in the air. "We bring the Buyer presents."

"How'd you get past our guards?"

Andrew thrust his thumb into his chest. "Me Choctaw. I know

hills better than white man, I think. Lived here since I be a boy. The Buyer know me."

The guard snickers. "Yeah, you look like an Injun, with your fat butt hangin' out for everybody to see."

"Only man who want see naked behind look at naked behind."

The guard steps up like he's going to give Andrew the butt of his rifle. A voice barks behind him, and he stops in midair. "Don't do it, Jack. It's just that drunk old Injun from down 'round Red Oak. I seen him in Riddle's Station a couple of times. Give 'em a bottle, and he'll give you no trouble. Just keep a fine bead on him, Jack. Never know about these poor worthless dawgs."

"I will, Zeph, but watch yourself, I don't know that other one either."

Zeph lifts my chin up and squeezes my behind. I kick at him, and he laughs. He does the same to Josie and then stops to put his hands on his hips. "Well, would you looky who we got here. Smith, that you?"

Smith steps up. "Yes, siree, sure good to see you again, Zeph. I brought this young'n in to make up for the one I lost in Austin and took this'n who happened to be runnin' from the law just 'fore I crossed into Texas. I fooled her into believin' I was gonna help her escape a posse. Worked, too."

"Well, dang, boy, ain't you steppin' up in the world and makin' yourself known, and a trickster to boot. Why, the Buyer is gonna be proud of you, especially for bringing the golden-haired one."

"Thought you'd be proud, and I want to y'all to know, I won't ever mess up—"

Zeph backhands him so hard Smith drops to his knees shaking his head. How he held onto the whiskey kegs is beyond me. "Shut your trap, boy, you got a face that'd sour milk. Speak when I tell you to, got it?"

Smith looks up through a furrowed brow but remains quiet.

Zeph laughs. "That's for miss gettin' that woman in Austin. The Buyer wanted her for himself. It was a payback thing Tom Kimbrell wanted to bring down on some feller named Lummy Tullos. You hear anythin' about that?"

"No…no, sir. Ain't never heard 'bout no Lummy Tullos. I just grabbed this young girl here named Josie and then captured the towheaded one over there that Andrew's got."

Zeph circles our small group and draws his knife. "Anybody follow you, anybody see you come up in here, Injun?"

Andrew steps forward. "If I can get by your guards towin' these sacks of horse apples behind me, then no, nobody ain't followed us here. Ain't a white man made any Choctaw can't slip by 'em." Andrew laughs. "Heck, my daddy told me I was smooth as a copperhead huntin' a mouse in these rocks when I was a child and that I could sneak up on ya with you lookin' right straight at me." He staggers a bit acting drunk and laughs hard at his own joke.

Zeph stops at Josie and plays with her hair. "Seen you before, girl." He smells of her hair. "Yeah, you still got the whorehouse scent on you. Thought we left you in Fort Worth a while back. You run off or somethin? What happened, Smith?"

Smith wipes the bit of blood from his lip. "That's right. She done runned off from the whorehouse owner's place, but I caught her. Thought if I was ever gonna get back in the good graces of the Buyer, I better not come back empty-handed." Smith sets the two moonshine kegs down. "And look, I brought somethin' a little extree special besides the two women. That's good ole homemade spring water shine as a gift from me to you boys. Y'all is the onliest family I got. I want back in. Will this do it?"

Zeph kicks at the kegs and Smith grabs them to keep them from rolling down the hill. "Yeah, all this should get you back in. Guess we gotta pay for it, right?"

Smith lowers his head. "Yeah, ain't got no money to pay for it. Bought from Andrew's friend, and he's gonna want to get paid. I'll get it to you when I get my cut from the Buyer for these two."

I'm seeing this boy in a whole new light. Smith surely knows how to play this game.

"Money we got, jackass. Ignorance we don't need. Just don't do what you did in Austin again, you hear? Austin cost the Buyer a lot of money, but...." Zeph looks at me like he's peeling off my clothes. "I might just buy this one myself."

Andrew stomps his foot. "Where's the Buyer? Me ready to get out of Robbers Cave. Way too many haints and too much bad blood in one place for me."

Zeph squints and studies all four of us. "He's in the cave, and he will reward you well, Injun. Take 'em inside." He turns and cups one hand to his cheek. "Eli, Zeke, get out here. We got company."

Two men, lanky and lean, trot out of the cave, pistols in hand. Eli asks, "What, Michael Angel and Little Dave Greasefire make it back from gettin' our horses reshoed?"

"Naw, they'll be along soon 'nuff. Got somethin' even better. Tell the boss he's got Smith back, and he brought gifts. Tell him that a drunk ole Injun is out here and needs to get paid."

Zeph takes me and Josie by the elbows and looks us over. "Straighten your hair, press out those wrinkles in your clothes. Look as good as you can, ladies. You'll want to impress the Buyer here in a minute." He yanks us toward the cave. "Eli, Zeke, bring Smith and the Injun. Jack, keep a sharp eye. We don't need no one sneakin' up on us."

A huge rock, big as a corral, slopes up on our left as we walk a trail no wider than a person to the cave entrance. We're near the top of this part of the mountain. I look back, and I can see for miles across green hills and forests.

Zeke yanks on the rope. "Turn around and look forward, girl, before I slap your face back around."

We enter the cave that continues the slanting rock on our left and a wall on the right with a path no wider than a yardstick. The room is large but brightened by sunlight. Bedrolls are lined up across the sloping rock. There's nowhere to lay flat except for the small path where a small spring trickles.

Zeke drags Josie and me across the cave floor like animals headed to a slaughter. Andrew refuses to be touched by Eli, but Zeph keeps pushing Smith along like a kid brother. They all have their pistols pulled.

Zeph stops. "Injun, you gonna keep that bow strapped down good on your back?"

Andrew nods. "Yes."

Zeph points down at the side of the quiver. "What'n the heck is that?"

Andrew stands tall as any statue I've ever seen. "That's a scalp. Choctaw don't take many scalp. Did last night on way here. Nosy man want know why me had two women and this boy. He ask no more question now."

Zeph turns to Eli and Zeke, grinning. "Ever seen one of those?"

Eli swallows hard. "Never even heard of anybody I know doin' somethin' like that. You, Zeke?"

Zeke walks over and squats down to get a better look. "Yep, my grandpappy, who fought in the Indian wars, had one as a souvenir. He didn't take it himself. I think he got it off some Comanche he killed while he was a Ranger in the Texas Panhandle. Nasty stuff, I say."

Zeph laughs. "Well, ain't that somethin'? Your grandpappy was a Ranger and now you'd be the outlaw he'd be lookin' for if he was still around." Zeke touches the scalp and Andrew slaps his hand away.

Andrew barks, "Never do that again. His power is now my power. Get your own scalp."

Zeke stands up with his palms up in surrender, snickering. "Sorry, Chief, it won't happen again. And yeah, Zeph, my grandpappy would whoop my naked butt with a sticker bush limb all week long then string me up if he knew what I'm doin' now."

Zeph eases over into a dark corner that has a small platform built against the sloping rock. The one-eyed man must be there sleeping. Zeph gently rouses him. "Boss, wake up. Smith is back. He brought you some presents. Thought you'd want to see 'em right off."

From the shadow on the wall that I can see in the flickering light of lanterns, the Buyer sits up like someone just doused him with a bucket of cold water. "What'n the—!" He draws a pistol, cocks it, and aims it at Zeph's head.

Zeph throws up his arms. "No, no, boss, it's me, Zeph, and they're all tied up. That 'un will bring a pretty penny come auction time. Smith here has done good by makin' up for losing that pretty one down in Austin."

Muffled whimpering comes from back farther into the cave. The cage is barely visible in the faded light beyond where the Buyer sleeps.

The Buyer rubs his bad eye under the patch as he stares at me like the Medusa trying to turn me to stone with his good eye. It works when I cower like a scared little lamb. He snickers in delight. I'm doing exactly what he wants and what I need to do to weaken his defenses. This man's weakness is enjoying lustful power over weak and defenseless women. He'll find out just how weak and defenseless I am come reckoning time. I just hope Rainy, Lummy, and Sted have things well in hand outside the cave entrance. What am I saying? Of course they do. I hope.

The Buyer gets up, stumbles across the cave floor, and asks as he rubs his head, "What's with the Injun garb? You a chief or somethin'?"

"No chief, just warrior. You know who I be."

"Yeah, I know you. So you like playin' warrior?"

"Not often Choctaw get to capture enemy and bring to other enemy."

"So I'm your enemy too?"

Andrew smiles and nods. "You good enemy. You pay gold for Andrew hard work."

"Yeah, I will do that." The Buyer fumbles around looking for his boots. He starts to slip them on. "Zeph, give this man a double eagle for the pair. That should do—"

Andrew speaks up, "And gold for moonshine. My cousin make it. Need pay him too."

"All right, all right. You're a persistent one." The Buyer waves his hand to be rid of Andrew. "Give him two double eagles and run him outta here. I'm done talking to him." He pulls his boots on. "Somebody bring me a cup of coffee. Make sure it's hot."

Zeph pulls a bag from a chest from under the Buyer's bed and sorts out the coins. He flips two double eagles to Andrew and barks, "Be on your way."

The Buyer waves his hand to soften Zeph's words. "Next time, bring more women. And thanks for bringing the shine and Smith with you."

Andrew looks at Smith and spits. "Had he not been your man, would scalp him too."

The Buyer laughs and waves his hand. "All right, all right, you made your point. You're a great warrior and yeah, yeah, see you next time."

This is not working how we'd hoped. The Buyer isn't the cutthroat I was hoping he'd be. He's actually treating Andrew well, not slapping us around, or worse. But now, Andrew can't give the war whoop signal to our men outside because he's being thrown out too soon. Dang it, there's just never an easy plan. With Zeph, there's four men in the cave, counting the Buyer, Eli, and Zeke.

Zeph gives Zeke a wink and a side nod toward Andrew. "Take him outside and send him on his way." That nod is a signal for what I hope it doesn't mean.

Andrew looks straight ahead as he passes me. He side-eyes a wink at me. He knows. If he can take Jack and Zeke, that will leave only Zeph, Eli, and the Buyer in the cave. Lummy, Rainy, and Sted will be there with Andrew to take care of Jack and Zeke. They leave the cave, and I hear Andrew give a three war whoop yell that sends shivers down my spine. Now, it's quiet as a church at prayer time.

The Buyer gets up to come see me and Josie. "Drunk Injun. Andrew, that can't be right. What's his real name anyway?"

I laugh. "Don't you know, cyclops, that's Nobody. Nobody brought you me and this girl." I thumb point at Smith. "Him? He ain't nothing. Just a boy who lucked up and got the drop on me back in Texas."

The Buyer drops to squat. "Well, ain't you the sassy one. You're gonna bring a fine price."

"Not if I snatch the other eyeball out of your dog-faced head first."

He stands and snickers. "I like 'em feisty." He kicks me hard in the side. "Just means I get to tame you like a wild mustang." He turns to Zeph and laughs as I moan a bit. He stomps his foot. "Yeah, you gotta break 'em, beat 'em, ride 'em, hump 'em, beat 'em some more, but once they get tamed, if you dress 'em up pretty and make 'em smell all pretty, feed and water 'em good, they'll serve an army of men in every way they can think of. Yeah, broke mustangs get used to it after a while, don't they, little Josie?" He kicks at her shoe, and she slinks back like the girls in the cage. She plays her part well.

The Buyer scoffs, "Yeah, thought I didn't recognize you. I gotta good memory, little girl, like an elephant, and I never forget a pretty face, or an ugly one, for that matter. My luck is good. You're both lookers."

I kick dirt and rocks back at the Buyer, dusting his boots. "Well, too bad, 'cause your face ain't on the smiling end of a mule, that's for dang sure."

He looks down at his boots and chuckles. "That's all right, little darlin', I'll just have you lick the dust off here in a bit and then dry 'em with your hair." He looks at Zeph. "Wait a minute. Ain't somethin' like that in the Bible? Somethin' about a woman cryin' and washin' Jesus's feet with her tears because she'd been a bad girl, and then dryin' them off with her hair?" He squats down and jerks my head back by my hair. "You been a bad girl, blondie?"

I grind my teeth. "I'm just getting started being bad, you whorish man. And besides, you two make more racket than an empty wagon rolling on rocks."

Zeph laughs as he looks down on me. "I don't know if the story about the tear washin' is in the Good Book or not, boss, but sounds like fun to me."

"Maybe later," the Buyer barks. "Eli, bring me a lantern." He walks to a dark corner where the cage made of wood and rope imprisons several women. They huddle against the wall away from the door. The Buyer rattles the door. The women shrink back and cry. "The only way out of here is to be prepared to make yourselves pretty, spread your legs, and make money, understand?" Whimpering and sobbing fills the room.

"And shut that cryin' up. I'm sick of hearin' it." He kicks the cage and the women cry out. I want to jump and rip his throat out. Maybe I will. At just the right time.

The Buyer asks, "Zeph, how many does this make? Enough for an auction, you think?"

"Let me get a good count, boss." He holds up the lantern and tells the women to line up. He counts on his fingers and returns. "Looks like we got fifteen in the hold and these two. That's seventeen, I think."

The Buyer laughs. "Yeah it is, you lop-eared mule. It's seventeen. Didn't you go to school?"

Zeph drops his head and kicks the dirt. "My pappy said the only schoolin' we needed was hard work, goin' to church, and a good strappin' every day."

"Is that what you did?"

"Yeah, till I killed him when I turned fifteen."

"Well, blonde lady over there's got you beat. She at least might know some stories that I heard in my six years of schoolin' back in Missip."

What? He's from Mississippi? Maybe this is a way to soften his lust-crazed spirit. In the sweetest, syrupiest Southern drawl I can muster, I whisper, "Don't mean to interrupt, but I'm from Mississippi, don't you know?"

"Oh, really? And what did you say your name is."

"Nobody. Just like the Choctaw you just sent packing."

Agitation strains his voice. "Okay then, Nobody, where are you from?"

"Down 'round Natchez way." I regret saying that the moment I turn loose of the words.

The Buyer unfurrows his brow and a devilish grin creeps across his face. "You say, Natchez? Under-the-Hill, Natchez?"

Now I'm sure I shouldn't have told him.

"Heck, I've been there many times. Even worked on a steamboat outta there when I was just a pup." The Buyer spouts story after story about his exploits in sin city and then stops abruptly. "Wait a minute. Haven't I seen you before?"

I shake my head. "Don't think so." I'm praying he hasn't.

"Oh, the sweet smile you have, silky voice, and that bit of defiance that I really like. I knew a girl once with silky blonde hair, like you, but only a younger woman at the time, if I remember right. Sure that wasn't you, Marion?" He laughs and laughs, holding his belly.

The weight of a thousand boulders drops on my heart as it sinks into the abyss of my soul. How does he know me? Wait, what?

The Buyer glares at me with the eye of Satan himself and starts humming that song—the song that haunts me still. The humming ends as he steps closer. "Do dah, do dah." His belly laugh echoes throughout the cave. He screams, "Doo dah!"

I want to rip my hair out of my head. It can't be him. I want to scream. How could it be him? I want to fight. Why did it have to be him? I want to die. But I can't. This can't be over. My face is hot. My arms and legs tremble. My resolve thickens. My anger turns to rage. I'm feeling weak. I'm getting dizzy. I take a deep breath and blow it out silently. I steady myself. I start to get up and take my chances with this rascal but in a dark corner, two eyes flashing blue blink three times. As the Buyer steps a bit closer, the light reveals the old man we met in the desert. The old man who sat beside Lummy in the saloon in Fort Worth and warned us about the two men following us. The old man who... Uncle Silas.

Uncle Silas shakes his head once and then up and down three times like the blinks. He whispers, *"No fear."* He holds up three fingers. *"Lummy, Rainy, Sted."* He vanishes, but his presence reassures me that I am not alone.

I whisper, "And this ain't over." I sit still. Giving up on doing this my way and allowing Creator to sort it out, well, it's the hardest thing to do for me not to take charge. But as Uncle Lummy's voice in my head reminds me, it'll be all right. Even still, I struggle to trust. I whisper without even thinking the words, "And at that time shall Michael stand up, the great prince which standeth for the children of thy people... and there shall be a time of trouble...."

"What did you just say? That makes it so." The Buyer spits. "Yeah, took me a minute, but I do recognize you. I was gonna buy you or take you, either way, I was gonna have you all to myself." He hums that familiar tune. The tune that sends shivers down my spine and makes me tremble. He laughs. "Yeah, you better tremble. You cost me my eye, you Bible quotin' witch. Yeah, you were quotin' those same words the night I lost my eye."

It all comes back to me like walking out of a dark, shadowy forest into a blazing, bright sunshine grassy plain. Scenes I thought I'd thrown into the fiery pit of hell, and images I wanted sunk to the bottom of the Mississippi River, never to resurface again, flash in my brain like a hundred ribbons each a different color of a separate memory. It was him. He was humming that song, "Camptown Races," as he tried to force himself inside me. I was quoting that same verse from the Book of Daniel. I had nothing else at the time. My hope had drained to nothing. I was spent. I look up at him, the man Uncle Silas snatched from on top of me when he rescued me from the whorehouse in Natchez. All I remember was the song, his stinking breath, and him screaming "my eye, my eye" after Uncle Silas grabbed me up, threw me over his shoulder, and carried me down the stairs and out the back door. The smell of the silty brown river filled my lungs as we dropped into the alley that night. Freedom was mine for the first time since I had left the orphanage. We were home free, I thought, until the whorehouse owner dashed out of the shadows with a cane sword and slashed at Uncle Silas. Without a yell or a misstep, Uncle Silas whipped out a blade, long and gleaming in the night, and ended the threat before it became one. I don't remember much after that. I passed out, Uncle Silas later told me.

"Ain't no Michael the angel or nobody else comin' to help you now, Marion." A slap that feels like an ax handle laid across my face knocks my head sideways. Dizzy, I struggle to stay upright. "You're the reason I started this whole thing. Chasing women who needed to be taught their place, who need to learn that it's a man's world and women are for men's pleasure and nothing more. You, you did this. Look at me! He screams as he lifts the eyepatch to reveal a socket that's dark as an abyss.

"I've been hopin', searchin', and believin' you would cross my path one day. I just had to keep stealin' women until you showed up. And now I have you." He slaps me again. This time he lays me out on the floor. I sit up and glare with the ferocity of a cornered catamount. He laughs. "That's just the beginning of your troubles, blonde whore. By the time I'm done with you, nobody will want you."

"So kill me now, you weak old hound. You got no power over me or any of these girls. You're nothing but a dirty, rotten sack of snakes, easily thrown out of this cave and down into the rocks."

The Buyer looks around at the caged girls, who whimper and writhe in fear. He turns back with Satan's grin and with a demon's laugh he hums the song, finishing with, "Doo dah, doo dah." He shakes, he's so happy. "I'm lookin' forward to 'doo dah-ing' you, Marion."

"Is that all you got?"

"Well, Nobody, it ain't, but that's all you'll ever be… is Nobody." He pulls a knife from his belt from behind his back and licks the blade. "I'm gonna take this Arkansas toothpick and make you the next cyclops, you know, a female version of me." He throws his head back and laughs. "Think of that, Mister and Missus Cyclops, married up by a preacher and everythin'. Just imagine what our children will look like. Maybe they'll have just one eye in the center of their foreheads like in the story. Yeah, I got learnin' too. I just don't have to show it to have it." He holds the knife high in the air and pulls a pistol with the other. "I'm the smartest man to ever hit these parts." He lifts his voice to the cave ceiling, "Everybody is afraid of the Buyer." He laughs loud and almost hysterically. "Heck, I even scare myself sometimes."

"Don't let your alligator mouth overload your hummingbird butt." This man believes his own lies. "Power and might don't make intelligence, you ignert fool."

"What did you just say to me? I'm here, and you're there all tied up, and you're sayin' that I'm stupid? Let's just see who has the power and might, the intelligence you're talkin' about as I pluck that pretty, sky-blue eyeball out of your head."

"It'll be a cold day in hell with your father the Devil before that happens."

"The Devil gave me this sword. It will be his demons who give me the strength to take your eye and break you, Marion."

I snicker. "There's a flaming sword coming for you, cyclops, and no amount of prayin' to your god Poseidon will help you."

While Zeke and Eli laugh and poke fun, three shadows form on the cave wall behind them. One shadow arm rises, wielding a large blade I recognize from my own belt. Lummy's knife. Saint Michael, the Protector of God's people stands up.

"Then do your worst, Lucifer, for you're about to burn."

Lummy, Rainy, and Sted race from the shadows and head for our captors. I sweep my leg around with all my might and catch the Buyer behind both knees. He topples to the ground. He's back up in a flash, but it gives Lummy just enough time to get at him. I'm wriggling free when gunshots pour in from behind our three saviors.

The Buyer shouts, "We have you now. That's my men returning from town. Throw your guns down, and I'll make peace with you."

Lummy fires a well-aimed shot that sends a rock chip into Zeph's face, drawing a stream of blood. Zeph stands and screams in pain, "I'm comin' for you, tall man."

Sted turns to fire back toward the mouth of the cave. Now it's three against two—the Buyer, Eli, and Zeph against Lummy and Rainy. Lord only knows how many Sted is fighting off. Where's Andrew? My hands shake as I get my hands free. Lummy and Rainy are handling themselves well, ducking and dodging between the rocks as the outlaws fire a shot or two. The gun battle just outside the cave rages on.

Zeph crosses the cave floor like a scampering rat at a speed I never would've expected. About the time Lummy stands to meet him, they tear into each other like two wildcats with their tails tied together and set on fire. I shiver with the horror of it all but get myself together. I sneak over to Smith who is holding Josie in his arms to protect her. He's already untied Josie's hands, and I point to a far corner where they can escape the bullets.

Zeph and Lummy are going at it and Rainy takes carefully aimed shots at the Buyer and Eli. Everyone has forgotten about me. I crawl to the darkest edge of the cave and make my way around behind where the Buyer and Eli crouch. Neither they nor Rainy chance any shots at the two mad dogs rolling around on the floor. It's hard to tell who's winning. Zeph is younger and probably quicker, but Lummy is experienced, patient, and with his broad frame, stronger. I keep a steady pace at my crawling until I'm right behind the Buyer. He doesn't know I'm here. Now then, who's got the power, the might, and the intelligence? Here I am sneaking up on the one who thinks he's the smartest and sneakiest of all men.

Rainy lifts his pistol barrel to stop shooting and the Buyer turns his head just enough to see that I'm behind him. The only weapon I have is the ball of twine Rainy gave me. It's enough. I throw the ball of twine at him but keep ahold of the end, wrapping it, doubling it, giving myself just the right amount of slack.

Before the Buyer can get around quick enough to face me, I hop on his back and slip the twine loop around his neck, and I pull it tight with all of my might.

Eli stands up and puts his pistol to my head. The Buyer cackles like the Devil himself, "Now you die, darlin'." As the hammer clicks back, Eli is blown against the wall. Rainy dashes over and stands perfectly still.

Rainy steps forward to help, but I yell, "No! He's mine."

Lummy walks up, pistol in one hand, the knife his father made for him in the other. He stops. Blood drips from the blade. "That one back there is dead." He speaks in the voice of the avenging angel he is as he studies me choking the Buyer. "A man's got to kill his own snakes." He wipes Zeph's blood on his pants and sheaths the knife. "But in this case, it's a strong and determined woman of the Most High killin' this serpent."

I bear down on the twine, straining with everything I've got. The Buyer gags, he chokes, he kicks, and curses hoarsely, but to no avail. He grabs the twine and pulls it away from his neck just enough to say, "How'd you get behind me, how'd you get loose?"

I yell, "Some run from what they fear. I run straight at it. And I don't hide who I am, you weak little boy who has to hide behind some fancy name that gives you no power, no might, and certainly no intelligence."

I jerk the twine hard and his fingers slip out from under the tightening string. "I am a woman! I am not weak and defenseless. I was not made for your pleasure or to cower on my knees before you. Strong, brave, and true, I fear no man, for I have the power of Creator, and I have good men with me."

I strain as hard as I can, and I can feel the life draining from the Buyer's body. "You tell Satan, we're coming for him next. Tell him who we are. Tell him we're bringing hell to Hades!"

I hold on to dear life as I take his. He tries to roll over, but I spread my legs and dig my boot heels into the sandy soil of the small path. He claws at the rope, and my heart breaks for a moment. But I don't stop. I twist the twine and yank as hard as I can, and I hear a pop. He stops struggling and gives up. He's dead. I relax as his body slumps.

DEATH OF A CYCLOPS

*"All men's souls are immortal, but the souls of
the righteous are immortal and divine."*
—Socrates

Sense of all time lost, September 6, 1886

I STAND OVER the one-eyed man. The Buyer lies lifeless, staring into the darkness with his one good eye swollen shut. "He looks so small to have lived so big."

The Buyer's one good eye blinks. I back up. He's not dead. He's trying to move his head, but it doesn't respond.

"Well ain't that a shame? Can't feel my arms and legs. I can't do nothin' except move my eyeball. Well, I reckon I'm done in, and you did it, little girl." His good eye scans the range he's allowed with a broken neck searching for something. Then it fixes on my face, and I feel the Devil's stare cutting at my soul, trying to whittle me down. "I know who you are, but all this excitement I can't remember your name." In the sweetest, slimiest voice, he coaxes me, "What is your name again, girl? I want to take it with me when I leave here. Show a little mercy, will you?"

I don't move. "Mercy is for those who have shown it."

"But that God of yours is merciful no matter what, ain't he?"

"Yes, the Lord is merciful… whether I am or not. And today, I'm not."

Rainy whispers, "You've been judged and found lacking, demon."

The fear in the Buyer's eyes grows. He whimpers just a little.

Lummy squats down beside him. "You don't need to know her name." He draws his knife to start something I'm sure I would not want to see. "Like she said, mercy is reserved for those who have shown it. You get none." Lummy thumbs the end of his blade and licks the thin red line. He leans over to do God knows what when Rainy takes him by the shoulder. Rainy takes the knife from Lummy's hand and hands it to me. I sheath it.

The Buyer snickers. "Go ahead, big man, I ain't gone yet, and I'll be comin' back for you… all of you. I'll haunt you till the day you die."

Rainy holsters his pistol. "Her name is Atalanta."

I snatch my head around. "What?"

Rainy mouths that he will tell me later.

The Buyer barely squeaks out, "Atalanta? What kind of name is that?" He groans from the back of his throat. He's clearly on his way out.

Lummy stands and studies the helpless outlaw who once claimed to be the one-eyed man who was king in the land of the blind. "The kind of name that always gets her man, and brings him down."

"She'll get hers, and I'll see her in hell someday."

I've had enough. "Angels of the Lord only see hell from a distance, like now."

I nod for Rainy to step back. I yank out the knife Lummy's father made for him when he was just a kid—the razor-edged weapon that took Dawg Smith's head off and the stone-sharpened blade that gutted Tom Kimbrell from crotch to throat.

The Buyer smiles, his teeth glistening with blood. "See, you ain't nothin'." He hums the "Camptown Races" song, finishing with, "Doo dah, doo dah." He laughs as best as his broken body will allow.

I stand still as a statue, knife in hand.

The Buyer looks at me in terrified disbelief. "What're you gonna do to me now, Atalanta?"

I don't move. I know what's coming for the Buyer. I sense the evil in the room as the lanterns flicker in the damp darkness.

An unholy, ungodly bellow purges itself out of the Buyer's mouth like the sound of a tornado wind. "What are those sharp claws clutchin' on me, tearing at my flesh?"

I shout, "Yeah, you can 'doo dah' all the way to hell, cyclops!"

The Buyer lets out a blood curdling scream, "Somethin's pulling me down a dark hole. I can't hold on to anything. The fire, the flames, my skin's burnin' off. It hurts!"

I yell at the top of my lungs, "Good, when you finally get settled, tell them I sent you. Tell them all that Atalanta is my name! Tell your master that I'll be sending more of your kind to the eternal torment of fire and brimstone."

The Buyer's body shakes and shivers, then squirms like a worm thrown into a campfire. How, I don't know. His eyes pop wide open, and he screams, "It won't stop burnin'. Make it stop. Please. It's dark. Where am I? I can't see. What's that? Wait. Who's that laughin'? Oh, God no-o-o-o! I'm in hell." He wails in agony.

The Buyer fixes his eye upon me. He hurls curses and insults, begging the Evil One to bring misery upon my life. "Satan, I don't care what you do to me. You can have my soul. I give it to you." He stops like he's listening to a voice from the pit. "What do I want in return? I want you to torment Atalanta's life until she arrives here. Make her life on Earth a living hell. Give her no rest from her work. Let it never end until she is old and gray, sufferin' from all kinds of disease and misery. When she gets here, let me hold the door open with hell's bells ringing for her then you give her a double portion of punishment!"

The wind kicks up something fierce with an eerie howl that sounds like a thousand souls being dragged into hell. The voice in the abyss howls, *"It shall be do-o-o-o-one,"* like tree limbs racking against each other in a tempest storm and then scream like so many demons loosed from the deepest part of hell. I shudder but fix my feet and stand my ground.

An even stronger blast of wind sweeps through cracks and crevices in the rocks and into the cave that has the appearance of man with a sword. Like the sound of rushing water, the wind blasts a sound like ten thousand voices, *"Be gone!"*

And the Buyer's one eye closes to open no more in this world.

The man with the sword says, *"He sees clearly now,"* and vanishes.

I glance at Lummy. "Did that just happen?"

He shrugs. "Now that you ask, yeah, it happens all the time. You just have to have eyes to see and ears to hear. Granny Thankful told me that."

"Whew, what have I gotten myself into here, Uncle?"

"You never got yourself into anything. A good heart was given to you at an early age but then the evil lurking and slithering in this world took a good thing, fed it a piece of fruit, told it to trust itself rather than the one who made you. It was thrust upon you almost without your consent. I want to have a word with Creator about that one when I pass through the thin veil and see him. But you doin' this? It ain't nothin' Creator ain't ever done himself or called other people to do long before you came into this world. Creator called you for his purpose, and then chose you to take on the mantle."

"How do you know that?"

He points at the knife still in my hand. "Has not the sword of justice been handed over to you with no argument, with no naysayers?"

I roll the hilt of the knife around in my hand and sheath the blade.

Rainy kicks the Buyer's boot. "And the one-eyed man who thought he was king in the land of the blind, well, he's dead."

Lummy sits on a hogshead barrel and sighs. He cries. "Another saint of the Lord of the Great Angel Armies is soon to step through the thin veil. I weep for our loss, your loss, Marion, but I weep for the world. It will not be a better place without him. Take a wicked soul, give up a good soul." Lummy wraps his arms around his shoulders and screams to high heaven, "Is that how it always has to be? Susannah for Dawg Smith? Poole for Lester? Old Bart for Tom Ford? J. A. for John West? Is this how it's always been? One good soul for a bad soul? Ahhhh! I can't stand it anymore!" He wilts into his own quiet thoughts.

What is he talking about, my loss?

Smith cries with Lummy, "But, can't you see, Mister Lummy? We all made it, safe and sound."

I whisper, "Uncle Silas for the preacher, voodoo witch, and carpetbagger. Trading souls, I guess it is the way of this fallen world… what?" It hits me. "Wait a minute, what do you mean, another saint is on his way home?"

A bloodied figure of a man stumbles into the cave. "Andrew!" In the fray, I'd lost all sense of what was going on outside—the shots from the men outside the cave, Andrew taking out the guard named Jack, and Zeke, and…. "Where's Sted?" I race to Andrew. He looks up with the most pitiful eyes I believe I've ever seen.

"You best hurry. He has little time." Andrew collapses, and I gently lay him down. Smith and Josie scramble to Andrew and start taking care of him.

I pull back bloody hands and scream, "Sted!"

I race like a jackrabbit to the cave entrance into the bright sunshine. I stand for just a moment to let my eyes adjust and frantically search the hillside for bodies. I run to one, Zeke. Then to another, but it's not Sted. It's that Jack. I shield my eyes and squint to see two more bodies down in the rocks, one with an arrow in his neck and the other with a clean shot to the forehead. Lummy and Rainy rush out, pistols waving in every direction trying to find any possible threat to cover me as I start shaking like a leaf.

Lummy asks, "Where is he?"

A small moan wafts up from behind a large boulder. I dash to one side of the rock and drop to my knees where Sted lies gasping in a puddle of blood. I gently unbutton his shirt. "Oooh no, Sted, my darling, Sted."

A wound to his chest pumps bright red blood bubbles each time he takes a troubled breath. Lummy and Rainy ease up behind me and sit on the ground, heads held low. Sted wheezes in and out, trying to say something. I hold back my wailing and put my ear to his lips.

Sted coughs and chokes a bit, but whispers, "I wanted to marry you, sweet Marion. I'd done anythin' for you."

My tears drip onto his wound. "And I would have said yes." He starts to fade. "Sted. You can't go, you just can't."

He comes back from the other side. "Just one thing before I go, please."

"Oh, Sted…."

"Just one more kiss to remember you by?"

I gently press my lips to his and hold them there until the breath of life, his very soul escapes what no longer is to be, our life together on this earth.

A welling up from the deepest part of me bellows out like I've never experienced. "Why?" My strength leaves me, and I have no more to say.

Rainy wraps his arm around me as I bawl like a baby. He whispers, "The kiss that lasts an eternity."

WHEN ALL YOU CAN DO IS JUST SIT

Sometimes, all you can do is sit on the ground next to Job, throw dust on your head, scrape your bloody sores with a broken piece of pottery, and wait on the Lord.

Midmorning, September 6, 1886

WE SIT FOR what seems an eternity. I savor the last kiss given to the first man I ever loved. Why, Lord? Why did Sted have to be the one? There is no asking why. It's like what Uncle Lummy asked, "One good soul for one bad soul?" There's no asking why because there is no reason why. And no answers why. Good and evil. It's just the way it is, and right now, I'm feeling pretty evil.

I peer up high into the rocks above the cave entrance and a voice wisps its way down to me in a piney scented breeze. *"Do what must be done to salve your soul or your soul will not survive,"* says Uncle Silas.

I jump and bolt into the cave, Lummy's knife in hand.

Rainy, slower getting up, yells, "Whoa, wait a minute, Marion, where are you going?"

I hear Lummy scream, "Marion, no!"

I get to the wretched, contorted body of the Buyer and drop to one knee beside him. I raise my knife and stab what's left of his good eye. "Now you're the blind man living with the king of the fiery land of the blind, whose demons will torment you forever, who have many eyes and many ways to torture you!" I stare down at the bloody socket and decide it's time to take this man apart, piece by piece, and scatter the parts in all directions.

I raise the knife high to make my first cut when a hand grabs my wrist and holds it fast. Uncle Lummy whispers, "Not like this, Marion. Please, not like this."

I snap my head around and jerk my arm from his grasp. "You did it!"

He hangs his head. "I did, and it cost me dearly. It never goes away."

Rainy walks up, hat in hand. "He's right, Marion. We both know what will happen if you do this. We suffer for our own sins every day."

Lummy squints. "They never go away. You say you have sins that need grace and mercy. Don't add this one to the list. He's dead, Marion. The Buyer is dead."

Rainy squats. "He is in Satan's hands now forever. Let him go."

Lummy takes a knee. "Let it all go, sweet niece."

Rainy pats my shoulder. "You will be glad you did."

I collapse from exhaustion like a pile of old clothes thrown on the floor. "Why am I so tired?"

Rainy offers, "Restraint to do the right thing takes much more energy than to do that which is wrong."

"I'm sure you must be right. And right now, I'm weak as a popcorn poot."

Lummy takes my hand and nods to Rainy who takes me by the elbow of the arm that wields the knife. "We have another way. One that will help get your strength back."

They gently lead me to the cage filled with fifteen frightened women and girls, cowering in the far back of the cave. I stop, smile at each of them, and pull away. "I can do this myself." I walk to the cage with the knife that Lummy's father made for him as a child, the one that took the head of Dawg Smith. I smash the lock on the door with the butt of the weapon and swing the door open.

"You're free! All of you. Come on out. The Buyer is dead and all of his demons have been sent back to hell from whence they came. We are your friends."

They start out of the cage in single file and huddle in the middle of the cave like little birds that don't know they're no longer in the birdcage.

"Smith, Josie, how's Andrew?"

Smith yells, "He'll be all right with a bit of patchin' up, Atalanta."

I whisper, "Why's he calling me Atalanta?"

Rainy snickers. "Tell you later. Let's get to what needs doing."

"All right then, Josie, get over here and let's get these ladies ready to travel. We've got a ways to go, and I want to get them back to their families quick as we can."

Josie pats Smith on the shoulder and asks, "You got this?" He nods as she kisses his forehead. "Coming, Marion." Josie trots to the ladies and asks, "Now, what can we do for you?"

Rainy leans over to Lummy. "I saw that coming—Smith and Josie, that is."

Lummy shrugs. "Things happen, good and bad. A found love and a lost love. An all too common occurrence in this world. I just hope they don't have to experience both."

"They won't if I have anything to do with it," Rainy says and winks.

"Lummy, Rainy, there's something I need to do. I'll be outside."

They both say at the same time, "You be careful."

I noticed on the way into the rocks this morning that several people had etched their names in the limestone at various places. I want to leave my mark as well.

I pull my knife and scratch a circle. It doesn't take too long. I think about what to put inside the circle. I only have time to etch one letter into the soft rock. Should it be an A for this new name Atalanta that seems to be sticking, or Marion, my real name? I whisper, "Nicknames fade, real names are eternal."

I stand back and admire my work. A perfect *M* surrounded by a perfect circle. "*M* for Marion, surrounded by the host of heaven led by the eternal circle of Saint Michael, the Protector of God's People and his angel armies."

✱ ✱ ✱

WE START OUT of the rocks on horses the Buyer once used to bring captured ladies into his lair. Now we use them to set captives free.

I speak aloud the words of the Lord. I have to. I have to find myself again after all of this. "The Spirit of the Lord is upon me because…." I cry for a moment when Sted's perfect face flashes in my mind. "Because he hath anointed me to preach the gospel to the poor… and hath sent me to heal the brokenhearted to preach deliverance to the captives"—I look around at the string of horses carrying the captured ladies out of hell—"and recovering sight to the blind." I think on that last one for a moment. The Buyer surely sees more clearly now, but I want the land of the blind to know there won't be any more stealing, buying, and selling of women in any form from now on. The eyes of those who live in the land of the blind are about to have their sight recovered. "And… how does that last part go… yes, I have it… to set at liberty them that are bruised."

Lummy adds, "To preach the acceptable year of the Lord. Oh, how I've longed for that."

Rainy snickers. "Good words, Marion. Are you going to become a preacher like your old raggedy-butt uncle over there?"

"Oh, heck no. Not me." I snicker. "But I do believe more I'm on the path of a clear eye than I have been in a long time."

Lummy laughs and eases his mount close. "I believe Marion has learned that not all preachin' is done with words by a loudmouth standin' in a church house hopin' for a good collection."

Rainy leans over. "It seems like I remember somebody turning over a bunch of tables in the temple in anger one time."

"You say we're bein' like Jesus, Rainy Mills?"

"I never claim anything the Devil is sure to topple at some point with ease. I am not a pious man, you know that."

"No, Rainy, you ain't. You just want to sound like you are."

Rainy sits up straight and laughs. "Well said, preacher, well said."

Lummy snickers, "Go to hell, Rainy Mills."

He grins. "Been there already, old friend, right alongside you."

"Ain't that the truth?"

Rainy licks his lips. "I think we should probably take a break from the flames, what do you say?"

Lummy shifts in his saddle. "If it involves good whiskey, I'm in."

I smile at both and say, "Me too." I love these two men with all my heart.

Rainy leads the way with Andrew's horse in tow. "Let's get this good man back home and hand off these sweet flowers rescued from Satan's scythe, then head to Skullyville. There's a man there I need to see."

I don't want to ask, but I want to know. "Who is it, if I can ask?"

"For now, I'll just say it's seeing a man I've needed to talk to for a long time. Just now found the wherewithal to do it with your help, Atalanta."

"You keep calling me that. Who in the heck is this Atalanta y'all keep calling me?"

Rainy gently goads his mount. "After I speak with my man, I'll tell you."

Leaving Sted buried in the same patch of rocks as the Buyer and his men rattles my heart, but doesn't shake my soul. Sted will guard those outlaws for eternity with the help of Saint Michael, the Protector of God's People. He would've wanted it that way.

We took everything of value—all the money, guns, horses and accoutrements, even the moonshine whiskey we had brought. It'll go a long way to helping these ladies get back home to their loved ones. And give peace to our weary minds.

RED OAK RETREAT

In saving another, you save yourself.

Midafternoon, September 6, 1886

HARDLY A WORD was spoken the twenty miles back to Edwards Store near Red Oak. We settle into our old camp by Brazil Creek not far from Edwards Store to rest and wait for Captain Charles Leflore with the Choctaw Lighthorse police and his partner, Sam Sixkiller. I try to stay busy, tending to the girls. We take them down to a secluded place along the creek so they can wash themselves and their clothes. They wander almost aimlessly back to camp—except by me and Josie's leading—clad only in blankets. It's a sight. Fifteen young women, shivering naked under blankets, wondering if they are safe, even still, and what their next steps will be.

After feeding them and getting their clothes dried by the fire, we have them dress and Josie asks, "Now, how can we help you?" I like that about her. Truly a servant of the Lord, that one.

One by one the ladies perk up, and they all say essentially the same thing. I ask with the best smile I can muster, "Y'all all want to go home?" They smile, even get a little giddy with hope flashing in their eyes.

Lummy eases over and says, "You might find out which one is the girl from Red River Station, if she's here."

I'd forgotten about her in the rush. I cross my fingers with hope. "Anyone here from Red River Station, a Carol Ann?"

A not so noticeable girl close to my height with curly dark brown hair steps out from behind the others in her boy clothes given to her by the Buyer. She clasps her hands together like no one could pry them apart. I slowly reach out my hand. She hesitates. Clearly this girl's mind is troubled. She takes a step forward and then runs into my arms, crying hard. I wrap my arms around her, and she lets it all out, the hurt of being kidnapped, abused, and treated like an animal. I hold her and nod for Josie to come take her.

Josie pulls Carol Ann's arms away. "Come with me. We're gonna get you home."

We sit on logs around the fire and Rainy records each ladies' name and from where they were taken. We can't get them all back home, but I'm sure Captain Leflore will be happy to get them where they need to go. All the ladies are fed and snuggle together under warm blankets to ward off the slight evening chill. It's not long that there's not an open eye between them.

Lummy, Rainy, and I sit together, sipping a bit of whiskey and talk about what just happened in the past twenty-four hours. Smith and Josie sit away from the fire on two empty barrels, whispering and laughing.

Rainy grins. "Those two have just started courting and don't even know it yet."

Lummy pulls a half-smoked cigar from his pocket, lights it with a burning ember from the fire, and blows a smoke ring that hangs in the air for a long time. "Yeah they do. Them two's makin' plans. They need somewhere to go to start their new life together. A place where a very influential and prosperous good-hearted man could make things a lot easier for them to get started."

Rainy asks, "Didn't you tell me on the way here from Skullyville that Josie is from Natchitoches?"

Lummy flicks the end of his cigar. "I do believe I did."

Rainy sips his whiskey and says, "As one of Winnfield's finest upstanding and most Christian of citizens, I believe it's my duty to initiate those two fine young people into the genteel society of Winn Parish."

Lummy coughs, chokes, and spits, sending his cigar flying from his mouth straight into the fire, he's laughing so hard. "Dang it, and I was countin' on gettin' at least a couple more puffs out of that thing. What I wasn't countin' on was you thinkin' so highly of your own sorry behind. I'll be speakin' to the Missus about you, brother, a certain Missus Mary Jane Mills, if I recall correctly?"

Rainy pulls a cigar quickly from his coat pocket and lights one. He hands it to Lummy. "Oh, no you don't. That woman will take me down a notch or two just for thinking like that."

Lummy takes a long draw on his new cigar, snuffs it out, and puts it in his pocket. He chuckles. "Ain't it somethin' how a woman can take the worst that the human race has to offer and make somethin' useful, even decent out of him?"

Rainy is not to be bested. "Seems like I remember a Missus Martha who had a knack for taming a wild and uncouth animal into a productive and occasionally likable human being."

Lummy takes Rainy's extended hand. "That's for dang sure, my good friend."

I laugh and punch them both in the shoulder. "You boys ain't got a snowball's chance in hell of gettin' through life without a good woman. Why you both…." Then I remember, Rainy goes home to a loving, caring wife and Uncle Lummy goes home, or wherever he's headed, to no one.

"I'm sorry, Lummy, I didn't mean to be insensitive."

He swats the air. "No harm done, niece. If I never have another woman, I've had the best Creator could've brought me."

Rainy lifts his hand. "Amen to that. Susannah, who I didn't know, but Martha who I did know, loved this man with all their hearts, and he will see them again."

Lummy stares into the cedar limbs across the creek, nodding his head.

He smiles and whispers, "I know, my darlings, I'll be along soon enough. Susannah, Martha, I will always love you both."

I jerk my head over just in time to see two figures melt into the forest, but an old man's face appears beside the trunk of a cedar. He gets up, waves to me, and disappears behind Susannah and Martha.

I turn around to find Smith and Josie standing together in the firelight like two kids caught sparking behind the church house. Smith looks to Josie then back to me. "Miss Marion, we was just thinkin', Josie and me. We'd like to offer to take Miss Carol Ann back home to her folks, it bein' all right with you and everythin'. We would just like to get her home and—"

"What, and get yourselves hitched?"

Lummy and Rainy laugh at the looks on Smith's and Josie's faces. "What? How'd you know, Miss Marion?"

"Boy, we were over here taking bets on how long it'd be before you got brave enough to tell us." I turn to Lummy and Rainy. "Y'all two are the only folks ever been married around here. What do you say?"

Smith and Josie dance a little step, they are so excited.

Lummy says, "Well, they're gonna need a home, but a preacher first, you know, so they can be legal and all."

Rainy smiles. "And if I've been informed correctly, somebody is from Natchitoches, right?"

Josie yells, "Yes, yes, that's me! I'm from Natchitoches! I still have family there, I hope. We want to go there, yes, we do."

Josie jumps up and down like a grasshopper. Smith covers his mouth with happy embarrassment. They wait like a sentence is about to be pronounced on them.

I nod to Lummy and Rainy then turn to Josie and Smith. "All right then. You get a preacher to get you hitched somewhere on the way to Red River Station and get Carol Ann home safe and sound. Then you get your hind ends over to Winnfield and Uncle Rainy will get you squared away. How's that sound?"

I don't have much in the way of money, so Lummy stands and pulls his money purse from his belt. "Smith, can you get Josie and the girl back to the train at Limestone Gap and then to Red River Station?"

"Yes, sir, no problem doin' that. For my young years, I've been on many a trail."

"Good, take Miss Carol Ann home, and you and Josie backtrack to Limestone Gap on the trail, and then come meet us in Skullyville. Should only take you three, at the most, four days. Think you can do that?"

"Yes, sir, I do."

Lummy counts out a stack of coins and hands it to Smith. "This'll get you there and back to Skullyville. Make every dollar count but eat well and do what needs doin'. Make sure your horses are secure and keep your eyes open for those two outlaws we missed. What were their names?"

Smith straightens his jacket like he's girding up his loins for war like in the Bible. "Michael Angel and Little Dave Greasefire. We will do just that, Mister Lummy."

"All right then. Y'all take off first light and go on down there with Carol Ann. We'll be waitin' for you in Skullyville."

Smith fumbles around, and then rushes to Lummy, wraps his arms around the big man, and holds on tight. "Thank you for savin' my life." He turns around. "You, too, Miss Marion and Mister Rainy. I will not let you down."

I smile. "We know that, Smith."

Josie gives the three of us each a kiss on the cheek. "Thank you."

They hug and jump up and down. They are so happy. A bit of good envy seeps into my heart for what they have. They rush around to gather what few things they have and huddle together whispering, Josie giggling, and Smith puffing his chest out like a toad, as it should be. Lucky pair, those two.

I look to the sky and whisper, "Thanks for the moments we had, Sted. I'll never forget you."

Rainy leans over. "Granny Thankful just told me your help is about to arrive."

Horse hooves shatter the late afternoon's silence. We jump up, weapons in hand. Andrew hops down from his pony and walks like he's never been wounded.

I ask, "Andrew Flying Hawk, shouldn't you be in bed at Edwards Store where we left you? You're still mending and—"

He throws up a war whoop. "You do not know the power of Choctaw holy man medicine. I'm good as new, well, a little of that whiskey would do me good right about now."

I ask, "Who you got there with you?"

Andrew snickers but grabs his side, the bit of laughing paining his wounds. "Your friend and savior, Captain Charles Leflore, and his trusty companion, Sam Sixkiller."

I hold out my hand. "So glad to see you, Captain. We certainly need your help."

After the men exchange handshakes and greetings, Captain Leflore plants his feet and rests his palms on his six-shooters. "You folks did some mighty fine work from what Andrew has told me. I want to hear all about it."

Rainy points to the fire and says, "Find a comfortable spot to sit, and we'll serve you the best moonshine this side of Choctaw County, Missip." He laughs. "And all the coffee you can drink to help with the headache you're gonna have in the morning."

Seats are found, drinks are served all around, and I wait for Rainy or Lummy to start the story. They don't.

Captain nods to me. "Well, Marion, it's for you to tell us the story. After all, Andrew here said you masterminded the plan and kept these yahoos together and going in the same direction."

My heart swells to the size of the beaming sun in the morning. Lummy and Rainy grin and nod, and I tell the story.

"And that's the way it was, Captain, the long and short of it. Rainy, Lummy, did I miss anything?" They shake their heads.

"Helluva a tale, helluva story, if you ask me. You folks did good, and you will be rewarded." He rubs his chin. "I do have a question I'll need to answer in my report. Since you have no prisoners, and that's not a problem, what about two bad characters we've been tryin' to capture named Michael Angel and Little Dave Greasefire?"

Rainy and Lummy look at me, and I ask Smith, "You mentioned them back in Red River Station. I don't believe they were in the bunch who fought outside the cave while we battled the Buyer inside. If they were there, they musta hightailed it out of there like a couple of jackrabbits before we knew they were there."

"I-I didn't see either of them in the bodies we buried in the rocks up there."

Andrew hangs his head. "No Angel and no Greasefire were there."

Smith agrees, "He's right. They were counted not among the dead."

I plant my hands on my gun belt. "Dang, it never ends, does it?"

Captain Leflore whispers, "Doin' the Lord's work ain't got no end. When one demon on this earth is killed, there's ten waitin' in line for their turn."

"Well, there's good angels waitin' in line to meet 'em head on too."

"All right then, I'll get a reward voucher written up by morning, and you can take it too. Let's see…." He turns to Sam. "Didn't I tell them a few days ago that the nearest gov'ment office is in Skullyville?" Sam agrees and the captain smiles. "You can cash it right there. I'll wire the main office to make sure it's there when you arrive. Should be a hefty sum to split amongst yourselves. Look for my men in the saloon. They'll have badges."

"Which saloon?"

"Ain't but one. You'll know it when you see it."

"Thank you, Captain. Now about the loot we brought with us taken from Robbers Cave. We brought any and everything of value we could carry."

"It's yours to do with as you wish."

"We were hoping you'd say that. We want all of it, the money, and with all the goods and stock sold, to be distributed to help get these girls back home and hopefully with a little jingle in their pockets."

Captain wipes a tear from his eye and turns to Sam Sixkiller. "If we had ten of these warrior women and men, we could clean up the entire Choctaw Nation in a heartbeat."

Sam hands him a kerchief. "Maybe we could talk one or two of 'em into joining the Choctaw Lighthorse." Sam smiles at me. "We'd be right proud to have you, Miss Marion, and any of you men, of course."

I purse my lips then say, "No, not right now, but I'm grateful for your offer. I need time to get over a few things and take some time to rest and clear my head. You understand?"

"Yes, I do. I need a little of the same to get past the thing we did in Muskogee yesterday." He rubs his arm.

I ask, "Y'all catch up to those Black Hoyt and Nicholson fellows y'all were lookin' to catch?"

Sixkiller rocks his head from side to side. "Yeah, well, kinda. We tried to arrest them peacefully, but they were both drunk as skunks. Nicholson shot at me, creasing my arm. Hurts somethin' fierce, but anyway, the captain here shot and wounded Nicholson before he could get off another shot. He escaped, but we did arrest Black Hoyt. It's just a matter of time before we capture Nicholson. That is, if he doesn't die of his wound first."

I sit back. "Well, for your sake, I hope he's already dead."

"Yeah, us too. After we get these ladies on the way to their homes, then we'll track Nicholson down."

We finish drinking, talking, laughing, and telling stories. We each go to our respective places to sleep. It's not long until all are resting peacefully.

I roll over after a short nap, like I often do in my fitful sleep each night, to see Andrew sitting by the fire, softly singing a song in what I'd guess to be in Choctaw. I wrap my blanket around my shoulders and sit by him. He stops his tune.

"What's that song about, Andrew?"

He turns with tears in his eyes. "I had to tell my brother that his daughter was not among those we brought back." He straightens up and draws in a deep breath like he's trying to inhale the Universe. "Tonight

I sing for her soul, to be happy and free wherever she is and that our God, and your God, will protect her, and someday free her, if that can be done. I can say no more about it, Miss Marion. I'm sorry. I must go find my own place in the cedars."

"I understand, Andrew. See you in the morning." He nods and walks away. He's carrying something weighty in a sack. I ask, "What's in the bag, Andrew? Choctaw medicine?"

He turns with a glare that could burn right through me. "You could say that." He opens the bag and pulls the Buyer's head up for me to see. "I told you I wanted his head. It will serve as a warning to all who believe they can harm innocent Choctaw women and girls."

I shudder as he turns. "Andrew?" He stops and resacks the head. I nod and say, "I'll be seeing you again."

He grins like a mule eating briars. "I know. That old man over there in the cedars told me. He wants to speak with you."

I wander over to the edge of the creek, careful to take the most solid rocks as my stepping stones. I sit on a big rock just on the other side and out walks Uncle Silas holding something in his hand.

"You did well in the work given you by Creator, Marion. You kept your head with the help of those you came to trust while the enemy lost his head."

I hold my head in my hands. "It was the hardest thing to do, not carving that man up into a thousand pieces so he could never be put back together, even in hell."

"All is done, all is right, all shall be well."

"Until next time?"

"There is always a next time for those who understand their calling and answer it."

"Why did Sted have to die, Uncle Silas?"

"The ones most loved are the one Satan seeks to take from us. The pain is not Sted's now. It is yours. The Evil One knows that. He will never let you forget."

"So what do I do?"

"Holding a grudge in your heart builds a wall no man can climb over. You must release hate and replace it with love as you now have enjoyed."

"I don't know if I can do that. Sted had become someone I could trust, with all that's happened."

"Trust one, trust another." Uncle Silas fades into the shadows of the cedar boughs.

"Marion," a gentle voice behind me whispers.

I jerk my feet up and pivot around to find Sam Sixkiller standing across the small stream with his hands folded in front of him.

"I'm sorry to disturb you, but I just want to say something before you leave tomorrow. Please come back. You are a person I would like as a friend."

I shake my head. "Sam, I just lost a man I loved, and I'm not sure what I'm gonna do. I need some time."

"I want a friend. I'm asking for no more than that. I will be here should you return."

I look to the sky and then to Sam. He's gone. A man of manners and respect. I like that, and I need friends. I'm sure Lummy and Rainy need to get on with their lives as do Smith and Josie.

My heart so aches over Sted being gone. I look into the dark but star-filled sky. A lone shooting star races across the sky glowing red, then orange, and finally yellow. I whisper a word to chase the star. "Go with God, my love. I will see you again someday, Stedman Walker."

ON TO SKULLYVILLE

Love that is eternal is love that has been set free.

Daylight, September 7, 1886

MORNING COMES QUICKER than I wanted. We're loaded and ready to ride. Smith and Josie left before dawn with Carol Ann in tow. Captain Leflore and Sam have the girls loaded and ready in a large wagon to take to the train station in Limestone where they'll start sending them home. I speak a word to the Good Lord for their safe travels.

Captain Leflore and Sam Sixkiller step out of Edwards Store to see us off. I think about what the captain and Sam talked about last night, about what they do here in the Choctaw Nation. They are committed, determined, and seem to have their rage in check. I need to be around men like that. Men much like Lummy and Rainy.

Sam Sixkiller is a man I would like to get to know better, but I can't right now. Sted's death is way too fresh in my heart.

The captain pulls me to the side before I mount. "Marion, you've got guts. If you need somewhere to live out your code of justice, you can always have a place with the Choctaw Lighthorse, you hear me?"

I bat my eyes like a little girl. "Why, I do hear you clearly, Captain, dear."

He laughs. "Dang, girl, you could kill a man just by lookin' at him. Get out of here before I arrest you for loitering and disturbing the peace."

I laugh and slap him on the shoulder. "Yes, sir, Captain, sir."

"Actually, she has the face that makes a man's heart hurt." Sam Sixkiller grins. "Be seein' you, Miss Marion Tullos." His dark eyes capture my soul, but I turn away for a moment.

Then I look up at him through a furrowed brow as he leans against a pole on Edwards Store porch. "I'd like that, Sam Sixkiller. You take care of yourself."

We ride east on the trail that leads to Skullyville, and I'm surprised even at myself thinking about Sam Sixkiller. Sted's gone, and I guess I need time to let that piece of my heart ripped to shreds mend. It does make me hesitate wanting to get into another friendship that can be snatched away in the flash of a bullet. Sam Sixkiller might be a good man to work with, but I have no eyes for any man right now. I need to get more of my soul back before I do anything else. He is good-looking, though.

Rainy leads the pack followed by Lummy and me. We ease along at a snail's pace. We've got nowhere to go in a rush. It's nice just to amble along. Gives me time to sort things out.

"Uncle Lummy, how do you do it?"

"What do you mean? About what?"

"You know I was starting to love Sted, and—"

"No, girl, you were *in* love with Sted."

"All right, yes, I was. But how did you get past Susannah to love another like you did with Martha?"

Lummy looks into the woods as we pass a pile of rocks, and he smiles. "I guess in this life, you love who you can, the best way you can, in the time you have together."

"So, I should leave my heart open for the next love that comes my way?"

Rainy drops back to ride beside us. "Mind of I answer that one, Lummy."

"Be my guest. You found love at just the right time when you weren't expectin' it, if I remember right?"

"You remember right. Marion, I watched this man recover from the first and best love of his life. He even had a child with Susannah, a constant reminder she will always be with him. He even sees her from time to time, like we see Granny Thankful, and you see your Uncle Silas. Sted will always be with you and if he truly loves you, as I believe he did, he wants you free to live a good life."

Lummy nods. "Exactly. Marion, physical love, heart and mind love, they are for this world. But it's that love of the soul you have for a person that lasts throughout eternity."

"How do you know that?"

"Well, I don't believe the Father would've allowed his Son to die without a love that will last forever, do you?"

"No, I don't."

"That's the love I'm talkin' about."

"What Sted has for you now can never be taken away, and he has no hold on you in this place except to have you be happy until we all walk through the thin veil and meet on the other side."

"So what you're saying is that he would want me to be happy, and that's true love that transcends the grave?"

Rainy slaps his thigh. "You've got it, Marion."

Lummy leans up to adjust his behind in the saddle. "Right, and don't be surprised if Sted comes to you and sets you free, because in setting you free, his love becomes eternal."

Rainy throws his arm out into his thespian pose. "And all the Universe shall know that Stedman Walker is the love of Atalanta's, alias Marion Tullos's, life."

Lummy stops, as do we. "Marion, Susannah came to me years ago and set me free. Then I was given Martha. I love them both. They both love me. It's far above the flesh, this kind of love."

"Thank you, both, and I will look for Sted, when the time is right."

"You'll know it when it happens."

✳ ✳ ✳

WE RIDE ON through the day with little said among the three of us. We all need time just to think and not have to deal with each other's feelings right now, I'm sure. It's an easy trail through mostly flat land flanked by not so big mountains. Lummy said Skullyville is right at fifty miles on the trail to Fort Smith.

The sun starts to sink low. "Time we start looking for a place to stay the night."

Lummy nods. "I'm for stayin' out in the woods. Don't want to be around people."

"I agree," Rainy says, "and it'll be safer. It hasn't been that long since we killed those men, and those men had friends, two that we know of for sure."

I ease off the road into a pine thicket that leads up to a stand of rocks. "Let's try there. Looks like we could defend ourselves there on the high ground with those rocks at our backs."

Lummy follows. "Good thinkin'. I'll start gatherin' firewood."

Rainy dismounts and hangs back. "I'm going to cross the road and sit in a thicket for a while. I want to know if we're being followed."

I wave and take his horse's reins. "Good idea. I'll put supper on to cook here in a bit."

Lummy drops a load of wood by the rock circle I made for the fire. "I'll take care of the horses."

"Thanks, Uncle." These men are no strangers to work, or danger, and they mix them well together for the best protection I've enjoyed in some time.

Just after dark, Rainy waltzes into camp. "No sign of anyone following, but just the same, I say we douse the fire after we're done cooking. Won't be so cool tonight that a good blanket won't ward it off."

"I agree." I start filling plates with beans, fried salt pork, biscuits made in Lummy's little cast iron oven and a fresh pot of coffee to wash it down with.

Lummy takes his and looks to the sky mumbling a few words. He looks down at his plate. "You know, I never tire of this kind of food, even if I have to eat it every day."

Rainy speaks through a mouthful. "Vicksburg?"

"Yep. Vicksburg."

I take my first bite and savor it like I haven't eaten in days. "What was it like? Being in a siege, I mean?"

Lummy takes a full bite and muffles out, "You don't want to know, and this ain't the time." He sets his plate down and sips his coffee, all the while pressing the owl claw into his wrist, trying not to let us see.

"Sorry, Uncle Lummy, I won't do that again."

"I'll tell you in time, Marion. I just need to get some distance between what we just did and…." He goes back to eating.

I say no more. I glance at Rainy who winks and nods as he keeps eating. The rest of the night we're silent, just enjoying the crackling of the fire for another hour before Rainy throws water on it. I wrap up in my blanket and shake a shiver off. I think about what a siege was like. I think about Sted, what he would've been like. I think about Sam Sixkiller, that dark-eyed Choctaw who certainly has eyes for me. I…."

I WALK TO the edge of the tiny stream just down from camp to wash myself. It's been too long. I strip off my britches and open my shirt. I squat to gather up water from a small pool when the familiar sound of a rattler buzzes to my side not two feet away. I slowly reach for the Derringer, but it's gone. The rattler strikes the side of my butt, and I yell out.

A hand pushes my shoulder. "Marion, wake up."

I sit up quick, feel my butt and for the Derringer that's supposed to be around my neck. It's gone. What did I do with it?

"Marion, get up, we need to leave in a few minutes."

I feel all around, check my shirt, my coat, pants pockets, it's nowhere. "Uncle Lummy, have you seen my Derringer?"

Lummy hands me a cup of hot coffee and a cold salt pork biscuit left from the night before. "Yes, here it is. It slipped out of your shirt while you were sleeping the night before we killed the Buyer. Sorry, but with the plan we came up with, that you came up with, I couldn't risk them finding it and maybe using it on you."

"You should've told me."

"Would you have listened?"

"Probably not." I slip the rawhide cord around my neck and dangle my secret weapon over my heart, right where it needs to be. How did I not know it was gone? I won't let that happen again.

"We should get moving."

"Where's Rainy?"

"He's been out by the road since before first light checking to make sure no one is around. When we leave, we'll skedaddle for a couple of miles then walk our horses. If someone's waitin' for us, better we're already in a light gallop if they come."

I get up, careful not to spill my coffee. "Agreed." I wolf down a biscuit and wash it down with the cooling coffee. The horses are saddled and ready to go.

Lummy smiles. "Boots and saddles, Atalanta."

I smack his shoulder, and before I can ask, he hops on his mount like he must've done a hundred times in the Mounted Rifles during the war.

We slip out to the edge of the road and Rainy waves for us to come on. We trot down the lane at a fair pace, and I keep looking back. No one comes and after a couple of miles we slow to a walk.

I finally have a chance to ask, "How far we got till Skullyville?"

Rainy scratches his head. "Oh, about twenty miles, give or take a couple."

"Good because, Uncle Lummy, now you will tell me about the siege."

"All right, I will, but you have to do something for me too."

"Oh, yeah? What's that?"

"Tell me all you know about Uncle Silas before he died."

I look into that far-off place where there is no sight, no sound, no feeling, no…. "All right, I will. He was your uncle, too, and you need to know the kind of man he was to my sister and me. The kind of person I want to be."

Lummy grins. "From what I can tell, you and Uncle Silas were cut from the same cloth and go together like biscuits and gravy."

We share our stories all the way to Skullyville. It's not just the stories I love to hear, but the lessons Uncle Lummy learned, and the wisdom he shares when the story is finished. I try that when it's my turn, and he compliments me on it.

"Marion, one of the most important things Uncle Silas did was to help me make sense of the world through his stories. Stories of my ancestors are the pegs that hold fast the tent of my life when the storms come."

I decide then and there, the stories will be my pegs, too.

SKULLYVILLE

Gettin' paid means the work never ends.

Just Before Noon, September 8, 1886

SKULLYVILLE. WHY COME here except to cash in the reward voucher Captain Leflore gave us? It has something to do with Uncle Rainy's past, I just know it.

Rainy sniffs the air like he's walking through his own front door at home hoping to smell a good supper cooking but finds the beans have burned. "Yeah, it still stinks, and still looks the same. Not much has changed." He slows his mount to a crawl as he passes by a run-down old building that used to be a saloon. He stares at it like he's reliving a moment. He turns his head back forward and proceeds without a word.

We dismount in front of what looks like the only remaining mercantile that doubles as a saloon and a café. Rainy looks around, surveying the scene like he's looking for someone. Maybe he is.

Two other horses are hitched to the post. Probably Captain Leflore's men. A farmer's wagon is pulled over to the side. We take the porch steps slowly with our hands near our weapons, my right hand on my pistol and the other on Lummy's knife. We step up to the batwings and give ourselves a few seconds to allow our eyes to adjust before entering. We can't walk in blind, not when the one-eyed king who ruled in the land of the blind has only been dead a few days. Besides, those horses might belong to the captain's men, and they might not.

We step through one at a time and ease up to the counter to order drinks and food. Four men huddle in a corner and the farmer stands at the counter waiting for the owner to fill his order for supplies. He sheepishly gives us a side-eye look and turns back hoping we didn't see him eye us. He's a bit nervy. Something's not right here. The store owner's hand trembles as he reaches for an item on a high shelf. He turns and immediately gives us a look like he knows he's about to die and hopes we're his salvation.

A voice from the back corner chuckles and says, "Takes two men to give that girl a run for her money?" The four slap each other on the back and snicker. The mouthy one asks, "How 'bout it, honey? Tired of tryin' to keep warm with those two old men?"

Lummy turns to Rainy who smiles and says, "Let's let her take care of these knotheads. We're here if she needs us."

"Agreed. Marion?"

"Thank you, uncles." Not to be outmatched, I reply, "The four of you couldn't hold a candle to what either of these men are capable of, but if you have to know, they're my uncles. I'm pretty sure I know how they're taking in what you're suggesting." I turn to Lummy. "Uncle?"

Lummy nods. "Just a bunch of bootlickin' little church choir boys who have a bad case of the red rooster, if you know what I mean, boy."

"Yes, sir, I know exactly what you mean, a lot of crow and well, not much.… Do I have to say it?" The mouthy one yanks his pistol that looks to be the biggest handgun I've ever seen.

"No, no, you don't." Rainy snickers as he slowly pulls back his black coat to reveal a six-shooter already trained on the man. "That's a big gun for such a little boy.…" He turns to me and asks, "But ain't that what they say? A big gun makes up for a very small rooster?"

The mouthy one yells, "Take it back, or I'll—"

We all turn on a dime and have our weapons in hand. I ask, "You'll do what?"

The miscreant smiles at me like he's studying a finely cooked steak he's about to devour. "What's your name, little darlin'?"

I say nothing.

He starts with the top of my head, and I can see he's undressing me all the way down with every word. "Surely, you got a name to go with that silky blonde hair and those—"

It came out of nowhere. "Atalanta. My name is Atalanta, you ignert fool."

He looks at his friends and laughs. "You mean, Atlanta, like in Georgia?"

Rainy growls, "That could be Atlanta in Winn Parish, Louisiana, where your heathen friend Tom Kimbrell's brother and the West-Kimbrell Gang were taken down, but it's not."

I take a step forward to give myself room to fight if it comes to it. "Make no mistake, my name is Atalanta, and I'll be having your name now."

Before the outlaw can speak, the batwings burst open so hard they break off at the hinges. Two Choctaw Lighthorse hold pistols out aimed at the four men in the back and the leader shows them his badge pinned to his shirt. "Michael Angel and Little Dave Greasefire, I'm Jim Walking Bear and this is Jasper Gray Fox. You're under arrest for murder, kidnapping, thievery, and for just general unpleasantness. Drop your guns." The outlaws don't move. Jim shouts, "Drop them, now, or we'll drop you."

The mouthy one, I see his face and neck more clearly now. So that's Little Dave Greasefire Smith told us about.

Greasefire grins like a boy who just got a free stick of candy. "There's four of us, and only two of you." The other three men rise slowly, their revolvers already in hand. They turn them up ready to shoot from the hip. The farmer throws up his hands and sneaks around the end of the counter to duck behind it with the store owner. They say nothing.

Greasefire throws out his arm and points at us. "This is none of your affair. You stay out of it, you hear, old man. Already dressed for your funeral, ain't ya?"

Rainy pulls his gun up and aims as Lummy and I pull ours. "Oh, yeah, I hear just fine for an old man." He nods and winks at the Lighthorse. "But, dang, boy, staying out of this is, well, that's going to be a problem, you see. When we left Red Oak yesterday, Captain Charles Leflore of the Choctaw Lighthorse forgot to retrieve our duly sworn in badges he gave us when he deputized us to...." Rainy barks, "Kill your evil cyclops boss, the Buyer!"

Greasefire has a worried look on his face. He must know that if he's arrested he will hang, both he and Michael Angel. The standoff seems like an eternity. No one moves but eyes dart back and forth like so many bats chasing mosquitoes.

Jim asks, "What's it gonna be, boys? We got you five to four, and if I'm right, Mister Jenkins back behind the counter has his sawed-off double-barreled shotgun loaded with buckshot with the hammers cocked. Two loud clicks break the silence. Jim snickers. "Well, he does now."

Little Dave Greasefire side-eyes his companion, Michael Angel, and in a flash they grab the other two men with them, shove them forward, and start shooting. The two men who find themselves as shields try to fire but are riddled with bullets and a two-barrel shotgun blast slams them both against the wall. Greasefire and Angel duck out the back continuing their pistol fire until they dive out the back door. Greasefire yells, "I got your name, Atalanta. I'll be seein' you again!" Bullets splinter the back door as they slam it shut on their way out.

I yell to the two Lighthorse, "We got these two on the floor. Go after them before they get away."

A couple of shots ring out and the two Lighthorse return. Jim shakes his head. "Those two were smart. They hid their horses in the back. Dang it, I wanted to capture them."

I smile. "At least you got these two."

He kicks at the corpses. "These two are new to the territory. Probably came to meet and get acquainted here for the first time to plan somethin' together. We don't even know their names."

Rainy whispers, "And probably never will."

I think, so that's why the more experienced outlaws hid their mounts in the back. I tuck that away for future use.

Jim and Jasper gather the two bodies, and we help carry them to the outlaws' horses and tie them down. Jim snickers. "Guess these boys won't be needin' these mounts anymore." He turns to us. "Let's wash our hands of death, get a drink, and then I do believe we have some business to attend to."

THE LIGHTHORSE THANK us again as they leave to take the bodies to Fort Smith for identification. We cash in the voucher and after taking care of the expenses I paid on the way here and what Lummy gave Smith and Josie, Rainy counts out five equal shares from the reward money. It is a hefty sum for each of us.

He looks up from his counting. "Everybody happy with the divvying up?"

We nod and raise a glass to salute our fine work. Before we toast, I ask, "Let's honor Sted first." We each pour a sip of whiskey on the floor beside our chairs in his honor. I grin sadly. "To a good man gone too soon." We touch glasses and sip.

Rainy lifts his glass again. "To men and women who worked together to save God's good people and allowed us the honor and privilege of doing it." We repeat the toast and down our drinks.

Lummy pours another. "One more. Here's in hopes that young ladies everywhere are safe tonight forevermore in the land of clear eyesight, who no longer live in the danger of the one-eyed king who only thought he ruled in the land of the blind." We drink. Lummy grits his teeth. "May he burn in hell forever."

Rainy holds up his glass. "Here, here."

And we sit silent for a very long time.

A NEW NAME

The stranger the name, the deeper the meaning.

1:15 p.m., September 8, 1886

"ALL RIGHT, YOU two old codgers, what'n the heck is this Atalanta business? Now that I've started calling myself that."

Rainy pats the air with his palms. "All right, all right, Marion, let's order our food first. We've got nowhere to go until Smith and Josie get here. Let's relax a bit. I promise to enlighten your troubled mind." He snickers and rubs the back of his neck. "But first, I have one thing I must do, and I'd like to take care of it right after we eat, if you don't mind."

I'm impatient. "I know we don't have anywhere else to be right now. That's my point. So let's get on with this Atalanta business."

Lummy laughs as he stirs sugar into his coffee. "You're not gonna make her wait, Rainy."

Rainy adds a little cream to his. He takes a sip and smiles. "Trust me, you're gonna like it."

Before I can fuss more, the store owner lays out a full spread of ham, grits and fresh eggs, hot biscuits and gravy, butter and jams that hardly leave room for our coffee cups. We dig in like there's no tomorrow. Food never tasted so good as it does now that the Buyer's death is behind me.

I sit back in my chair and undo the top button on my britches. "Whew, that was good."

Lummy takes his last bite, sips his coffee, and lights the stub of his cigar. "Food that good makes you wanna go lie down somewhere."

Rainy snickers. "I could do that," he says as he lays his silverware down.

I wag my finger in the air. "Oh, no, uncles, you got unfinished business sitting right here in front of you. No time for napping, you old lazy hound dawgs."

Rainy shifts in his seat. "I know, and it's time."

The store owner waddles over to our table. "More coffee, anyone?" We all take another full cup. He sticks out his hand to me first. "I'm Don Iskuli, owner operator of this mercantile, café, saloon, and barber chair."

Lummy smiles. "You're Choctaw, aren't you?"

"Yes, sir, I am. I happen to carry the name of this town, at least the skully part. My father worked with the government agent to dole out supplies and such to our people, that is, before the Buyer's men murdered him ten years or so ago. He's buried in the Skullyville cemetery up on the hill just out of town." Don fidgets a little and takes in a deep breath.

I ask, "What's skully, or better said, Iskuli mean? Did I say it right?"

Don grins. "You did. It means 'piece of money' in Choctaw. It kinda fits with this being the place where money allotments were handed out to our people by the government."

Lummy sighs. "Never woulda had to hand out money if the government woulda let your people alone in the first place."

"True." Don reflects for a moment. "I've been listening to you good folks, and I hope I'm not too far out of line to tell you that I've been writing down your story. I'm an amateur author and well, this is a good story." He fidgets a bit as he shakes Rainy's and Lummy's hands. "Be all right if I write what happened here down too?"

Lummy doesn't turn loose of Don's hand. "On one condition."

"Anything," the store owner offers as he slides into the empty chair and lays his pencil and paper on the table.

"Make me a copy of whatever you have written so I can send it to my niece in Choctaw County, Missip. She's writing a book about our family and certainly would want all of this."

"Agreed." He sets his paper down and sharpens his pencil.

I turn to Lummy. "I didn't know that."

"Yeah, I've been writing down my story, better said, our story, since I left Choctaw County. I promised my niece, Mary, who is a schoolteacher, and a writer, that I would."

Rainy agrees. "I've sent her a few stories myself, and from what Lummy says, she keeps every scrap of paper that has any historical value to it, like letters, telegrams, newspaper articles, and such."

I turn to the store owner. "Then by all means, write what you hear, the truth of it, and leave nothing out."

"Happily, Miss Atalanta." He grins.

I slap the table with my palm. "All right, Mister Black Britches, your turn."

Rainy stares off into space for a bit, then returns with the look of a professor. "You know I received pretty good classical education down at the school in Natchez. I believe you went there for a time, didn't you, Marion?"

"I did."

"One of the areas our teacher was most versed in was Greek and Roman mythology and others as well. What attracted me to the culture, the stories, and quotes from philosophers and kings I throw around from time to time—they often gave me context for my own life, and often the wisdom to see more clearly. It's like the Bible, Marion. Same thing. I use that, too, but that's not the only wisdom in the world. I've learned to live by a phrase Lummy and I have discussed on occasion, which is, truth is truth, and all truth comes from God, then what does it matter who says it?"

"Yeah, Uncle Lummy told me about that. Makes sense."

Don writes furiously and Lummy asks, "Goin' too fast for you?"

He doesn't even look up and keeps writing. "If y'all go any faster, yes."

Rainy taps his index finger on the table. "We'll slow down." He stretches and then lays his hands on the table palms down. "Much of how we've made sense of all of this has been to relate what we've been experiencing in Greek heroes and villains."

"Yeah, Uncle Lummy and I have spoken on that a couple of times on the way here."

Rainy turns his hands palms up. "Yes, like the cyclops and Odysseus, and such. Well, that got me thinking when it became clear who you really are, what you're doing, and how you're going about it. You're the real-life Atalanta in the flesh. No myth here. Only the truth about what needs to happen and by whom."

"So who was Atalanta?"

Rainy takes a sip of coffee. "Centuries ago in what's now Greece, newborn Atalanta was left on a mountaintop by her father to die but was saved by a she-bear and later raised by hunters."

"That'd be like Uncle Silas saving me and my sister, right?"

"Yes."

"So, what does Atalanta mean?"

"In Greek, something like, 'equal in weight.'"

Lummy chuckles. "Well, that certainly fits, and I ain't talking about bone and muscle."

Rainy side-eyes me. "Yeah, more than equal to her male counterparts, I'd say."

I straighten up and poke out my chest. "Dang straight I am."

Rainy continues, "Anyway, she was known to be a devoted follower of Artemis, goddess of the hunt, and a skilled and fast runner. She was the only woman who went with Jason and the Argonauts on their adventures and helped kill a giant boar. She was warned in an oracle not to marry but did entertain the idea only if a suitor could outrun her in a footrace. If she caught a prospective husband in the race, she killed him. Many men died trying to finish first. After being tricked by Hippomenes, with the help of the love goddess Aphrodite, she lost a race and married him. Hippomenes forgot to thank Aphrodite, which angered her, so she turned them both into lions. They wandered the earth together hunting and mating for all eternity."

Lummy laughs. "Now that's a tale."

I don't laugh. "Yeah, but for me, without Sted, it won't happen."

Rainy lays his hand on my shoulder. "You don't know that, Marion. Remind me, or ask Lummy, to tell you about how I found love and wasn't looking for it, or even expecting it."

Lummy sits up. "He's right, Marion. The only love you don't find is if you stop allowing the possibility of it finding you."

I'm amazed. "How did you two old worn-out loggerhead turtles come to know so much about love?"

Lummy and Rainy look at each other, laugh, and say together, "The hard way."

I contemplate the name. "So Atalanta it is. Always first and foremost the hunt, and if love catches me, I'll know it when it does."

Lummy nods and Rainy agrees, "Good answer, Marion.... I mean about the name."

Don finishes his writing and looks up. "It'll also protect you, wearing the name Atalanta, I mean."

"What are you saying?"

"Those men, Greasefire and Angel, their deepest pride has been, excuse my language, ma'am, pissed on, and you did it. They'll be lookin' for you from now on if you stay in these parts."

I breathe in deeply and let it out slowly. "I'm not one to slink away in fear, sir. In fact I believe the best way to face fear is to run straight at it and put a face on it. You can't let fear surround you like a ghostly fog that will swallow you up. No, put a face on your fear and then you know who you're fighting."

Don jots down every word I say. "I wish I had your fire in my heart, lady."

I remind him, "And if those words find their way into a book someday, you write that it was Atalanta who said them."

He looks up and grins. "Oh, make no mistake, I will."

RAINY'S BUSINESS NOW MINE

It may not be my business right now, but it is coming.

Late afternoon, September 8, 1886

WE REST A bit just outside of town by a small stream that bubbles along just right to help me doze. I wake with a start to see Lummy and Rainy discussing something just out of earshot.

"What're you boys conjuring up over there?"

Rainy frowns, rocking his head from side to side. "Oh, nothing really, just discussing a little business I need to take care of now that I'm ready. You sure had a fitful nap, in and out of it, I might add."

"Yeah, I was dreaming about what happened up in the cave. Sted... and some other things that either plague my mind or bring it peace, you know?"

Rainy smiles. "I do know. One of my favorite authors once wrote, 'They who dream by day are cognizant of many things which escape those who dream only by night.'" He lets that hang in the air for a moment.

Lummy asks, "Mark Twain?"

"Edgar Allen Poe, I believe it was."

I add, "It's true, what he said." I stand up and press the wrinkles out of my clothes and stretch. "So what's the business you need to take care of, if you don't mind me asking?"

Rainy clears his throat. "I don't mind, in fact, I was hoping you would come with Lummy and me."

"Where are we going?"

"To a little cemetery that's just a short walk from here. We can leave our horses here."

We start down the road that leads to Fort Smith and make a right turn just out of town into a grove of oaks that offer dark shade. Grave markers made of stone and wood are scattered about in this small place devoted to the dead. There are some very nice and ornate stones but more so, simple blocks of sandstone with no names. Rainy searches around as Lummy and I lean against a tree waiting.

Rainy squats down and clears away old dead dried grass and brushes away the dust from a stone. "Here it is. I found it."

We walk over to where Rainy stands staring down at a flat sandstone with an inscription etched into it. It reads,

JOHN RATLIFF
KILLED BY HIS OWN SON
WHO WORE BLACK
1859

Rainy doesn't move. Lummy says nothing. The ground is bare and there are no flowers on this grave. We stare down at the tomb of the man who fathered Rainy.

Rainy looks into the sky. "This man killed my real father, Thomas Mills, and then raped my mother, but made possible me being born. I was raised by a good man, taught the skills of the gun trade by another good man, and have long enjoyed the company and friendship of this good man, Lummy Tullos." He lays his hand on Lummy's shoulder.

"I should hate you, John Ratliff, and I have for a very long time, but not today. Because of my friend who stands with me today, I understand now that no one does things like you did without having had some pretty bad things happen to them. I understand that something really terrible must've happened to you when you were little to turn out the way you did." Rainy wipes a tear and says, "I wish you had been a better man, but you weren't." He sniffles and straightens up.

"But today, I forgive you because the only way I can be forgiven is if I forgive, and I do that for you. I'm not a praying man, but if I was, I'd ask the Lord to forgive your wrongs, snatch you from punishment, and seat you in heaven so that you will see who and what you were supposed to be, but also that I am your son, and I turned out all right."

We stand there for a long time. Lummy wraps his arm around Rainy's shoulder, and I wrap my arms around his waist. Lummy prays, "Lord, you've heard his words. Who would you be if you do not honor his merciful request for his father who deserves nothing but the flames? We ask this for we know we all stand in the spot that needs Jesus to set us free. Free the captive that he might have his eyes opened to who you really are, Creator."

The sound of a thousand whispering breezes passes through, shaking the trees and fluffing the dry grass. A figure wearing a long flowing white robe glides across the ground and stops before the grave.

Granny Thankful.

"I come for the man who took the life of my cousin, your father." She reaches into the ground and John Ratliff follows into the trees, disappearing.

Rainy kicks the dirt like a little child wondering what he's supposed to do next. He offers another quote, "What you leave behind is not what is engraved in stone monuments, but what is woven into the lives of others."

Lummy asks, "Did my ancestor, Marcus *Tullius* Cicero say that?"

"No, but not far off. It was Pericles."

I ask, "How about a shot of good whiskey?"

Rainy nods. "That sounds good right about now."

We sit in Don's store, sipping a libation with a fine flavor.

"What happened here, Uncle Rainy?"

Rainy shrugs. "It's pretty simple. I found out who John Ratliff was after all those years, tracked him down, and killed him in that abandoned saloon just across the street there. That's about it."

"Nothing simple about that, Uncle. It took a lot of courage to form those words today, say them, and mean them."

Lummy pours another round. "She's right, Rainy, and you know I know that."

"I do, and I did mean them. It took two killings to even get started on the path that led here today. It took a lot of thought to get to where I'd even consider it, but a man does that as he gets older, I guess."

"He does." Lummy takes a sip from his glass. "Yeah, why carry somethin' around that's only good for slowin' a soul down?" He downs the rest. "I still have a few of those yet to deal with myself."

I sip my whiskey. "I have to say, Uncle Rainy, I don't know if I could forgive like that. I felt some terrible stuff when I bent down to start carving up the Buyer's body. I'd-a done it, too, had y'all not stopped me."

Lummy grins. "Yeah, I think Rainy and I both have had people stand in that same place for us, to help us stay sane in the craziest of moments when we needed help the most."

Rainy raises his glass. "Here, here, and I say amen to all of that." He giggles a little.

I laugh. "Are you on your way to getting drunk, Uncle Rainy?"

"No, I believe I have arrived, thank you very much."

Lummy looks at his glass. "This is pretty good stuff. I'm feeling a bit on the wobbly side myself."

"Then I better slack off so I can keep an eye on you two old boar raccoons. The things I do for two raggedy-ass old…." I can't help but laugh.

Rainy holds up his glass and smiles. "And we thank you very much."

"And I'll drink to that," Lummy says, as he tries to pour another shot but spills half of it on the table.

I take the bottle. "All right, you boys have had enough already."

Rainy looks to Lummy. "Dang, she'd make somebody a fine wife. She's already bossy enough, don't you think?"

"I'd say I'd drink to that, but she took the bottle away from us."

I hand the bottle back to Don at the counter and say, "We're going to need a pot of strong coffee."

He belly-laughs. "Not a problem. Just keep them in their seats."

"Don't think that'll be much of a problem. They both have already slumped over in their chairs."

WE SIT UNTIL two pots of coffee are polished off and the whiskey wears off. We stroll down to camp to wait for Smith and Josie under the shady oaks.

Rainy goes across the small stream and when he returns, he's no longer wearing black. He throws the black clothes into a fire Lummy started so I can cook another meal over the flames. He likes food cooked over an open fire. This time it'll be fresh beef, boiled potatoes, with beans and cornbread fritters. I even picked up a few sweet cakes for after. The luxury of quiet stillness is not lost on these two. They've seen enough trouble that just the sound of a crackling fire is noise enough. I'm coming to appreciate that myself. I have a thousand questions for these two, but I leave them with their thoughts.

THE WAY HOME

The way home is not so much to a "where," but to a "whom."

Noon, September 11, 1886

WE FINISH A fine meal and stretch out under a couple of oaks to rest and let our stomachs settle. It's been good to just lay around, talk, and do nothing for a couple of days. Just after noon, Josie and Smith ride in with the biggest grins I've seen on two faces in a long time.

I have to say, "You two are married, aren't you?"

As Josie hops off her mount, Smith laughs. "You better believe it, and legal too."

Rainy and Lummy step out into the sunlight from their shady rests and wave.

Smith and Josie take one of my hands each, and Josie says, "Just want you to know, our first son, well, we'll be naming him Stedman. And if a girl, Marion."

Tears well up, and my throat chokes, but I manage to get out in a raspy voice, "That'd be just all right with me. Thank you."

Rainy asks, "Any trouble or notice any suspicious characters on the way?"

Smith plants his feet like a man. "No, sir, we got Carol Ann home, and I brought us right back here. We made extra sure nobody was followin' us."

Rainy breathes a sigh of relief. "First, I'm glad you're back with us safe and sound, and second, that you didn't bring trouble with you. Good man, and good woman to you, Josie. Y'all did a fine job. You must be hungry. Marion has been doing some mighty fine cooking lately."

Smith holds out his hand to Lummy. "This is all we had left from our trip, Mister Lummy. It took all but twenty dollars to get us there and back."

Lummy smiles. "Consider it my wedding gift."

Smith looks to Josie who jumps up and down like a puppy. "Oh, thank you, Mister Lummy, oh thank you."

We all laugh until we can't anymore. Lummy walks away and waves for us to come along. "Y'all come on over, let me show you something." Rainy hitches Smith's and Josie's mounts to an oak limb, and we join him at a rock where he's laid out a map.

"Mister Iskuli let me borrow this map. See this place called Dallas in Polk County, Arkansas? I figure we can ride there then go our separate ways. I'll go south to my daughter Rosey's home. Rainy, you and the lovebirds can strike out for Winn Parish from there as well. Not sure what you're gonna do, Marion, but you can go anywhere from there, and it's kinda off the well-beaten path, if you know what I mean."

"I do."

"We won't tell Mister Iskuli which way we're going so he can't field a question he has no answer for. Rainy, you good with that? Smith, Josie?" They nod.

I straighten my hat. "All right then, I say we leave first thing in the morning and be on our way." All agree, and we turn in early for a long but peaceful ride.

WE EASE INTO Dallas, Arkansas, early afternoon not quite three days from leaving Skullyville ready for a break. Rainy looks around. "I don't know, this looks to be a pretty nice place."

I suggest, "Let's find a place to stay in a real bed and get baths, some café-cooked food, and let our horses rest a day or so."

We pass three mills, a couple of churches, and leave our horses to be cared for at the second livery stable we come to. Josie and Smith dance off together to visit the three stores scattered around. They're like a couple of kids at a county fair. The freedom they have is freedom hard won, and worth every ounce of pain and blood we gave it.

I look to the sky. "Lord, give Sted an extra special portion of reward for providing that for those two lovebirds."

Lummy and Rainy start toward one of the boardinghouses that look inviting. Lummy asks, "You comin'?"

I look around, and I see things in a different way. I'm not the little girl with a devil's grudge against the world. I don't need to be angry and sad in the same moment. I've experienced love, even if only for a little while, and I have friends—real friends—who love me and hold me dear to their hearts. I have a calling from the Lord himself and a story that goes back thousands of years.

I stop, lift my arms up, and speak out loud in the middle of the street. "I am Atalanta, and I hunt men and women who break the law." I wait for a round of applause. All I get from the few people in this small town are strange stares, a couple of dogs yelping, and a mule that hee-haws one time, almost like it's laughing at me. So I add, "Charles Dickens once said, 'I have been bent and broken, but, I hope, into a better shape.'" I'm not exactly sure why I did that, but it sure as heck felt good.

Rainy and Lummy settle into a bench on the porch steps to sit for a moment. I walk up the steps where they whisper to each other and smile.

"All right, what're you two talking about?"

Rainy lifts his chin. "I was just complimenting the fine declaration of your new personhood and the Charles Dickens quote you rolled out in such a superb way."

Lummy nods. "And I believe your Uncle Rainy here was about to discuss the merits of your ability to carry out your so-called profession."

I place my hands on my hips. "Was he now?"

He turns to Lummy. "Yes, yes, I was. I'm trying to decide if it will be a problem, you know, a hindrance to the performance of her duties."

Lummy asks, "The face, you mean?"

"Exactly, it's the face that's a problem."

I get my hackles up even though I know these men aren't trying to rile me. "What's wrong with my face? Got dirt on it, or what?"

Rainy looks left and right, up and down, anywhere but directly at me. "Oh, oh, nothing, no, not a thing, believe me, nothing wrong with the face."

"Then what's the problem?"

Rainy stops still and his eyes bore into my soul. "Had you walked out on the veranda when the ships were launched to go retrieve Helen of Troy, Menelaus would've told his brother Agamemnon to turn the thousand ship fleet to turn around because your beauty far exceeds that of some nobody named Helen."

I'm speechless. No one has ever talked to me this way. I don't know what to do with myself. I fidget like a little girl about to have to sing by herself in front of church.

Lummy turns a little red in the telling, "Marion, your beauty is heavenly, like an angel. You're like a bouquet of flowers. Just nice to look at."

Rainy squints. "Yes, but your loveliness goes much deeper than outward beauty. You're an avenging angel bent on righting the wrongs you believe Creator gives you to deal with. That's beauty of the soul."

Lummy nods. "Yeah, but before we get carried away, she's almost too pretty for a job like this."

"Yeah, though that face will get her into doors that I certainly could not."

Lummy rubs his chin. "Well, yeah, now that you mention it, I do believe you may be right about that."

Rainy laughs. "Say it again. You don't tell me I'm right very often."

"That's because you're rarely right about anythin', and—"

I laugh and pop both in the shoulders with my palms. "Oh, stop it.

You boys are as pretty as men come. You're just a bit old and decrepit, dumb but funny, that's all." They both reach out to grab at me, but I'm too fast for them. "Like I said, two slow old men."

I grab the knob on the boardinghouse door. I've never been around better people than Lummy and Rainy.

Both slowly rise. Rainy laughs. "You say it, or I will."

Lummy grins. "Now that you've announced yourself to the world, please do us all a favor, Marion, and go take a bath! You still stink!"

"Stink or no stink, my name is Atalanta." I shake the door back and forth, the little bells ringing like they'll never stop. "And hell's bells are no longer a problem for me."

ANTHONY WOOD grew up in historic Natchez, Mississippi, fueling a life-long love of history. Not long after high school, he lived and worked in Alaska for several years. He returned to the South and ministered for nearly three decades among the poor, homeless, and incarcerated. Leading an effort that planted five urban churches inspired him to co-author *Up Close and Personal: Embracing the Poor* about his work in Memphis, Tennessee. He also authored a number of articles and stories about inner city ministry.

Anthony is a member of Turner's Battery, a Civil War re-enactment group, the Civil War Roundtable of Arkansas, and the White County Creative Writers group. His short stories and poetry have won multiple awards and have been published in *Saddlebag Dispatches, The Vault of Terror,* and *The Avocet: A Journal of Nature Poetry,* and a number of anthologies. One of those stories, "Not So Long in the Tooth," won a Will Rogers Medallion in 2021. Anthony was also the Arkansas Writers' Hall of Fame inductee for 2024.

When not writing, Anthony enjoys roaming and researching historical sites, camping and kayaking on the Mississippi River, and being with family. Anthony, and his wife, Lisa, live in Arkansas.